D1000376

THE TERRORS OF ICE AND DARKNESS

Also by Christoph Ransmayr

The Last World

THE TERRORS OF ICE AND DARKNESS

A NOVEL

Christoph Ransmayr

TRANSLATED FROM THE GERMAN BY JOHN E. WOODS

GROVE WEIDENFELD
New York

Published by Grove Weidenfeld
A division of Grove Press, Inc.
841 Broadway
New York, NY 10003–4793

Published in Canada by General Publishing Company, Ltd.

Credits appear on pages 227 and 228.

Library of Congress Cataloging-in-Publication Data

Ransmayr, Christoph.
[Schrecken des Eises und der Finsternis. English]
The terrors of ice and darkness : a novel / Christoph Ransmayr ; translated from the German by John E. Woods. — 1st ed.
p. cm.
Translation of: Die Schrecken des Eises und der Finsternis.
Includes bibliographical references.
ISBN 0-8021-1152-1 (alk. paper)
1. North Pole—Fiction. I. Title.
PT2678.A65S3713 1991
833'.914—dc20 90-25549
CIP

Manufactured in the United States of America

Printed on acid-free paper

Designed by Irving Perkins Associates

First American Edition 1991

10 9 8 7 6 5 4 3 2 1

For Pizzo

Contents

Above All

What has become of our adventures—the ones that led us over icy passes, across great dunes, or often simply down highways? We could be seen making our way through mangrove forests, across prairies, windswept wastelands, and glaciers, over oceans, passing on through cloudbanks, moving toward ever more remote destinations, external and internal. We were not content simply to go adventuring. We also made our adventures public, at the very least in postcards and letters. But above all in reports and accounts, profusely illustrated and secretly fostering an illusion: that even the most remote and distant spot is as accessible as an amusement park, a twinkling Coney Island; that the world has grown smaller with the rapid development of our modes of transportation; that a trip around the equator or to the poles is now merely a question of finances and coordinating flight schedules. But that is a mistake! Airlines have allowed at best for an almost absurd reduction in travel time, but not in distances. Those remain as immense as before. Let us not forget: The line of flight is only a line, not a road. From a physiognomic viewpoint, we are pedestrians and runners.

I

Removed from the World

Josef Mazzini often traveled alone and mostly on foot. For him, walking made the world not smaller but larger, so large that he finally disappeared in it.

Mazzini, thirty-two years old and a hiker, got lost in the glacial terrain of the Spitsbergens during the arctic winter of 1981. It was a private death, to be sure. Another missing person, nothing special. But when a man is lost and leaves behind no tangible remains—nothing to cremate, bury, or cover with a mound of dirt—we apparently need the stories people begin to tell about him after his disappearance if he is to be removed from this world. No one has ever gone on living in such stories.

I've often thought it uncanny how the beginning of every story, as well as the end, if you follow it far enough, gets lost at some point in the expanses of time. But since everything that might be said can never be said, and since a century must surely be sufficient to explain a man's fate, I shall begin at sea and say: It was a clear, windy day on the Adriatic coast in March 1872. Perhaps then, too, gulls stood in the wind above the wharves like dainty kites, white rags gliding in a blue sky turbulent with the season's tattered line of clouds—I do not know. What is recorded, however, is that on that day Carl

Weyprecht, a lieutenant on a battleship of the Imperial Austro-Hungarian Navy, gave a speech outside the harbor-master's office in the city the Italians call Fiume and its Croatian inhabitants call Rijeka. He spoke to sailors and assorted harbor folk about the perils of the far north.

I have long clung to the notion that in the course of Weyprecht's lengthy speech there was a sudden burst of spring rain, its gentle rush allowing a few sailors in the audience to move away without arousing the suspicion that they had taken fright at the scenes conjured up by the naval lieutenant. Weyprecht described a remote world and a cold summer sun that circled above the navigators for months, never setting; but in autumn its light dimmed and those regions once again fell under the darkness of polar night—and nameless cold—for months on end. Weyprecht spoke of the desolation of a ship frozen in pack ice and drifting through an unexplored sea, at the mercy of arbitrary currents and forces of compression that could burst the tons of covering ice, piling ice boulder upon ice boulder into towers! Forces that had often crushed the steel-reinforced bellies of schooners and frigates like balsawood models. He told how the frozen swells of the Arctic Ocean would groan and screech until a traveler who had penetrated its waters might sometimes feel his most hidden fears thrust upward, and yet he would have to stay on in that world, often for years, locked inside walls of pack ice, his own energy his only solace.

But now Weyprecht's speech took a surprising turn that cast a different light on all those terrors and apparently so fascinated at least several sailors that they came to see the lieutenant afterward in the harbormaster's office:

The bleak monotony of an arctic journey, the deadly boredom of endless night, the gruesome cold—those are but the various catch-phrases with which the civilized world is accustomed to express its pity for the poor traveler to the poles. But the only man to be pitied is he who cannot resist the memory of the pleasures he has left behind, who bewails his hard fate, counting the days that must pass until the hour for the homeward journey comes round. Such a man would do better to remain quietly beside his hearth, relishing others' sufferings, perhaps exaggerating them in his own imagination. To those who are interested in the forces of nature, the cold is not so fierce but that they can bear it, or the night so long but that it will one day end. Boredom, moreover, is felt only by the man who bears it within himself, incapable of finding pursuits to prevent his spirit from hatching its own miseries.

In the Bremerhaven shipyard of Teklenberg and Beurmann, a ship was being built—so Weyprecht concluded his speech—the *Admiral Tegetthoff*, a three-masted, 220-ton bark equipped with an auxiliary steam engine and every safeguard against the ice. The *Admiral Tegetthoff* would set out that very June, taking a course for North Cape, and from there sail ever farther into the unexplored seas northeast of the Russian archipelago Novaya Zemlya. Any able-bodied seaman present who had no fear of those icy waters and was prepared to leave all familiar faces behind for two and a half years should register with him at the harbormaster's office—as a member of the Imperial Austro-Hungarian North Pole Expedition. On board the *Admiral Tegetthoff*, he, Weyprecht, would be in command; on land, however, his comrade First Lieutenant Julius Payer would give the orders.

While wage negotiations and preparations for departure took their tedious course beside the Adriatic, back in Vienna a Polar Committee of aristocrats, at their head a great lover of adventures named Count Hans Wilczek, looked to the financing of the expedition. And First Lieutenant Julius Payer wrote letters to South Tyrol.

My dear Haller,

I'm glad I have at last found you and that you have replied so promptly.

I propose to go on a journey of some two and a half years, to very cold regions, where there are no human beings but great numbers of polar bears, and where the sun shines without interruption for several months and then not at all for several more.

I am, you see, going on a North Pole expedition.

1. I shall pay your way, with no deductions, from Sankt Leonhard to Bremerhaven, where we shall embark.

2. Your term of service would begin at the end of May, you would have to be in Vienna by that time.

3. You would have to remain with me for two and a half years.

4. I would provide your clothing, weapons, and board, and you would receive, apart from any bonuses for special achievement, 1,000 guldens in banknotes, partial payment of which you can claim prior to departure.

My good Haller, would you please look about for another mountaineer—he should be a decent fellow, good-natured, industrious, one who would lose neither heart nor stamina though the hardships prove ever so great, he should be a good hunter and would receive the same compensation as you. Upon our return, I shall present you with a fine Lefaucheux rifle (double-barreled, breechloader).

Do write me at once, but at all events look about for a second man who you can guarantee would be of use.

There will be cold and dangers—does that alarm you? I have returned home safe from two such journeys, and what I can do, you can do as well.

Your friend Payer

2

The Missing Man—Personal Data

Josef Mazzini came into the world in Trieste in 1948, the son of Kaspar Mazzini, a Viennese paperhanger, and his wife, Lucia, a native of Trieste and a painter of miniatures. In the first days after his birth an argument that had raged in the paperhanger's home for several weeks reached its climax. Lucia, a zealous Italian, tried to block the German name Josef, but to no avail. The paperhanger—who even then was having eye trouble and growing increasingly irascible as his sight worsened—cast all such objections and pleas aside in this instance, too. Josef Mazzini was raised in an apartment separated from his father's workshop only by a sliding wooden door, and his upbringing—in both his parents' native tongues—was so rigorous that despite his father's determination that his heir enjoy a *better future*, he very soon began to live a life not only counter to paternal intentions but counter to all proscriptions whatever. He proved *difficult*.

In his mother's earliest stories the world was an album to be paged through. Lucia Mazzini née Scarpa was always trying to pacify her son. She told him many tales. In the afternoon hours the present was often nothing more than an intermittent sound emerging from beyond the sliding door—someone working. At the kitchen table, however, the past was overwhelming and picturesque. Many Scarpas had been sailors, so the story went, helmsmen, captains! Lorenzo, for instance—he had sailed around the world seventeen times before being murdered in Port Said. Or Antonio, his great-great-uncle, Antonio Scarpa!—a member of an Austrian expedition (although almost all of the sailors had been Italian, if the truth were known) that had sailed clear to the North Pole and discovered mountains of ice and black stones, a shining land beneath a sun that never set. But the ship, covered with layer upon layer of crystalline ice, was frozen fast, and Antonio had finally returned from the wilderness by crossing a solid sea on foot. And had suffered a great deal. When his mother told of Antonio Scarpa's agonizing trek across the ice, she sometimes clapped her hands above her head and a strange light came into her eyes. Italy was great. Italy was everywhere! And Lucia, who no longer took any joy in her paperhanger from Vienna, comforted herself and her son with those truths. As a schoolboy Mazzini learned all about "heroes." And about the sad fate of handsome General Umberto Nobile from Avellino, who figured, one may be sure, in many of Lucia's dreams. In May 1926—accompanied by Roald Amundsen, the conqueror of the South Pole, the American millionaire Lincoln Ellsworth, and twelve others—Nobile had taken off from the Spitsbergens in a dirigible and flown over the North Pole to Alaska, and landed unscathed in his gold-embroidered parade uniform. And two years later Lucia had been there—a girl all in white, waving her little flag!—when people gathered in Milan for Nobile's departure on a second polar flight. What a gala occasion! Even the Duce had been there. But the April day dragged on, passed, and Nobile's dirigible *Italia* did not lift into the Milanese skies. Late that night it was still tied down, and the crowd had gradually drifted off. Then, at last, the massive cigar of the

Italia gently slipped its chains and rose into the darkness, a vast, dull shimmer. Lucia had held out until that one wonderful moment, had stood there on tiptoe, raising her paper banner into the night, biting hard into the white knuckles of her fist. But Lucia's hero had returned from his adventure much changed—a castaway spurned by public opinion, a man whom the miniature-painter had difficulty remembering in his old splendor. It was the one disaster that Josef Mazzini heard about in the paperhanger's home. The crash of the *Italia* may have occurred long before—the dead were long since dead, the surviving heroes as good as forgotten, and the Second World War had reduced all adventures in the Arctic or anywhere else to absurd games of chance—but nevertheless, it was the first disaster in Mazzini's life to affect him and give him bad dreams. For the story about the failure of the *Italia* expedition made Mazzini realize for the first time that there was such a thing: being dead. And that terrified him. What sort of sea was that, where heroes could be transformed into scarecrows, captains into cannibals, and dirigibles into icy tatters?

I assume it was about then that Mazzini (was he twelve, was he younger?) began to arrange his first rough ideas of the Arctic into an image of a cold, glittering world of monsters, a world so disquieting and empty that simply everything was possible—even in the secret, rather old-fashioned dreams that he dared dream about it here in the paperhanger's house. It was not a beautiful image. But it was so powerful that Mazzini took it with him from childhood into his later years.

The paperhanger did not like to hear the stories his wife told his heir. He cursed Lucia's heroes as "idiots," sometimes he would call Nobile a fascist, and yet for years he permitted a postcard-sized photograph to remain tacked to the workshop's sliding door: the general standing beside his dirigible's anchor mast in Ny Ålesund. When the photo was finally taken down it left a bright rectangle on the door, like a window onto another world. Josef Mazzini, however, had long since left for Vienna. With his departure from Trieste he was at last rid of his family's pointless bickering about his future, and in the course of his increasingly infrequent visits he refused their attempts to reestablish him in his proper position of "heir." Mazzini's move to Vienna may well have been motivated in part by his father's own fantasies of running off, for on his bad days he would curse Trieste and talk about returning to his hometown. Or it may have had something to do with a distant and dusty relation, an aunt who sold domestic and tropical fruits in her shop on Thaliastrasse and halfheartedly supported her Italian nephew for a while after his arrival. Whatever the reason, Mazzini was in Vienna and, apart from packing for grueling excursions, made no move to indicate he was ever going to Trieste or anywhere else. He had settled down here—*"hier niedergelassen,"* he would say if he happened to be speaking in his father's German.

Mazzini furnished a room he sublet from a stonemason's widow, drove a truck now and then for a moving company where a friend of his relatives held down a job as a bookkeeper, made some under-the-counter money dealing in antique Oriental porcelains, jades, and ivories, and read a lot. The stonemason's widow sat her days away at a bulky knitting machine, offered her lodger the oddest woolen garments, and stared out the window for hours on end at her husband's unsold gravestones stored in the back courtyard. Moss grew on the stones.

I became acquainted with Josef Mazzini at Anna Koreth's apartment. She was a book dealer, a woman who found her way into academic circles after writing an ethnological study of a Samoyed tribe living on the arctic coasts of Siberia. She went on to make ethnohistoric works and travel books her shop's specialty. In her dark, roomy apartment on Rauhensteingasse, the book dealer occasionally gave dinners for her best customers. These were evenings with much discussion of manuscripts and rare editions and much drinking of cheap Italian wine. On Rauhensteingasse you learned the most incredible details about how various works came to be published, about edition dates, designs, and bindings, but almost nothing about the people who read such works. Mazzini—Anna Koreth had introduced him to her evening circle of friends as "my Josef"—was an exception. He talked a lot about himself, in a polite German clearly influenced by emigration. When Mazzini was still new to Rauhensteingasse, he used terms like "picture palace," said "howbeit," "high-hearted," "peradventure," "trunk call."

At the time I misread his vocabulary, spoken as it was with no accent, as part of a concerted campaign to score conversational points, especially since the things he talked about seemed odd and offbeat in Anna Koreth's circle. He said he was redesigning the past, as it were. He would think up stories, invent a plot or a course of events, write them down, and then check whether there had ever been *real* precursors of his imaginary figures in the distant or recent past. This was no different from the methods of science fiction writers, Mazzini said, except that he was traveling back in time. He had the advantage of being able to test the truth of his inventions by historical research. He was playing a game with reality. He assumed that whatever he fantasized must have happened at some time or other. "Aha," the Rauhensteingasse guests said to the Italian, sitting there pontificating at the table in his oversized pullover and swilling red wine, "aha, that's nice, sounds familiar," but it would be impossible to differentiate between a made-up story that had actually happened at some time and a basic account of the event; no one would know to value the fantasy since everyone would think it was a purely factual report. That was unimportant, Mazzini replied, he was quite content with his private, secret proof that he had invented reality.

I assume it was Anna Koreth (she was a good head taller than Josef, than *her* Josef) who finally convinced the inventor to abandon the privacy and secrecy of his mind games and offer his stories to a wider public. (At any rate, they occasionally appeared in the few magazines stocked by Koreth Books, ambassadors of the present amid solid rows of historical works.) Mazzini continued working part-time as a driver for the moving company, went on supplying middle-class clients in need of antique statuettes, and wrote stories set in places that usually could be located only approximately on a map. He would send fishing boats to the bottom of remote seas, set wildfires raging on far-off Asian steppes, or provide an eyewitness account of battles and streams of refugees in Greater Somewhere. The border between the lands of Fact and Fiction was always invisible.

"The wish to be entertained is always the same in any case," Mazzini would write in his arctic diary, which the oceanographer Kjetil Fyrand later sent back to Anna Koreth from Longyearbyen, a mining town in the Spitsbergens, ". . . Once we have closed up shop for the day, surely it is always the same embarrassed desire to break away that makes us dream of marches through jungles, caravans, or glistening floes of ice. We send our deputies where we cannot go ourselves—reporters who will tell us what it was like. But usually it was *not* like that. And whether the report is about the destruction of Pompeii or some current war amid rice fields, adventure is adventure. Nothing moves us anymore. Nor does anyone truly inform us. No one moves us, they entertain us. . . ."

The more the notion took hold of Mazzini that he could actually rediscover his phantasms in reality, the more often he would lay the scene of his tales in uninhabited barren landscapes and northern wastes. An invented drama that unfolded in an empty world was ultimately much more probable and conceivable than some tropic adventure that required you to take into account a multifold nature or the rituals of a strange culture. And so Mazzini pushed the characters in his fantasies ever northward, to arrive at last in a place where not even Eskimos lived—the pack ice of the pole. The inventor thought he had found a connection with the rigid, icy scenes of his childhood; later, however, it turned out that it was also a connection with his end. Indeed, the prelude to Mazzini's disappearance began in the antiquarian section of Koreth Books when he discovered a description of an arctic voyage—an account more than a century old, so dramatic, so bizarre, and ending so improbably that only his fantasy could match it. It was the report of Sir Julius Payer concerning the Imperial Austro-Hungarian North Pole Expedition, published in Vienna in 1876 by Alfred Hölder, Stationer to the Court and the University.

Josef Mazzini was fascinated. The expedition had spent more than two years in the pack ice and on a brilliant August day in 1873 had discovered at 79° north latitude a hitherto unknown archipelago in the Arctic Ocean—some sixty islands of bedrock, a chain of basalt mountains almost totally buried under the cover of a massive glacier, seven thousand square miles of lifelessness. Four months out of the year the sun did not rise on this island empire, and from December to January total darkness reigned, with temperatures reaching −95° Fahrenheit. Julius Payer and Carl Weyprecht, the commanders of the expedition, had christened this horrible land Kaiser Franz Josef Land in honor of their distant monarch, thereby erasing one of the last blank spots on the map of the Old World.

I can imagine no other reason why the report of this expedition so piqued Josef Mazzini's fancy than that he believed he had found in Payer's account a "proof" for one of his own invented adventures. One thing is certain, however: with almost fanatic zeal Mazzini began to reconstruct the confused course this journey of discovery had taken. He wandered through archives. (The frayed log of the *Admiral Tegetthoff* as well as the unpublished letters and journals of both Weyprecht and Payer lay preserved in the naval section of the Austrian War Archives; the diary of the expedition's machinist, Otto Krisch, and the "wordless," monotone notes of Johann Haller, the hunter from the Passeiertal, were in the map collection of the National Library. . . .) It was as if the undertow that had already pulled Mazzini's imagined characters into the far north had now grabbed him and was dragging him away. Mazzini raced off in search of an obsolete reality. Archives were too small, too narrow for his race. Mazzini traveled to arctic waters. Mazzini celebrated the chronicle of the Payer–Weyprecht expedition against the backdrop of reality—the violet sky above the ice floes must be the same one beneath which the crew of the *Admiral Tegetthoff* had despaired more than a century before. Mazzini hiked across glaciers. Mazzini disappeared.

No, I was not one of his friends. Looking at that slight, almost dainty man, who would probably have followed even a mirage with the energy of a fanatic, I sometimes felt the peculiar enmity one might feel when confronted with someone all too like oneself. Without wanting to, I had stumbled into his life—a passing acquaintance. In fact, I first took real notice of Mazzini only after he had disappeared in the ice. The enigmatic and disquieting nature of his disappearance worked its way back into his existence, until gradually everything the man had ever done or concerned himself with became enigmatic and disquieting. All the same, at first it was nothing more than a game to try to reduce the circumstances of his disappearance to some sort of explanation, any explanation. But every clue yielded a new unanswered question. Quite involuntarily I found myself taking one step after the other, entering biographical details, data, and names into a kind of crossword puzzle, until Mazzini became my *downfall.* I ended up doing further research on the same arctic history he had so doggedly pursued, losing myself more and more in his work and neglecting my own. Mazzini's sketches and diaries from the Spitsbergens, which Anna Koreth handed over to me, became so familiar I had no trouble quoting the most muddled passages by heart. I could not get the sentences and images, the most meaningless fragments, out of my head. Even when I wanted to, I could forget nothing now. Cumulus clouds mirrored in a shop window became calving glaciers, patches of old snow in city parks became great floes of ice. The Arctic Ocean lay at my window. Much the same thing must have happened to Mazzini. It still perturbs me to recall that day in March—I was on my way to a geography library—when I suddenly realized that I had taken up residence in another man's world. It was an embarrassing, absurd discovery—I had more or less taken Mazzini's place. I was doing *his* work and moving as mechanically through *his* fantasies as if I were some piece in a board game.

It rained that day, a steady rain that did not stop until late at night. Long puddles foamed and closed again behind passing cars moving along the street to the rhythm of the stoplights. The rain turned the old blackened snow into a glassy morass. It was cold. Mazzini was dead. He *had* to be dead.

3

Roll Call for a Drama at the End of the World

Lieutenant Commander Carl Weyprecht from Michelstadt, Hesse	Commander of the expedition on water and ice, ranking officer on the *Admiral Tegetthoff*
First Lieutenant Julius Payer from Teplitz, Bohemia	Commander of the expedition on land, cartographer to the Kaiser
Lieutenant Commander Gustav Brosch from Komotau, Bohemia	First officer (on board), purser
Midshipman Eduard Orel from Neutitschein, Moravia	Second officer (pilot)
Dr. Julius Kepes from Bari, Hungary	Medical officer
Captain Pietro Lusina from Fiume	Boatswain

Captain Elling Carlsen from Tromsø, Norway	Ice master and harpooner
Otto Krisch from Kremsier, Moravia	Machinist
Josef Pospischill from Prerau, Moravia	Stoker
Antonio Vecerina from Draga, near Fiume	Carpenter

Johann Orasch from Graz	Cook
Johann Haller from the Passeiertal, Tyrol	First hunter, medic, and dogsled driver
Alexander Klotz from the Passeiertal, Tyrol	Second hunter, medic, and dogsled driver

Oesterr.=unga
„Tegetthoff" vom Eise besetzt 8. August 1872
Brosch
Kepes.
Carl Weyprecht
Schiffslieutenant
Lusina
Höfer
Catarinich
Lukinovich
Stiglich
Sussich
Palmich
Lettis

… 50jährigen Jubiläum der

… Nordpol-Expedition 1872—1874.

Antonio Scarpa from Trieste	Able seamen
Antonio Zaninovich from Lesina	
Antonio Catarinich from Lussino	
Antonio Lukinovich from Brazza	
Giuseppe Latkovich from Fianona, near Albona	
Pietro Fallesich from Fiume	
Giorgio Stiglich from Buccari	
Vincenzo Palmich from Volosca, near Fiume	
Lorenzo Marola from Fiume	
Francesco Lettis from Volosca	
Giacomo Sussich from Volosca	
Lead dog Jubinal from northern Asia, bought in Vienna	Sled dogs
Gillis, origin unknown, bought in Vienna	
Matochkin, origin unknown, bought in Vienna	
Bop, origin unknown, bought in Vienna	
Novaya, origin unknown, bought in Vienna	
Zemlya, origin unknown, bought in Vienna	
Zumbu from Lapland, bought in the wild	
Pekel from Lapland, bought in Tromsø	
Torossy from the Arctic Ocean, born to Zemlya on board the *Admiral Tegetthoff*	
Two cats from Tromsø, nameless	
Josef Mazzini from Trieste	Follower

SUPPLEMENT: EXTRACTS FROM THE PERSONAL FILES OF THE COMMANDERS

WEYPRECHT, Carl, marine lieutenant, polar explorer. Born September 8, 1838, at Michelstadt im Odenwald in the Grand Duchy of Hesse-Darmstadt; from a prosperous

middle-class family; secondary education and trade school in Darmstadt. At age eighteen joins the Austrian Navy as a provisional cadet. In 1856–59 naval training on board the sailing frigate *Schwarzenberg*, the corvette *Archduke Friedrich*, the frigate *Danube*, and the steamship *Curtatone*; transoceanic voyages. In 1860–61, serves as officer, full cadet, on board the frigate *Radetzky* under the command of Wilhelm von Tegetthoff (later Admiral Tegetthoff); in 1861 is promoted by Tegetthoff to midshipman. In 1863–65 is training officer on board the brig *Husar.* Distinguishes himself for prudence and bravery aboard the ironclad frigate *Drache* during the battle of Lissa; awarded the Iron Crown third class and promoted to marine lieutenant during a voyage in the Gulf of Mexico, 1868. Before 1871 makes several voyages to Asia and America; cruises the coasts of Syria and Egypt and completes a comprehensive mapping of the Dalmatian coastline. Excellent knowledge of languages—Italian, Hungarian, Serbo-Croatian, French, English, and Norwegian. In 1871, together with Julius Payer and Count Hans Wilczek, undertakes a preliminary expedition to the Spitsbergens and Novaya Zemlya aboard the frigate *Isbjørn* to study weather and ice conditions in the northern Barents Sea; in 1872, at age thirty-three, commissioned as commander of the Imperial Austro-Hungarian North Pole Expedition.

Numerous publications on nautical science, meteorology, geomagnetism, and oceanography, including *The Metamorphoses of Ice, A Practical Introduction to the Observation of Polar Lights,* and *Future North Pole Expeditions and Their Certain Outcome.*

Knight of the Order of Leopold; awarded Iron Crown third class, Royal Prussian Order of the Red Eagle third class, Officer's Cross of the Royal Italian Order of Mauritius and Lazarus, Silver Laurel Wreath of the City of Frankfurt, Gold Medal of the Paris Congress of International Geography, Founders' Gold Medal of the London Geographical Society, etc., etc. (cf. Payer's decorations); honorary citizen of the cities of Fiume (Rijeka) and Trieste.

PAYER, Sir Julius von, first lieutenant, cartographer, alpine and arctic explorer, painter, writer. Born September 2, 1841, near Teplitz in Schönau, Bohemia; son of a riding instructor for the uhlans. Graduate of the cadet institute in Lobzova near Krakow and the Theresian Military Academy in Vienna Neustadt; in 1859 fights as an ensign of the 36th Infantry Regiment in the battle of Solferino; awarded the Cross for Distinguished Service in Battle and promoted to the rank of

first lieutenant. Stationed variously at Mainz, Frankfurt, Verona, Venice, Chioggia, and Jägerndorf; teaches history at the cadet institute in Eisenstadt and later works under Field Marshal von Fligely for the Military Geographic Institute. Spectacular mountain expeditions exploring the South Tyrolean Alps and the Hohe Tauern; mappings of the Lessini, Pasubio, Glockner, and Venice groups; more than thirty first-climbs in the Brenta, Adamello, and Presanella groups. In 1865–68 participates in systematic exploration and trigonometric survey of all sections of the extensive branches of the Ortler group; conquers sixty summits. In 1869–70 member of the Second German North Pole Expedition to Greenland as geographer, orographer, and glaciologist; discovery of Tyrol Fjord and Franz Josef Fjord while exploring 350 miles of the east coast of Greenland on foot. In 1871, along with Carl Weyprecht and Count Hans Wilczek, advances to 78° 48′ north latitude in the Barents Sea; supplementary mapping of the Spitsbergens. In 1872, at age thirty, assumes command on land of the Imperial Austro-Hungarian North Pole Expedition.

Numerous publications on cartography, geography, and arctic adventures, including *The Adamello–Presanella Alps, The Bocca di Brenta, The Ortler Alps, The Austrian Preliminary Expedition to Explore the Novaya Zemlya Sea, Concerning Cold, The Interior of Greenland, The Austro-Hungarian North Pole Expedition of 1872–74*, etc.

Awarded Iron Crown third class, Gold Medal of geographical societies of London and Paris; honorary member of geographical societies of Vienna, Berlin, Rome, Budapest, Dresden, Hamburg, Bremen, Hannover, Munich, Frankfurt am Main, and Geneva; honorary member of the Meteorological Society of Algiers, the Nautical Club of Hamburg, and the Earth Studies Association in Pressburg; honorary member of the French, English, and Italian alpine clubs; Knight of the French Legion of Honor; Royal Prussian Order of the Red Eagle third class, Royal Swedish Order of the North Star, Royal Italian Order of Mauritius and Lazarus, Order of the Italian Crown, Royal Portuguese Order of the Town and Sword, Order of the White Falcon of the Grand Duchy of Saxony; D.Phil. h.c., University of Prague; honorary citizen of the cities of Brno, Fiume, and Teplitz; enjoys the reputation of being the best dogsled driver of his time born below the Arctic Circle.

4

Chronicle of Farewells, or, Reality Is Divisible

In 1868, during my survey of the Ortler Alps, a newspaper containing a report on the German expedition undertaken by Koldewey reached my remote mountain tent. Around the evening fire I lectured my companions, shepherds and hunters, about the North Pole, sharing with them my amazement that there could be men with a capacity far beyond that of others for enduring the terrors of cold and darkness. At the time I had no idea that a year later I myself would be part of a North Pole expedition, no more than Haller, my sharpshooter at the time, could know that he would accompany me on my third journey. (*Julius Payer*)

Where did the farewells begin? And when? There were so many points of departure—the railroad platform at Vienna West Station, the floodgate at Geestemünde, the harbor of the northern Norwegian city of Tromsø; and a century later, an airport and a runway.

Five sailors on the *Admiral Tegetthoff* left families behind. As they said their good-byes, did they repeat the promises made to them? *We will discover new lands*. Did they talk about the pay, better than on other ships, and the grand life they would live on their return? *One thousand two hundred guldens in silver, equipment, and free board for two and a half years, maybe even three, maybe—but no, that could never happen—forever.* Those left behind did not know much more than that things were very different and cold in the place where their sons, brothers, and fathers were going, that no one had ever been there before, and that it would take a long time—longer than usual.

On Corpus Christi in the year 1872—May 31, a Friday—the Austro-Hungarian North Pole Expedition, including sled dogs, moved out as a unit for the first time. They boarded the train for Bremerhaven and left Vienna West Station at 6:30 p.m., wrapped in a cloud of smoke of which there is no record. It was not a grand departure. For two days they watched as the landscape passed their compartment windows, rolling back to where they had come from. Trübau in Moravia, Budweis, Prague, Dresden, Magdeburg, Braunschweig, Hannover, Bremen—at some stations they passed delegations extending their best wishes, with hands raised but not voices.

Each man senses, though without saying it, that difficult days lie ahead; and each is free to hope today for whatever he wishes; for the future lies open to no man's gaze. Yet we all feel, are keenly aware, that we serve the glory of our fatherland in a battle for the advancement of science and that at home our steps are followed with liveliest sympathy. (*Julius Payer*)

Sailors in their new clothes, standing at the compartment windows or lying back in their seats, bottles of brandy between their knees; the hunters Haller and Klotz, both in typical Passeiertal garb—embroidered loden jackets, wide-brimmed hats, and knee-length deerskin trousers (Payer had wanted his hunters in folk costume for their departure)—what did science and glory mean to these men compared with one thousand two hundred guldens in silver? One thousand two hundred guldens in silver, plus bonuses and a new land! They sit now in the train, getting acquainted in the dialects of four different languages. Italian will be the language on board ship. But ahead of them lies a day when Alexander Klotz, the tough Tyrolean, will sink beneath the snow of Franz Josef Land; emaciated, his furs in rags, his feet frozen, he will break into sobs, no longer responding either to exhortation or to comfort. And another day they will carry Otto Krisch, the twenty-nine-year-old machinist, across the ice in a coffin made by Antonio Vecerina. There, between basalt columns below the cliffs of that new land, they will cover him with stones. *Indescribable solitude lies over these snow-clad mountains . . .* Julius Payer will write in his diary. *When ebb and flood do not lift the groaning and straining drift ice, when the sighing wind is not brushing across the stony chinks, the stillness of death lies upon the ghostly pale landscape. People speak of the solemn silence of the forest, of the desert, even of a city wrapped in night. But what a silence lies over such a land and its cold glaciered mountains lost in impenetrable, vaporous distances—its very existence must remain, so it seems, a mystery for all time. . . . A man dies at the North Pole alone, fades like a will-o'-the-wisp, while a simple sailor lifts the keen and a grave of ice and stones waits for him outside. . . .*

But in the conversations on the train, it is only solemn and distant whiteness coming toward them; and if they should discover an island on their journey through the sea of ice, it will certainly be a beautiful land, silent and gentle.

At the time we pictured its valleys adorned with meadows and alive with reindeer undisturbed in the enjoyment of their asylum, far from all enemies. (*Julius Payer*)

The world outside the compartment windows grows steadily more foreign. But keeps its green. Fields of hops, poplared lanes, meadows, thatched brick houses. One summer begins.

On June 2 the expeditionary team arrived in Bremerhaven, and it found itself on the wharves of Geestemünde by evening of the same day. And there they stood—

some awed, others anxious—before the *Admiral Tegetthoff.* What a ship. And how new everything was. No algae or barnacles on its planks, no salty crust; it smelled of varnish, tar, and fresh wood. With iron plates mounted below the waterline, and an auxiliary steam engine built by Stabilimento Tecnico Triestino and capable of a hundred horsepower, this bark could move through drifting ice even in a calm; provisions for a thousand days had been delivered by the firm of Richers in Hamburg and by Carstens, a Lübeck canner; there were 130 tons of coal good for twelve hundred hours of steam-driven power—twelve hundred hours independent of wind in the sails. But how long would their journey through polar seas take? And how big was an iceberg? The *Admiral Tegetthoff* was 105 feet long and 24 feet wide. What good were three masts and a hundred horsepower against ice floes so large you could build palaces on them? It was cramped aboard ship; cramped in the officers' cabin, oppressive in the seamen's bunked quarters. The officers' mess was decorated with an engraving of a fancy phrase in Arabic: *In niz beguzared*—This too will pass.

Ten days slip by as final preparations are made. A waiver is presented for signature in the harbormaster's office: In the event of shipwreck, the Royal and Imperial North Pole Expedition will expect neither search parties nor rescue. They would either return under their own power or not return at all. The document bears the signatures of the officers—heading the list Carl Weyprecht's, in an elegant Italian hand slanting to the right, and the almost youthful flourish of Julius Payer. I cannot recall the marks of the sailors. There must have been some X's, too. Not all of them could read and write.

Early on the morning of June 13, 1872, a day of summery warmth, the *Admiral Tegetthoff* is towed by a municipal tug through the locks of Geestemünde and down the Weser. Trees and meadows, one last time. Then Weyprecht orders the sails set. The sea opens before them. It is the first time the Tyrolean hunters have seen the ocean.

Undaunted, we saw all the charms of creation diminish and fade as land sank farther and farther behind us; by evening the German coast had vanished from sight. . . . The crew is in high spirits. The merry songs of the Italians are borne off by a light evening breeze, and the regular rhythms of a Dalmatian ludro awaken memories of a sunny homeland soon to be exchanged for an antithesis that remains a mystery even in their imaginations. (*Julius Payer*)

Near Helgoland there is no more singing. The *Admiral Tegetthoff* barely eludes the coastal shoals. Bad weather moves in. Heavy seas, rain, cold—no, this is no cold yet. *Haller the Tyrolean is quite seasick,* the machinist Krisch writes in his diary. This goes on for two weeks. Then the rocks of Norway rise up from the waves, the same blue-green as the swells. The wind slackens.

After a rather stormy voyage we anchored on July 2nd, 1872, at Tromsø, where the harpooner Elling Carlsen came on board, a man of sixty years and with considerable experience in ice seas, who had made a respectable name for himself circumnavigating the Spitsbergens. (*Gustav Brosch*)

Stormy weather had held us back at the Lofotens, so that we did not arrive in Tromsø until July 3rd. (*Julius Payer*)

Arrived in Tromsø at 11 p.m. on July 4th. Dampened our fire and anchored in Tromsø Sound. (*Otto Krisch*)

On the second, third, fourth of July: the origins of such contradictions about their arrival date can be reconstructed without difficulty. By conjecture, for instance, about the influence of the midnight sun, which can erase the difference between day and night; nor is there any doubt that someone keeping time in heavy seas can lose a day or two; or one man may have meant the entrance into the sound, another their setting foot on the dock. There are, moreover, definite clues for objectively dating their arrival, but I shall not speak of those. A day cannot be more real than in the consciousness of a man who has lived it. And so I say: The expedition arrived in Tromsø on the second, arrived on the third, arrived on the fourth of July. Reality is divisible. (Even among the small party on board the *Tegetthoff*, the journals kept by the lower ranks were so different from those of their superiors that it sometimes seems as if the men in the bunks and those in the cabins were writing chronicles not of one but of several wildly different expeditions. Each man reported from his own world of ice.)

Tromsø. It is cool here and the southern summer is only a memory. Sometimes fog rolls in. Once again they prepare for a departure, the most serious one, taking on equipment and stores, buying sheet iron, steel, and dried cod in a city built of wood. Weyprecht hires Norwegian divers to repair a leak; the *Tegetthoff* has taken on a great deal of water in the storms of the last weeks. The lieutenant waits in vain for the walrus hunters to return from their hunting grounds in the north. He will have to set sail without news about the limits and patterns of this year's drift ice. For the sailors of the *Tegetthoff* these last days in the inhabited world are also a time for modest attempts to practice the life awaiting them in fine salons if they are lucky enough to return from the wilderness—a life of honors and invitations, of unaccustomed conversation and deference. Andreas Aagaard, the Austrian consul in Tromsø, invites them to dinner; others follow his example. No voyage in their lives has ever brought the sailors such admiration as the mere intention to sail to the North Pole does now. The North Pole must be more desirable, then, more important than the coasts of America and India, which several of them have visited. Not until months later, deep in the ice and darkness of polar night, will Julius Payer enlighten the last of these innocents:

At temperatures of 20 to 30 degrees below zero (Réaumur), the seed of wisdom was planted in these sons of nature. But the climate proved unfavorable to its growth. To their painful disappointment they learned of the nature and worthlessness of the ''North Pole,'' that it is not a country, not an empire to be conquered, nothing but lines intersecting at a point, nothing of which can be seen in reality!

I have attempted to imagine what an innocent must feel when he suddenly realizes—on a ship frozen fast and drifting, surrounded by all the terrors of ice and darkness—that his goal is invisible in any case, a worthless point, a cipher. I got no further than the attempt; I could not re-create that feeling of painful disappointment. But they are still in Tromsø, getting spruced up for the reception at the home of the consul.

Invited to dinner with Herr Aagart on July 6th, remaining until midnight; the sun no longer sets now and we return on board in bright sunshine. Invited on the 7th by Herr Stiftsmann of Tromsø to his villa high in forests above Tromsø, returned on board at 2 a.m.

On July 8th visit Lapps in their gamma *beneath Kilpis-Jaure mountain, where they live with their great reindeer herds; each* gamma *is inhabited by a clan, whose wealth consists of 3–500 head of reindeer. The* gamma*'s exterior is covered with earth, its interior with reindeer hides. A cooking pot hangs from a chain. The people are clad in reindeer hides; they are quite illiterate, most of them heathens as well, believing in Jubinal or Aika.*

A multitude of herding dogs, their own special breed, likewise live with them in the gamma; *we bought one for 2½ talers specie and brought it on board; it was given the name Pekel, ''Devil'' in Lapp, but later rechristened Pekelino by the sailors.* (*Otto Krisch*)

Weyprecht is not particularly fond of dogs. Payer is quite pleased; with six Newfoundlands and two Lapland dogs he believes he now has a full sled team he can use to travel on the ice, just as he did two years before on the coast of Greenland. But despite the blows of the Tyrolean hunters, the dogs do not lose their wildness: *There were places belowdecks where only their friends could be certain they would not be torn to pieces.* (*Julius Payer*)

Accompanied by his hunters, the commander on land climbs the cliffs above Tromsø and from their heights checks the accuracy of his barometer. On July 10 they stand atop a peak their Lapp guide Dilkoa calls Sallas Uoivi. Below them, fjords, rocky broken land, and the sea.

From the summit we saw an immense black column of smoke ascending in the calm air to some 1,500 feet—the north end of Tromsø stood in flames. (*Julius Payer*)

From on board the *Tegetthoff* lying at anchor, things looked different:

On July 10th fire broke out in the northern part of town, reducing several houses and sheds to ashes; a boat with most of our crew and firefighting equipment was sent ashore. After 2½ hours of hard work, the fire was put out, whereupon the fire department commissioner expressed his thanks to Commander Weyprecht for the assistance. . . .

On July 11th, I made a tour of the town, which has few remarkable sights, all its houses and even its two churches being of wood, as is the concert hall, where a musician was performing on the harp.

On July 12th the steamer arrived; I received 3 letters in the post, from Anton, father, and Theodor; was unable to receive any that might be arriving later, as we cannot wait for the next steamer; at 5 p.m. I shall go to the steambath and then to a supper I have ordered at the Hotel "Nielsen."

At 9 a.m. on the 13th a mass was read for us in the Catholic church; followed by refreshments at the rectory; I then applied all the money I had for the purchase of 1/2 keg of wine and 40 bottles of beer, returning on board relieved of my last shilling, for we depart Tromsø tomorrow and in arctic seas we shall not need money, but a good nip of wine now and then; fire relit at 10 p.m. (*Otto Krisch*)

By midnight the *Admiral Tegetthoff* has full steam. Only now does ice master and harpooner Elling Carlsen climb the gangplank; he is the only man on board who owes no obedience to the Austrian kaiser. He enters the mess carrying a mighty walrus spear, a coat of polar-bear skins tossed over his shoulder. How old he is. The sailors here, even the commanders, could be his sons. The most precious items in Carlsen's pack are a white periwig to be worn on upcoming holidays and the Order of Olaf he was awarded for his circumnavigation of the Spitsbergens. How many walruses has he killed with that spear? He has lost count. Then it is morning, July 14, 1872, a Sunday.

On Sunday morning we left the quiet little capital of Europe's north. The passengers aboard the mail steamer from Hamburg, which had just entered the harbor, greeted us with prolonged cheers, and then we steamed through the narrow straits of the Qual and Grøt sounds, beneath the cliffs of Sandø and Rysø, toward open sea. Captain Carlsen served as our pilot. As we emerged from these narrows, fog came in and enveloped the massive tor of Fuglø. Here we dampened the engine fires and set our sails. On July 15th, we sailed to the north, the glacier-covered Norwegian coast still visible. On July 16th, in the blue distance, Europe's North Cape came into view. . . .

The ideal goal *of our voyage was the Northeast Passage. Its true purpose, however, was to explore the seas or lands to the northeast of Novaya Zemlya.* (*Julius Payer*)

I picture the black waters of a sound turned smooth again behind the *Admiral Tegetthoff.* Krisch's banner of smoke still hangs in the sky above Tromsø harbor when the passengers disembark from the mail steamer that morning. There is no wind. Breakfast is being prepared in the Hotel Nielsen. The topic of the day is the *Tegetthoff.* Where are they headed, did you say? To Japan? By way of the pole? There are letters for the crew in the mailbag, two of them for machinist Otto Krisch. They will be held in safekeeping for him.

And then I see Josef Mazzini walking around as if in a museum, surveying the equipment strewn across the floor of the room he rents from the stonemason's widow, and sometimes he doubts whether all this will protect him against the ice—the down clothes, the canvas boots, the sleeping bag, and all the other essentials for his masquerade. Outside it is July and hot. But he is preparing for the various stages of being catapulted out of summer into the cold—Copenhagen, Oslo, Tromsø, Longyearbyen—by air; and from Longyearbyen by ship to the northeast, into the Arctic Ocean, farther and farther, to the coast of Franz Josef Land and, if he has his way, on to the Bering Strait and Yokohama.

"You're crazy," Anna Koreth says. But she knows he is in earnest. I see Mazzini in Anna Koreth's apartment, trying to make her understand about his trip to the Spitsbergens. Her guests for the evening want to hear explanations, too. No, not serious ones, just in general. (The Italian doesn't leave it simply at "the Spitsbergens," and they would also have accepted "exploring glaciers" without any particular question, as a whim. But a trip following the route of some sailboat long since sunk in the Arctic Ocean? Who would go to the Arctic just to "imagine" what once was, what could have been?)

The guests sit at the table, are still sitting at the table, but Mazzini is alone with Anna now; he says what he has to say to her. Then they can no longer listen to each other, but they go on talking all evening—each from his own world of ice.

5

First Digression
The Northeast Passage, or, The White Way to India— A Dream Reconstructed

Roundabout the lonely crown of the North Pole stand stone pyramids, each marking a limit for the advance of the human spirit. A few gulls hover at its zenith, and its ice floes grant the safety of asylum to seals pursued by harpoons. But until now it has proven an unreachable goal for voyages of discovery.

Just as any development can only gradually ripen and progress to greater goals, so, too, the weak light of the cosmogonic dawn spread very slowly from the flat Homeric disk across the land of the Hyperboreans. Millennia passed before the thirst for knowledge overcame the North Pole's terrors—with which the Arabs once imagined Siberia to be filled. Around the sun-bathed Orient, however, the world lay buried for millennia beneath delusions and fables, whose crude and naive triviality was mitigated only by the ethical edifications of ancient poet-philosophers.

In that world ruled by the spirit of caste, no breeze of truth moved to scatter the phantasms of searing heat, killing frost, or plunging seas from which no sailor returned, of ominous gods ruling wind and sea or of ants guarding hoards of gold. The earth, after all, rested in the endless isolation of space, and the crystalline bowl of the sky rested upon the columns of its mountains—all of it unbalanced, since the rich vegetation of the tropics outweighed the sparse zones of the north. Such were the presuppositions: three mighty walls, unscaled for millennia, overgrown in time with religious dogma, and set in a ring around a small circle of knowledge.

Once men understood the earth to be a sphere, however, theoretical notions of climate and a very vague idea of climatic zones arose. Four centuries before Christ, these were given some scientific precision by Pytheas of Massilia and his theory of a polar circle. At almost the same time Alexander's drive to the wonderland of India created a paradise of commerce and navigation, and even now, 1,800 years later, we ought not shy from even the most upside-down shortcut to reach it—through the ice. (*Julius Payer*)

While my imagination pictures the *Admiral Tegetthoff* steaming past its first fields of drift ice and Josef Mazzini on his Scandinavian Airlines flight watching clouds tower up from below, I let myself sink gently back into the darkness of time, glide down through the centuries to the beginnings of a great longing. For even in those days, as the Italian sailors of the *Tegetthoff* set their sails, navigators in the Western world had not yet dreamed one of their longest dreams to its end. Somewhere along the polar coast of Siberia, holding steady to the northeast, there had to be a shortcut rimmed with pack ice and leading to Japan, China, and India, a route from the Atlantic to the Pacific—the *Northeast Passage.*

Prior to 1872 whole fleets had vanished in the pack ice without ever having found a Northeast Passage. Chroniclers had filled folios with accounts of catastrophes in the ice, with reports of ships departing laden with goods, gifts, heavy cannon, and letters of introduction to the emperors of Japan and

China, but arriving nowhere, never returning. In the end even the chroniclers no longer knew how many sailors had been lost in the search for the northeastern route. A thousand dead? A thousand four hundred or more? The statistical compilations of disaster were contradictory and incomplete, vain attempts to convert the horrors of the fabled route into numbers. (Officialdom was having difficulty with its categories: A fleet of walrus hunters freezes fast in the pack ice and drifts steadily northeast, well beyond Cape Chelyuskin in Siberia, only to sink, crushed between walls of press ice; were the dead and castaways in such a catastrophe to be entered as victims of the Northeast Passage, or were they merely run-of-the-mill victims of the Arctic Ocean?) The ships sank. The chroniclers wrote. The arctic world was indifferent.

Whoever goes in search of the prehistory of this northeastern dream must think in terms not of centuries but of millennia, must look for images of a cold sea on the far side of the year zero by Christian reckoning. He will have to try to imagine the northern voyages of Pytheas of Massilia or Himilko the Carthaginian, the dragon-headed boats of the Normans and their helmsmen—Bjarne Herjulfsson and Leif Eriksson, for instance, who sailed and rowed to the coasts of North America even before the turn of the first millennium. He will recall Erik the Red, lord of Greenland and Iceland; Ohthere, who sailed around North Cape and across the White Sea to the land of the Biarmians, to Siberia; or Erik Blodøks, the "Blood-axe," and others who set foot on the Spitsbergens and the lands of the far north long before the explorers of modern times. . . . But I shall stop this game of running time backward and halt at an era when these early arctic voyages were as scattered and forgotten as the achievements of classical cosmography, shifting my attention to a castle in Castile. It is the castle of Tordesillas. The year is 1494. It is June.

In this summer and this year a treaty between Spain and

Portugal was signed at Tordesillas, and sealed with a papal bull "for all eternity" by the father of Lucrezia and Cesare Borgia, Pontifex Maximus Alexander VI, a lover of whores and art. The New World and all its lands, both those already discovered and those still unknown, were to be divided between the peoples of the Iberian peninsula. The border was the meridian running from pole to pole 1,200 nautical miles west of the Cape Verde Islands; lands east of this line were ceded to Portugal, those west to Spain. The deal struck at Tordesillas, parceling up the globe like a piece of pasture, gave the Spaniards and Portuguese a monopoly not only on new lands but also on the sea-lanes leading westward across the Atlantic to where treasure abounded and the air was heavy with spices. Last but not least, the verdict of the Borgia pope Alexander was intended to force the losers at this game of avarice, the English and Dutch, to northern routes—into the ice. The events of the years before and the decades after the papal verdict are hardly worth specific mention.

For the plain truth about the age of discovery was recorded not by European cosmographers in their studies, but in reports like the Nahuatl text of the Aztecs that gives a good picture of the arriving Europeans. "The chalk-faced men were delighted. Like monkeys they weighed the gold in their hands and sat upon the floor, faces filled with pleasure and souls gathering new energy. They shone. Their bodies expanded at the sight; their hunger was hot. They were greedy for gold like hungry swine. . . ." No matter what the news brought home by the navigators, in the Old World people held on hysterically to the myths of an inexhaustible golden paradise. No desert was barren enough, no reality desolate enough to calm the madness. Sixteenth-century polar expeditions were sent out to look for yellow pebbles in the layer of arctic debris that covered icebergs. There had to be *gold*—a token of islands yet to be discovered beyond the walls of pack ice, richer than the new lands of Spain. (They will throw anything remotely nonessential overboard and load their ships with pyrites, with worthless stones.)

As always in such times of greatness, heroic figures dominated this early "awe-inspiring" period. They were the idols of the arctic voyagers who came after them and even now are more familiar to us than the cultures their adventures ultimately destroyed. Between 1492 and 1504, Christoforo Colombo of Genoa, alias Cristóbal Colón, undertakes four voyages west across the Atlantic Ocean. He sails away trusting the accuracy of a skewed, white-blotched map drawn by a Florentine cosmographer named Paolo dal Pozzo Toscanelli, and glad to be in the pay of Isabel of Castile, patroness of the Holy Inquisition and mother of Joan the Mad. (Is it coincidental or symbolic that Joan the Mad will later succumb to her idiocy in the castle of Tordesillas and die there?) In the course of his journeys, Colón lands on islands in the Caribbean and mistakes them for Japan, lands on the shores of Central and South America and thinks he is in India, discovers the estuary of the Orinoco and believes it to be the delta of the Ganges. He dies at last in 1506 in Valladolid without ever having recognized his errors.

In 1497, King Manuel I of Portugal commissions Vasco da Gama, Count of Vidigueira, to search for a sea route to the lands of spice. He sails around the Cape of Good Hope at the bottom of Africa and lands in the *real* India, opening up a paradise where colonial powers can display their might.

In 1520, Fernão de Magahães, sailing in a southwesterly direction, discovers a route that cuts between the South American continent and Tierra del Fuego and leads from the Atlantic to the Pacific. The following year he is killed in the Philippines. The Strait of Magellan endures.

While Magahães was still searching the coasts of the New World for a passage to the Pacific, Hernán Cortés began destroying the empire of the Aztecs. Little more than a decade later, the sailing swineherd Francisco Pizarro deals with the civilization of the Incas as per instructions of the Church and Spain. He has the Incas baptized and executed, crushes all opposition, and dedicates the massacre to the Lord Jesus and the Spanish crown.

But what the heroes of the Iberian peninsula had found on their western, southwestern, or southeastern voyages—new trade routes, gold, spices, and lands—could surely be found by way of shorter northern routes and on behalf of English kings and Russian czars. As early as 1497, Giovanni Caboto from Genoa, alias John Cabot, sailed in the service of Henry VII, departing from Bristol on a northwest heading across the Atlantic. Cabot reached the American continent thirteen months before Cristóbal Colón. He landed in the north of the New World, in Newfoundland, and like Colón, he thought he was somewhere else—in Cathay. In China. A procession of adventurers followed Cabot's route as well—the brothers Gaspar and Miguel de Corte Real, for example. They reached Newfoundland, too, and then vanished at sea. Then came Giovanni da Verrazzano, a Florentine commissioned by the French, the Spaniard Esteban Gómez, and even German captains such as Pining and Pothurst. . . . They brought back news of cold cliffs and icebergs but neither gold nor coordinates for a short route to the riches of the East Indies. With each voyage it became clearer that a massive land barrier, America, extended far to the north and blocked all sea-lanes leading west around the world. But somewhere, be it in the thickest drift ice, even this continent had to come to an end at some northernmost cape that a ship could sail around. There had to be a gaping crack between where the Old World ended and the New began, a cold strait, a waterway to the Pacific. Without ever having seen it, the cosmographers of the day dubbed this hope *Fretum Anianum*, the Anian Strait. Not until centuries later would such a strait actually be discovered and entered in atlases under the name of one of the first people to pass through it, the Danish navigator Vitus Bering. But long

after the voyage of the Dane, who had sailed from a Siberian harbor, the riddle remained how one might reach the Bering Strait from the shores of Europe. The game offered three possibilities:

Sail northwest across the Atlantic and then along the coast of the New World, holding steady to the northwest.

Sail northeast along the cliffs of the Old World and Siberia, holding steady to the northeast.

Sail hard to the north, always north, directly over the pole and then beyond it, beyond it to the South Seas.

Northeast Passages, Northwest Passages, walls of pack ice, ice-free straits, the end of the world, the Pacific!, stones and capes, islands, drift ice and a good wind—who wouldn't want to find a way through all the chaos and riddles, *ACROSS THE ARCTIC OCEAN* to paradise, and return with all the treasures of the East, to approach princes and lords of commerce and say: I was the first!

The first ships sent to search for a Northwest Passage have already vanished and the waves of cold seas have closed over unsuccessful explorers, but the idea of a Northeast Passage is still in the planning stage. In the spring of 1525 an envoy of Vasily III Ivanovich, grand prince of Moscow, arrives at the papal court in Rome. He calls himself Dimitri Gerasimov. At the behest of Pope Clement VII he is received by the historian Paolo Giovio. The scholar and the envoy meet, and their acquaintanceship results in a vague theory to feed the fantasies of Christian navigation. Gerasimov inspires his host to write a memorandum in Latin, which Giovio presents to a select public that same year. The historian says that according to Gerasimov the Severnaya Dvina River, bearing the water of countless tributaries, flows to the north with torrential force. The resultant sea is so broad that by holding to the

coast on the right one can in all probability sail to China, if no new land interposes. . . . The memorandum is translated into Italian and causes a furor—particularly since that year reports arrive from Augsburg about Muscovite travelers who have discussed with German scholars the possibility of a northeastern sea route to the lands of spices. Within two years the first rumors of this news from Muscovy have spread, and Robert Thorne, a cosmographer and merchant born in Bristol but living in Seville, appeals to Henry VIII in a memorandum of his own. Thorne commends to the English crown, along with routes no less adventurous, the passage along the Siberian coast. England would thus be able to reach the Spice Islands more quickly than the Portuguese or the Spaniards. But King Henry considers execution blocks more important than icebergs. And so two more decades pass before the undaunted faith in a Northeast Passage sets not just pens in motion but ships as well.

In 1549, Baron Sigismund zu Herberstain, Neyperg, and Guettenhag at last gives the northeastern dream the help it needs for a breakthrough. His treatise *Rerum moscoviticarum commentarii* is published in Vienna that year. In his account of his experiences in the East as ambassador of Kaiser Maximilian I to the Russian court, the baron not only provides a description of an empire known by few, but also includes journal entries of Russian travelers and geographical reports supplementing the information about a Northeast Passage furnished by Paolo Giovio and Dimitri Gerasimov. His supplements and descriptions are so convincing that they are published in variant accounts and translated into several languages. Four years after the first printing of Herberstain's intimations, the first navigator follows the dream to the northeast—where he freezes to death. His name is Sir Hugh Willoughby.

English businessmen found the Company of Merchant Adventurers in 1553, and that same year their mentor, Sebas-

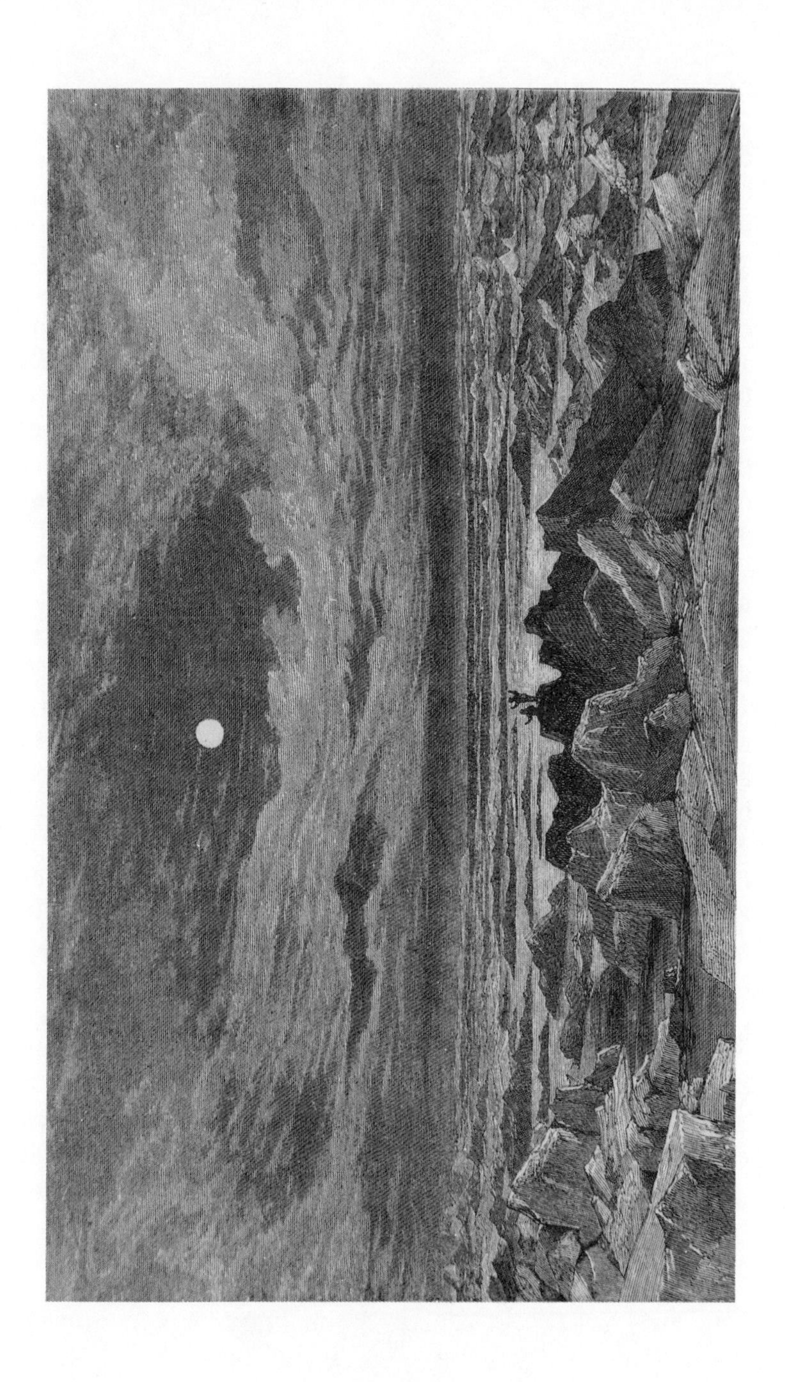

tian Cabot, son of John Cabot and pilot major of England, commissions Sir Hugh Willoughby to conduct a search for the Northeast Passage. Willoughby, who is given command of three ships—the *Bona Esperanza,* the *Edward Bonaventure,* and the *Bona Confidentia*—is so firm in his resolve to discharge his duties that while still on the Thames he has his ships lead-plated to protect against the shipworms of the Indian seas. They sail that summer. By September the ice along the Kola Peninsula of Russia is so thick that two of the three ships are frozen fast. Willoughby orders a camp erected on shore. The first arctic wintering by a European expedition begins. Willoughby and sixty-four crew members remain behind in their improvised shelter, but the crew of the *Edward Bonaventure,* under their officers Richard Chancellor and Stephen Burrough, manage to continue through the drift ice of the White Sea to the mouth of the Severnaya Dvina. Then the ice closes over the last open channels. The English take to land, and the Permiak inhabitants of these coasts accompany them to Moscow. There Czar Ivan IV, the Terrible, receives the navigators in the Golden Hall of the Kremlin. The following summer the *Edward Bonaventure* returns to England, riding low in the water from the goods it carries. Even before festivities can be held in London to honor the returnees, Russian walrus hunters find Willoughby's camp—a graveyard. The crews of both ships have died during the polar night, of cold, starvation, or scurvy. The walrus hunters report that they found the corpse of Sir Hugh Willoughby bent over the log of the *Bona Confidentia.* Willoughby's northeast expedition is the start of a dance of death that will continue into the time of Payer and Weyprecht and beyond.

6

Flights into the Internal and External Void

The road to the interior of the Arctic is a hard one. The wanderer who travels it must summon all his mental and physical energies to wring some scant knowledge from the mystery he hopes to penetrate. He must have unutterable patience to gird himself against disappointment and misfortune, to pursue his goal even when he has become a plaything of chance. His goal dare not be to satisfy his own ambition, but rather to expand our knowledge. He spends years in the most dreadful exile, far from friends, from all the pleasures of life, beset by dangers and the burden of loneliness. And therefore only the ideal of his goal can support him; otherwise he will wander, a victim of mental ambiguity, through an internal and external void. (*Julius Payer*)

While collecting and stacking the baggage that has slowly taken over his floor in the last few days, Josef Mazzini knocks over a half-full glass from the previous evening. I see him on the first morning of his trip, July 26, 1981, kneeling in his room to rub salt into the puddle of red wine soaking into the white wool carpet. He will brush away the salt when he gets back. Or so he intends. It will be dry and pale pink then. Two, maybe three months older, he will kneel on the carpet again, just like this, as if only the short time usually needed for such chores has passed between the strewing and removing of the salt—and for a moment he will recall everything that still lies before him now. Josef Mazzini starts several other small tasks this morning, without completing them—opens a tin of tea and doesn't close it, pulls a drawer out halfway and when he pushes it back in creates an incidental mess or two that he will take care of on his return. Such tasks, begun and then interrupted, will function as connections to the reality he is about to leave behind. Once he has departed, Josef Mazzini will be as far away from me as the crew on the *Admiral Tegetthoff.* That I knew him—and not the machinist Krisch or the boatswain Lusina—permits me little more than an opportunity to re-create probable situations, situations not recorded in Mazzini's journals. And so I arrange the few hints at my disposal, fill the lacunae with guesses, and arriving at the end of a chain of clues, feel how arbitrary it is to say: This is how it was. I feel as if Mazzini's departure is a transition from reality into probability.

I can recall an afternoon, long after Mazzini's disappearance, when with Anna Koreth I entered his room for the first time. The book dealer wore a smock and a kerchief, as if to protect herself from a great layer of dust. In reality, hardly enough particles had gathered in those months to leave behind a visible handprint on a desk or bookcase. Anna Koreth opened the window. The draft of cold air rolled smooth and steady over the windowsill like water over a weir, and a door slammed shut with such a bang that the stonemason's widow—as always busy with her business at the far end of a corridor—held her breath for a moment and the knitting machine fell silent. Anna Koreth opened a drawer, removed some nickel-plated cutlery, closed it, wrapped dishes (and the tea tin) in newspaper, and stuffed it all in a cardboard box. By evening the room had been emptied out. Salt trickled from the wool of the carpet as we rolled it up. The pale pink stain vanished like a clump of dirt on a snowball rolled across a winter meadow. By then I was already so familiar with Mazzini's journals that I tumbled from this red wine stain onto an ice floe: Mazzini had described how polar bears are hunted by helicopter and stunned by guns loaded with tranquilizers.

The animals rear up—the movement is inimitable and almost charming—noses held high to catch a scent. The helicopter closes in, and then something happens that hardly ever happens in the Arctic. The bears take flight, trotting off, picking up speed. Then it is no longer a trot, but an elastic, powerful gallop. They leap the wide cracks between the floes, swim canals, and change direction suddenly and unexpectedly. But then the helicopter is above them, the darts are shot, the gallop becomes a clumsy stagger. Then they are lying on the ice, a good distance apart. Three of them. A tooth is ripped from each mouth. Beside the skull, a puddle of blood seeps into the ice. A metal tag is punched in an ear with a pair of pliers; a thin red rivulet runs down the pelt, which is then sprayed with a large dye marker. This is how they gather information about the route the bears follow across hundreds of miles of ice. Crystals of ice quickly form over the bloodstain; it fades.

(And the stain leads to yet another memory: In the course of their adventures the crew of the *Admiral Tegetthoff* used their Lefaucheux rifles and Werndl carbines to kill sixty-seven polar bears. The cadavers were divvied up with axes and ice saws, and always in the same way: the brains for the officers, the tongue for Kepes the medical officer, the heart for Orasch the cook, the blood for men with scurvy, the loin and thighs for the common mess; skull, backbone, and ribs went to the sled dogs; the hide was put in a barrel and the liver tossed out as garbage.) The crystals of salt left on the bare wood floor reminded me of nothing. As we left, the stonemason's widow was sitting as always at her knitting machine; she barely looked at the money Anna Koreth gave her. It was late. Snow began to fall in the darkness.

In the months before this last summer and his departure, Mazzini had kept up a steady correspondence that gradually brought out the contrast between his own notions about the world of Weyprecht and Payer's polar voyage and present realities in the Arctic. The exchange of letters with the governor of the Spitsbergens, the representatives of the Norwegian Polar Institute, and the offices of the Store Norske Spitsbergen Kulkompani had begun casually, almost playfully, but eventually led to firm arrangements, turning Mazzini's fantasies about such a trip into precise plans. I do not think that at the very beginning he had definite intentions about the trip, had *really* wanted to take it. It looks more as if things took their own course and that only subsequently did Mazzini try to pass this off as *his* decision. By the end of this correspondence, the arrangements included both the confirmed shelter of a guest room in Longyearbyen and a reservation for a berth on board the *Cradle*, a trawler with 3,200 available horsepower and standard fittings for operating in ice. Nevertheless, the closer and more accessible the Arctic became, the more inhospitable, unfriendly, and sometimes even threatening it seemed. In the icy wastes of his fantasies and mind games Josef Mazzini had needed no down clothing, no protection against glaring sunlight, and no gun. But now . . . The world of arctic islands, which until then had served merely as the stage and backdrop for his imagination, took on harsh and bizarre forms that both frightened and attracted him the closer he got. And so he headed for it.

"Dear Herr Mazzini," Governor Ivar Thorsen wrote in his first reply from Longyearbyen, "although I have great respect for your interest in polar history, I doubt whether you have been sufficiently informed about conditions in the Norwegian Arctic. Please put from your mind as quickly as possible any intention of sailing in a fishing cutter from the Spitsbergens to the North Barents Sea. Such a plan would be a very risky venture at any time of the year. Besides which, there are neither fishermen nor boats here. Concerning your interest in joining one of the research expeditions of the Norwegian Polar Institute, I suggest you apply to the appropriate office in Oslo. But do not set your hopes too high. As you know, both Novaya Zemlya and Franz Josef Land are Soviet territory. Whatever your plans there, you will have to present them to Soviet officials and not to me. Enclosed you will find some basic information for tourists. Sincerely yours, Ivar Thorsen."

Information for Tourists

Svalbard is the collective name for all the islands lying in the Arctic Ocean between 10° and 35° east longitude and 74° and 81° north latitude; this includes the Spitsbergen group, Kvitøya, Kong Karls Land, and Bjørnøya (Bear Island). *Svalbard,* an old Norse name first recorded in the *Icelandic Annals* of the twelfth century, evokes the character of this land of basalt, metamorphic sediments, and red and gray granite. It means "cold coasts." But when the Dutch navigator Willem Barents reached the Spitsbergens in 1596, both the annals and the land itself had been forgotten. Barents is therefore considered their discoverer. Since 1925 Svalbard has been part of the Kingdom of Norway. The chief representative of government on the archipelago is the *sysselmann,* or governor. The address for his office is 9170 Longyearbyen. His instructions should be followed implicitly.

Travel Restrictions

Although passport or visa is not required, proof of the ability to survive in the open under arctic conditions is. There are neither hotels nor inns open to the general public on

Svalbard. Nor are there arrangements for having meals furnished. All travelers who have not arranged for housing prior to arrival must therefore bring with them equipment suitable for a stay in the wilderness: tent, sleeping bag, provisions, clothes appropriate for arctic weather, land and sea maps, compass, signal lamps, weapons, etc. Upon arrival, every traveler's equipment is inspected by local officials. Anyone whose equipment and supplies are inadequate will be denied entry and must leave the archipelago with the same airplane or ship on which he arrived.

Landscape

The islands of Svalbard are mountain ranges cut by deep ravines and indented with fjords. There is little vegetation. There are moss and lichens, even flowers, but no trees. Large areas are completely bare. The coastline follows along steep cliffs, palisades, and calving glaciers. Almost two-thirds of the archipelago's 62,049 square kilometers lies beneath glaciers. There are no paths or roads outside the settlements: Longyearbyen, Ny Ålesund, Barentsburg, and Pyramiden.

Climate and Light

Svalbard is one of the few areas in the high Arctic accessible by sea for longer periods during the year. A secondary current of the Gulf Stream keeps the west coast of the Spitsbergens free of ice during the summer. Even in summer months the air temperature seldom exceeds 10° Celsius; in winter it falls to −35° Celsius, on rare occasions to −40°. The summers are foggy, with weather conditions generally very changeable. In Longyearbyen the *midnight sun* shines from April 21 to August 21. The *period of darkness* lasts from October 28 to February 14. With each degree of latitude farther north, the periods of both midnight sun and polar night are six days longer.

Settlements and Flight Connections

The permanent settlements of Svalbard were founded by coal-mining companies—the Norwegian Store Norske Spitsbergen Kulkompani and the Soviet Trust Artikugol. Approximately 1,200 Norwegians and 2,100 Soviets are permanent residents. SAS flies routes between Tromsø and Longyearbyen; Aeroflot, between Murmansk and Longyearbyen. Passenger ships dock regularly in Svalbard in the summer. The frequency of flights changes according to the season.

Danger: Polar Bears

Polar bears migrate during the summer months, primarily in the eastern and northern regions, but one can run into bears on the west coast as well. They are usually very hungry and therefore very dangerous. Travelers should observe the following rules:

Always keep at a safe distance. Never try to lure the animals closer with food—either from a boat or even from the window in your lodging. Polar bears attack without warning.

In order to have sufficient warning of an approaching bear, always keep your garbage in a direct line of sight at least 100 meters from your tent or door.

Polar bears are protected by law, with no exception. Should it nevertheless prove necessary to shoot one out of self-defense, aim not for the head, but for the shoulders and chest. You thereby run less danger of missing your shot, and should the first one not prove lethal you gain time for a second. The killing of a bear must be officially reported. The hide and skull must be turned in to the Governor's Office.

* * *

And so on.

The bird species of Svalbard have been counted. The names of the lichens and moss are registered, their propagation cycles known. There are instructions for saving one's life in an emergency. The depth of the seas has been measured, the reefs and cliffs are studded with lighthouses, and even the steepest elevations have been mapped. The land for which Josef Mazzini departs is remote, but no longer one enchanted by myth. The Spitsbergens lie there in the Arctic Ocean, properly surveyed and administered—a cold raft, the last stony foothold on the journey to another time.

Mazzini leaves Vienna at noon July 26, feeling dazed, the way you feel when you wake up, grope about, and gradually realize that it was *this* room, this wall, the bed you're lying on that you were just dreaming about. Instead of melting away, the objects and props of the dream become clearer and more palpable on awakening.

As the plane to Oslo climbs to cruising altitude, the thrust presses him gently back against his seat. The slant of the horizon slices through the scene rotating in the frame of the cabin window. Then for a moment the machine is no longer ascending, but rather the world is sinking away, where it lies shimmering on the surface of the sea's green depths. Then the water ruffles. The cloud cover closes to white. No more ground. No land.

Even on board the airplane Josef Mazzini—like all flying pedestrians—tries to remain *below.* At each rare opening in the clouds he embellishes the flat relief of visible land with details and memories from earlier trips, and turns to the salesman beside him, who is on his way to a business deal and his "future." He strikes up a shapeless conversation about those hidden landscapes. The salesman talks about national borders and the cities they are flying over. He knows nothing about dikes and poplared lanes. In Copenhagen the salesman takes his leave, they wish each other good luck.

After this stopover Josef Mazzini has no memories of the land below to draw on. Whatever appears in the openings in the clouds is foreign to him now. When he stares at the back of the seat ahead of him, he sees the Tyrolean Alexander Klotz in Passeiertal costume at the window of a train compartment. Across the empty blue of the sky drifts the plume of smoke of a train heading for Bremerhaven, then the smoke from the funnel of the *Tegetthoff*. Sled dogs are yapping in the cargo hold of the DC-9. The distant rumble of the engines is the seething of keel water, a wedge ribbed by waves and spreading toward infinity—pieces of ice floating on it, and salty foam.

By early evening Mazzini is in Oslo. As he makes his way to his hotel, a warm, heavy summer rain begins. Other than the persistent daylight, which later keeps him from sleeping, nothing here matches his conceptions of the north. He can see the reflections of construction cranes in the glass façade of his hotel, and a balloon tied to the cranes hovers in the curtain of rain. Late that night Mazzini starts a letter to Anna, but the sentences veer off into mere diary entries addressed to no one and capturing nothing except the first remembered fragments of a journey. Mazzini crosses out "Dear Anna" and puts the sheet of paper with his journal. The rain continues until morning.

"We normally deny such requests," Ole Fagerlien said the next morning, repeating what he had written in a letter Mazzini had received while still in Vienna; "there are too many of them. The *Cradle* is not a ship for tourists. You have Fyrand to thank if I've made an exception in your case. But you know that." Still weary from his night in the hotel, Mazzini was sitting across from Fagerlien in a wood-paneled room of the Polar Institute, a courtesy call, and he remembered how Anna had scolded him for turning to Kjetil Fyrand of all people, one of *her* friends, and asking him for help—this was after that first, hopeless letter to the governor of the

Spitsbergens—in putting together a trip Anna thought was crazy anyway. Fyrand had been in Vienna to attend a convention and give a lecture on industrial pollution in the Arctic Ocean. He had shown up at one of Anna's soirees and drunk schnapps from a water glass. He was back sitting in Longyearbyen again now, pondering polar seas.

Fyrand's oceanographic studies were a project of the Polar Institute, and as a result of his intervention Fagerlien had in fact agreed to make an exception and let Mazzini take part in one of the *Cradle*'s annual research voyages. But his tone of voice that morning seemed to say he regretted his decision—after all, the *Cradle* was more or less the flagship of Norwegian arctic research, no, absolutely not a ship for tourists. It had cost the Polar Institute an immense sum to buy the trawler from a shipowner with cash-flow difficulties and refit it for scientific purposes. Every place on board was precious. . . . Mazzini had the feeling that Fagerlien was expecting him to apologize for his persistence in getting a cabin. He nodded at each of his host's statements, assumed the air of a pupil, and let the teacher teach. (After all, what did it matter that Fagerlien made sure he felt the casual disregard in which he held him? That was nothing compared with the fact that the *Cradle* would sail out of Longyearbyen harbor on August 10 with its course set for Franz Josef Land, and that he, Josef Mazzini!, would be leaning on the rail reliving a moment of discovery, 110 years after the *Tegetthoff* had drifted in pack ice.)

"So it's a book," Fagerlien said now, turning from his guest and staring out into the rain, ". . . another book. Every adventure results in a whole shipload of books, a whole library. . . ."

"And every library results in a new adventure," came Mazzini's modest attempt at rousing himself from silent and nodding agreement. But Fagerlien maintained his demeanor and had the last word: "Or in a tourist." Now he smiled.

Kjetil Fyrand had advised Mazzini to include in his petition to the Polar Institute (and Fagerlien *was* the Polar Institute) some perfectly obvious reason (a scientific project was best, historical research would do in a pinch, but no journalism!) for wanting to travel the Arctic Ocean above the routes followed by summer cruises. It took this correspondence to force Mazzini to declare that his interest was "research"—and so belittle it. But what reason could have sounded more plausible than suggesting he was working on a book about polar history? Work that demanded an experience of the world of ice undisturbed by the small talk and limited horizons of a cruise ship? No, a book about the Payer–Weyprecht expedition could not be written on a tourist steamer. (Mazzini tried these and similar explanations, at any rate, as he struggled to write the letters.)

But this morning, too, Ole Fagerlien was unimpressed by the plans presented to him by Fyrand the Guzzler's protégé—Josef Mazzini, sitting there so polite, almost servile. (Why had Fyrand lent his support to this Italian?) Fagerlien knew too many arctic chronicles all too well to share his visitor's astonishment at the adventures of a single expedition, one of hundreds. Besides which, he had his own heroes. His roomy office was rich in the relics of a much larger past. In the display cases lay fossils—snails, fern fronds, mussels, and tree bark, proof of how green and paradisiacal the landscape of the Arctic had once been—the Spitsbergens, a tropical garden. The walls shone with the dull luster of gold frames and the varnish of oil paintings, scenes recorded from icy seas of long ago: bear hunts beneath a sky whose colors were cracking now, billowing sails of ships in drift ice, and towering fountains rising white and blue above glaciers calving and crashing to the sea. In front of a wall map of the North Pole, hanging like a large tapestry between pictures, stood a bronze bust of Roald Amundsen, an altar. Amundsen! Fagerlien mentioned him several times that morning—what was anything this Italian visitor might say about Dalmatian sailors and the hardships of frozen saints, compared with the greatness of this one man? The conqueror of the Northwest Passage, the first man at the South Pole, Norway's hero, the mentor of a joint polar flight undertaken with Nobile—had not *he*, too, had a taste of Italians? Fagerlien's archive—"Here, look here; and here . . ."—also contained newspaper clippings that documented Nobile's ugly attacks on the paragon. After their joint polar flight the Italian general had written pamphlets intended to contest *his* fame, had pushed his way between Amundsen and the world's applause. Nobile may have built the dirigible *Norge* and Mussolini may have financed the expedition—but what good would all the money have been without the organizing genius of Amundsen?

"I know the story," Mazzini said.

And then two years later, when the general had made his own polar flight with the *Italia* and come crashing down on the ice, bringing his adventure to a sorry end—who but Amundsen would have had the greatness to fly off on a mission to rescue his foe? Amundsen and his five companions had been missing since the day of that flight, June 18, 1928. They had died for a highly decorated fanatic, a madman. After their last radioed message from above Bear Island (Fagerlien knew it word for word), there had been only silence—and a pontoon from their Latham later found on the coast of the Spitsbergens.

"I'm not Nobile," Mazzini said under his breath and in Italian (how long it had been since he had spoken Italian) as he stood up to say good-bye to his host. His clothes, wet with rain, had not dried during his courtesy call. It was late morning.

"Sorry?" Fagerlien had not understood.

"My name is Josef Mazzini," said his guest. For the first time—in a long time—Fagerlien looked unsure of himself.

At that moment he felt something like affection for this crazy little Italian who was so stubborn about sailing arctic waters. But perhaps it was only a trace of the magnanimity with which Amundsen had put Nobile to shame—a trace that ran like a crack through Fagerlien's view of the world. Sometimes the crack even seemed to widen into a moral principle.

"Give my regards to Fyrand." Fagerlien nodded to his visitor, banning the momentary affection and uncertainty. He was alone again at last—a bald, pudgy man in a pale blue suit.

The streets are steaming. The rain has stopped. Mazzini returns slowly to his hotel, taking the long way in the hope that this will give him a sense of Oslo—a tourist struggling with a fluttering map. He stands at each street corner, trying to picture the next stretch in his mind before moving on and finding himself refuted by the city's realities: a game. Only toward the end of his long walk do the views in his imagination begin to resemble those of the streets. What a quiet and subdued life people live here, producing hardly more noise than a holiday in some provincial town. The *Fram*, Fagerlien had said, Amundsen and Nansen's polar ship, the *Fram* in the shipping museum on Bygdøy . . . Mazzini changes his mind while still on the ferry to Bygdøy. No, he wouldn't go through the museum—no more visits, no immersing himself in other strange adventures that would thrust their way into his own and disturb it. Oslo should be the no-man's-land between the present and the timelessness of the arctic backdrop. A stopover.

The afternoon is spent shopping for the rest of his equipment. Every bookstore here has marine maps in any scale you want—his snow goggles, he left his snow goggles at home with the stonemason's widow. That evening Mazzini stands looking in his hotel room mirror. The black disks of a pair of snow goggles are fastened at his eyes (how secure he feels with his field of vision narrowed to a slit). The goggles' elastic band gathers his thick dark hair into a tuft. The clean-shaven face, the narrow, high cheekbones, the finely chiseled nose—they glisten with a film of salve to protect against frostbite. He stands there motionless for several minutes, taking aim with his gun, a double-barreled Ferlacher, sighting at the mirror through its cross hairs and the slits in his goggles. A spindly carnival fool.

Tomorrow he will be in Tromsø.

7

Melancholy

The sails are heavy with cold rain. Sometimes snow falls in great, wet flakes. Under the low-scudding clouds there is no difference between day and night. The horizon dissolves in scraps of fog and a gray, endless brightness. The *Tegetthoff* steams through a sea turning rough and violent. They have never seen swells like this. The breakers rolling down on the bark make a torment of every deck watch. The Tyrolean hunters take turns being seasick and can barely keep their legs. They nurse each other, offering words of encouragement. *The coastal waters off Novaya Zemlya will be calmer; we will see beautiful mountains.* That's what First Lieutenant Payer has promised. As the mountainous waves finally begin to abate and the wind no longer makes shreds of their ridges and combs, it turns cold. The tackle, the yards and masts, the network of shrouds all grow stiff—a mother-of-pearl rigging, a work of art in ice. Even in gentler seas and lighter gusts of wind, icicles break loose, splintering like glass on the planks of the deck. The jingling clatter drives the dogs wild. Barely two weeks have passed since they left Tromsø, but no one speaks about Tromsø anymore, about the candles and silver candelabra on Consul Aagaard's table, about vanished festivities. The sea pushes memories of land from their diaries. Sea birds—eiders, auks, and Ross's gulls—fall from the sky in a barrage of buckshot. Then Haller and Klotz sit beside buckets of hot water and pluck feathers. Time begins to pass more slowly. Weyprecht orders the crow's nest attached to the mainmast. That weak arc of light they have seen for several days now in the north-northeast—can that already be the *iceblink*, a sign that the open water will soon be strewn with floes and barriers of ice? This early? Last year at this time, on the preliminary expedition of the *Isbjørn*, the drift ice lay considerably farther north. The officer on watch in the crow's nest will see the ice before anyone else, will warn and guide the helmsman. On one special evening, it is calm and the commander plays his zither for the sailors in the mess. The man in the crow's nest, either Orel or Brosch, hears nothing. He is alone with his vigilance.

On July 25th, 8:30 a.m., the bitch Novaya dies whelping. At 10 o'clock she is lowered into her cool grave, at 7:30 on that same evening we see our first floes and greet them wishing they were the last. (*Otto Krisch*)

Surprised that the ice lay so far to the south, we were quick to comfort ourselves with the notion that we were not dealing with the closed ice-sea itself, but rather with a complex of floes that had perhaps drifted from the Kara Sea through the Matochkin Strait. Yet we were soon convinced that we were indeed within the conglomerate ice-sea, and that conditions for sailing in 1872 differed most unfavorably from those of the previous year. (*Julius Payer*)

Under full sail they pass fields of drift ice, still scattered and with broad navigable channels. Then the ice thickens; even the good strong wind no longer suffices. Otto Krisch and Pospischill, his fireman, are ordered to the boiler. They make laborious progress. But the fields gradually close to a white plain extending to the horizon. No more channels. On July 30 the *Tegetthoff* is held prisoner by ice for the first time; it is frozen fast. Not until the next day does the plain burst under the swells and warming air. Krisch is proud to see his ship making headway again under a cloud of smoke that casts a shadow larger than a riding ring. On August 3 they reach the west coast of the Russian archipelago Novaya Zemlya. Sailing and steaming ever so slowly, the bark makes its way along the rocky coast. The crew assembles on deck on Sundays. Then Weyprecht reads from an Italian Bible.

And take heed to yourselves, lest at any time your hearts be overcharged with surfeiting and drunkenness, and cares of this life, and so that day come upon you unawares. For as a snare shall it come on all them that dwell on the face of the whole earth. Watch ye therefore, and pray always, that ye may be accounted worthy to escape all these things that shall come to pass, and to stand before the Son of man. . . .

And when the day comes when the word of God is no longer mighty enough to calm those of little faith, Weyprecht's exhortations do, for he steadfastly reads all the signs of sea and heaven as favorable. We are prepared, he says. Nothing will surprise us.

For several days now we had entered a world totally alien to most men on board. We were often enveloped in thick fog. In their ragged garments of snow, the broken pinnacles of distant land stared at us inhospitably. All around us were the sermons of transience, for the gnawing sea reigns unabated and thaw is ever hard at work in the fields of this frozen world. There is no more melancholy scene than the whispering death of ice under the clouds of a night sky. In slow and proud ceremonial procession the white coffins are relentlessly borne to their graves beneath a southern sun. Every few seconds comes the steady sough of dying breakers as they roll beneath the hollowed-out floes. Water melts and seeps in monotonous whispers from the towering flards [*the larger floes*]. *Or a clump of snow, robbed of support, slides to the sea and dies with a hiss like a flame. The crunch and creak of bursting sections of ice never cease. Splendid cascades of thaw water, their brilliance veiled and muted, surge down the icebergs as they break with a burst of self-destructive thunder under the glow of the sun's rays. . . . Then day reigns again, and in its garish light the radiant dream of color fades to nothingness.* (*Julius Payer*)

To gain some notion of a ship's course in a sea of ice it is useful to imagine the flight of a housefly projected against a white wall. There is no easy line of progress, only a knot that unravels as the ship detours around icebergs, turns back before a solid wall of pack ice, runs aground on floes, breaks through again with a crack, and moves on at last through a maze of icy channels. Thus they negotiate the coastal waters of Novaya Zemlya. The guest in the crow's nest on the topmast shouts himself hoarse. "Open water! To luff, four tacks backboard, five tacks!" The wheel whirls under boatswain Lusina's hands. The rudder flutters through all its pitches like the wings of a panicky bird. The *Tegetthoff* lurches through a world of garish, glittering shards.

On August 12—they had thought they were completely alone now—a strange ship suddenly emerges out of the gauze of fog. The enchanting image is so small and diffuse that they might have thought it a phantom, except that the ship was sailing not keel up, as a mirage would, but as upright as reality itself. It is coming toward them, topsails hoisted, and if they close their eyes and open them again, it is still there. And then tiny stars, golden red flashes, cannon salutes! A frigate. But the most wonderful thing about the spectacle is in the flags that are now hoisted—of Norway . . . and Austria! The Austrian flag in a forlorn world, now filled with the hurrahs of sailors. Sailing from the Spitsbergens on the *Isbjørn*, Count Wilczek, their patron and friend, has followed them! Despite worsening ice conditions, he is determined to keep the promise he made in Vienna to leave a cache of provisions for the expedition on Cape Nassau, a first refuge in case the *Admiral Tegetthoff* should meet the same fate that befell the *Island* and the *Valborg* just days before and only a few nautical miles away. Both yachts sank after having been crushed in the ice. The count tells them about it, once he and his companions—Baron Sterneck, the court photographer Wilhelm Burger, and geology professor Hans Höfer—have boarded the *Tegetthoff* from their dinghy. How many dead? The count doesn't know. He has brought champagne.

For several days the *Isbjørn* sails farther northward in the wake of the *Tegetthoff*, as far as the Barents Islands, which Norwegian sailors call the Three Coffins. In case of emergency, the cache of provisions will be more accessible there than on Cape Nassau. With every nautical mile the danger of being encircled by ice increases, and with it the necessity of wintering in the stony and deserted wastes of Novaya Zemlya. The *Isbjørn* has a full crew and no steam engine. A winter here would mean death. But the count does not want to turn back, not yet. Near the Barents Islands the ice closes. Both ships are caught fast. Court photographer Burger stands motionless among the towering piles of ice and stares through his lens at the end of the world: barren, black cliffs, sky, and ice.

They use dogsleds to transport the emergency supplies—two thousand pounds of rye bread in barrels and a thousand pounds of pease sausage in soldered tin boxes—to the Three Coffins and deposit them there in ancient rocks for all eternity. Not one of them will ever come back here. Professor Höfer, the geologist, gathers fossils.

The animal world buried in the limestone of the Barents Islands is indisputable witness that a warm sea once extended across these high degrees of latitude, rendering it impossible for glaciers to have bathed, as they now do, in its tides. At that time this portion of the world, though now quite dead and buried by ice, enjoyed a period of abundant life. As our finds from that age on Bear Island and the Spitsbergens prove, its seas ran riot with multiform and often elegant fauna, and the land was crowned with giant palmlike ferns. We call this age in earth's history the Carboniferous. It was the richly blessed youth of the high north. It lived its life more quickly, hastened more nimbly toward its end, than southern zones now do in the full vigor of their daily interplay. . . . A short examination of the fossils buried here awakened in us a dreamlike scene of its once abundant life, a luxuriant organic creation, but a glance at the here and now of the Barents Islands aroused only gloom. (*Hans Höfer*)

As they lie stuck fast in the ice near the islands, Weyprecht orders that heavy, free-hanging beams be mounted on the ship's stern—swinging defenses against the imminent danger of being crushed by the ice. The idea is to distribute the pressure of the floes along the beams. Payer, Klotz, and Haller regularly harness the dogs to the sleds, racing them across the ice in an attempt to tame their fury. The dogs pull the sleds badly. And then the first polar bear is shot. A feast. The dogs are out of control.

On August 18th a grand banquet was held on board in honor of the birthday of His Majesty Kaiser Franz Josef I to which the gentlemen of the "Ice-Bear" [Isbjørn] were also invited. Count Wilczek provided the requisite champagne. At dinner Commander Weyprecht rose to offer a toast to the health of the Kaiser, surely the first time ever amid ice and in such close proximity to Novaya Zemlya. We also received a fresh shoulder of reindeer from the "Ice-Bear"; it was excellent. The menu consisted of: turtle soup, fieldfare with mixed pickles, reindeer roast with potato puree, chicken ragout with a salad of French beans, pancakes with stewed plums and raspberry marmalade, concluding with cheese, bread, and butter, then black coffee and excellent cigars reserved for special occasions. In our after-dinner conversation we recalled our homeland and our dear families. (*Otto Krisch*)

The sailors' meal is simpler, the menu unknown. They eat at separate tables. Even boatswain Lusina, ice master Carlsen, and the machinist Krisch are invited to the officers' table only on special occasions. But a time will come when there is neither table nor ship; they will crouch on the ice, their hands black, their faces cracked by frost, and chew the raw fat of seals. Under their shirts they will carry canteens filled with snow, and after agonizing hours of pulling their sleds there will be a swallow or two of flat water.

At 10 that evening we rose from the table and the gentlemen of the "Ice-Bear" departed ship. I too retired after recording these lines. (*Otto Krisch*)

On August 20th several changes in the ice appeared to make it possible for our voyage to be resumed; the following day, then, we boarded the "Isbjørn" to say farewell to Count Wilczek, Commodore Baron Sterneck, Professor Höfer, and Herr Burger. It was not an ordinary farewell. If it be true that parting especially touches the hearts of those who are already separated from the rest of mankind, then on this occasion there were most powerful reasons for sentiment. . . . Under gray skies and with a fresh northeast wind, we steamed northward away from the "Isbjørn," soon veiled in mist and vanishing from sight. . . . By afternoon we reached a "wacke" [i.e., open water rimmed by ice, a pond in the sea]. But during the following night solid barriers of ice prevented further progress here as well. (*Julius Payer*)

On August 22nd we are held by thick ice and dampen our fire at 4:30 a.m. While we wait for the ice to break, heavy snow falls. . . . One of the two cats on board died today of an intestinal knot. (*Otto Krisch*)

Waiting. Days. Weeks. Waiting. Months. Years. Waiting to the heart of despair. The trap will not open. Ever again. On the fortieth day out from Tromsø harbor, the frozen sea pushes in on the *Tegetthoff* from all sides. No open water anywhere. The *Tegetthoff* is no longer a ship, only a hut wedged in among ice floes, a refuge, a prison. The sails are useless rags. The steam engine mere ballast. The wheel an absurdity. An entry in ice master Carlsen's log gives the coordinates for their imprisonment: 76° 22′ north latitude and 62° 3′ east longitude. The snow that fell was granular and hard.

And now they drift along on their floe, an island of ice,

shrinking, growing larger again, and its wooden heart is their ship. They drift in a blinding void, in darkness, to the north, northeast, northwest, and north again—fully at the mercy of unknown ocean currents and the tortures of the ice. They are sailing for nowhere. Everything presses in on them, moves toward them. Two years, during eight months of which the sun does not rise. The loneliness and the fear. A cold that freezes wool blankets tacked to cabin walls for warmth under a layer of ice thick as a man's arm. Weak lungs fighting for breath. Frozen limbs—medical officer Kepes can stave off the fatal consequences only by agonizing amputation. With scissors they cut the rank flesh of scurvy from each other's gums; then they cauterize the wounds with hydrochloric acid. And finally, delusions and despair.

Most terrifying of all, however, is the howling rage of the ice floes, their shrieks as they wedge together, pile up in great towers, and threaten to crush the *Tegetthoff.* When the ice presses in like this, the crew waits belowdecks under emergency packs, listening for the warning cry of the watch on deck—*Move out! Move out! Life's goal is here!*—and then overboard once more, out into the darkness, onto the ice, water boiling up in black surges through the gaping cracks. And then it grows calm again, and there is no more water. A phantom.

But in the end, what are all such privations and torments compared with the immortality of a discoverer or—from the crew's viewpoint—the accumulating bonuses and wages? And what is the darkness of polar night compared with the marvels of light in the arctic heavens? Compared with the midnight sun, its rays refracted by veils of mist that multiply it to five or six suns? Compared with delicate fata morgana, with the shimmering vastness of the ring encircling the moon? Or the wavering splendor of the northern lights, before whose first appearance able seaman Lorenzo Marola sinks to his knees and begins praying loudly?

As they drift along with this floe they will experience every terror of ice and darkness that Weyprecht conjured up in his Adriatic exorcism outside the harbormaster's office in Fiume—yet these sailors from the south seem to have the strength to endure them all. It gratifies Weyprecht to know he was right, despite doubts and reservations expressed in the ranks of the Imperial Navy. No southerners, surely! they had said. For an arctic expedition, he needed to recruit Norwegians, Danes, or Russians. But in the darkness of winter night, when the wind is calm, it is Italians and Dalmatians who climb out onto the ice and play bocce by torchlight. He had taken these despised southerners along, Weyprecht will later write a ladyfriend, because they possessed the most precious thing a man can possess in the far north—a sunny disposition. It has always been of greater importance to him, Weyprecht will conclude his letter, to share that fact with the world than to spread the news of having discovered Franz Josef Land.

They drift along. Everything has been taken care of, they counted on being frozen fast, the commanders assure their crew. The *Tegetthoff* is a sound ship, built like no other for such seas, and come spring they will free themselves from the clutches of the ice and sail on, to a new, open sea, ever farther, perhaps to the Bering Strait and beyond. How confident their commanders are. Unshakable Weyprecht. And Payer defers to him. And although everything may seem to contradict their ever returning from wherever they are now drifting, Weyprecht keeps repeating: "We will return. I know it." No one wants to doubt it yet. Someone like ice master Carlsen ought to know a different truth. But he is silent.

So many have failed before us. We are drifting north, inexorably north. And then come latitudes where everything freezes forever, where no spring can come. No thaw. No navigable water. No one has ever returned from there. The Bering Strait is far and we are drifting, like everyone else, toward our end.

Who would have had the strength to speak such prophecies? No, death is only a figure in the mind. Julius Payer pictures a scene, as improbable as it is gentle: a naked man, defenseless against the cold of arctic winter. Unexpectedly, a cloud of fog forms around him, like the ring around the moon. If the light is just right, the edges of this cloud, which is nothing more than the body's moisture evaporating rapidly, shine in all the colors of the rainbow. Violet, blue, green, yellow, orange, and yellow-red. The rainbow gradually dissolves, color by color, each vanishing hue corresponding to a stage of death. A death beyond the threshold of pain, visible in the disappearance of that last, yellow-red arc.

Death, a play of color.

8

Second Digression
The Search for a Passage—
A Table from the Chronicle of Failure

(Selected Forerunners of the Payer-Weyprecht Expedition and Men Who Gave Their Names to the Capes and Waters of the Arctic Landscape)

Nota bene: Anyone lost in the ice on a fishing cutter, anyone who was not rescued but drowned, starved, or froze to death, has no claim to historical note. No one speaks nowadays of the missing whalers and other hunters of blubber—of mariners who sailed the Arctic Ocean every year but never gave their enterprises the emphatic name of an *expedition.* Whalers, too, made discoveries and spent their winters on islands that long remained unknown to cosmographers. They knew the ice and navigable routes better than did the representatives of the academies—but who, other than some scribbler in a commercial office, was to record their names?

What are ten lost frigates that set sail to club seals to death compared with a single expedition ship sailing under royal commission and sinking? The men who slaved away on working ships have no claim to glory. But there are monuments to expeditions, even the most unsuccessful.

SUPPLEMENT ENTRY: THE VICTORS

In 1878, four years after the return of the Payer–Weyprecht expedition, Baron Adolf Erik Nordenskiöld intentionally allows his ship, the *Vega*, to be locked in the ice, drifts with the floes through the polar night, is set free the next arctic summer, and sails on, passing through the Bering Strait to arrive at last on September 2, 1879, in Yokohama, where he receives an enthusiastic welcome. The first! The conqueror of the Northeast Passage! (A passage of no importance or value to commerce, since it can be used only at the price of being trapped in ice for years perhaps. . . . But that, too, will change—with the icebreakers of a still distant future. Like the gigantic Soviet ship *Lenin*, with 75,000 horsepower, or the tankers of Exxon and similar missionary vessels of an overpowering technology.)

In the years between 1903 and 1906, Roald Amundsen survives two polar nights aboard the *Gjøa*, drifting with the ice and reaching the Bering Strait via the Northwest Passage: a passage of no importance or value to commerce, since it can be used only at the price of being trapped in the ice for years perhaps, etc. etc.

But who would dare claim that the torments and sufferings endured in the search for a passage were pointless? Voyages to hell for routes of no value? At least they served science if not wealth and commerce, destroying the myths of an open polar sea, the myths of paradises in the ice. And myths are not destroyed without sacrifice.

Chronicle of Failure

Name	*Years in the ice*	*Goals not reached*	*Remarks*
Hugh Willoughby	1553/54	Northeast Passage	See "First Digression," Willoughby's death.
Martin Frobisher	1576/77/78	Northeast Passage	Sails to the southern tip of Greenland; returns home with a shipload of pyrites, with "gold nuggets" and several abducted Greenland Eskimos. During a second voyage, five sailors are killed by Eskimos. Frobisher reports that many Greenlanders drowned themselves to escape him; eventually he disappears in the Arctic Ocean.
Willem Barents	1594/95/96/97	Northeast Passage; Northwest Passage; direct route to the Pacific via the North Pole	First to circumnavigate Novaya Zemlya; rediscovers the Spitsbergens, once known to Permiaks and Icelanders; returns each time with pyrites. On the last voyage his ship is crushed by ice and sinks near the Three Coffins off the northern coast of Novaya Zemlya; Barents and four sailors die wintering on the coast. The remains of their camp are discovered centuries later by ice master Elling Carlsen.
John Knight	1606	Northwest Passage	Killed in Greenland by Eskimos.

Chronicle of Failure *(continued)*

Name	*Years in the ice*	*Goals not reached*	*Remarks*
James Hall	1605/06/07/08	Northwest Passage	Killed in Greenland by Eskimos.
Henry Hudson	1607/08/09/10/11	Northwest Passage; direct route to the Pacific via the North Pole	Sails to Greenland, the Spitsbergens, and through the Hudson Strait and Hudson Bay to North America; discovers the island of Jan Mayen on return trip; after two suppressed mutinies, is set in a dinghy with his son and seven crew members; vanishes. The mutineers return to England and are hanged.
Vitus Bering	1725–41	Northwest Passage; Northeast Passage; direct route to the Pacific via the North Pole	Hero of the czarist Great Northern Expedition planned and organized by Ivan Kirillovich Kirilov (with a total of seven divisions and six hundred members); first to pass through the Bering Strait. After a shipwreck off Bering Island, he dies there of scurvy.
Vasily Jakovlevich Chichagov	1765/66	Direct route to the Pacific via the North Pole	After returning from a first unsuccessful search for a passage, is forced to try another, in the course of which a majority of the expeditionary crew dies. (Coerced expeditions are typical of czarist polar explorations—the mariners therefore sometimes invent new lands and ice-free routes in order to avoid making a second voyage.)

John Franklin	1818/19, 1820/21, 1825/26/27, 1845/46/47	Northwest Passage; direct route to the Pacific via the North Pole	After surviving three difficult polar expeditions, vanishes on the fourth, along with 129 crew members and two ships, *Erebus* and *Terror*; a search of many years has no success. In 1859, however, Captain McClintock finds the remains of his camp and mutilated corpses.
Elisha Kent Kane	1850/51, 1853/54/55	American Route (via Smith Strait on the west coast of Greenland to the North Pole and the Bering Strait)	Sails from New York Harbor on his first attempt to reach the Pacific via the American Route. This first trip is unsuccessful, and only a portion of the crew survives the second; Kane dies shortly after his return as a result of the hardships.
Charles Francis Hall and Emil Israel Bessels	1860/61/62, 1864–69, 1871/72/73	American Route	Hall takes a family of Eskimos along as guides and advisers, and dies in 1871 from the rigors of a dogsled trip across the ice. Under Bessels the crew attempts further probes to the North Pole. A portion of them are separated from the drifting ships, and their floe drifts for seven months before reaching the Labrador Sea. The entire Hall expedition is still considered missing when the *Admiral Tegetthoff* departs.

9

Shifting Scenes of a Landscape

July ends tomorrow. It is Josef Mazzini's third day in Tromsø. The arctic sea dissolves in mists; the high humidity hides any views into the distance. The daytime high does not exceed 50° Fahrenheit. The sky is white. The breeze just above the rocky landscape is barely enough to ripple the surface of standing water, of a pond, although sometimes it creates dainty wavelets and a calming rustle in the tops of stunted birches, the distinguishing mark of a light breeze for meteorologists. A hang glider traces elongated gentle loops against the cliffs of the Fragernes, the mountains towering above Tromsø. The pilot hangs like an opossum below the garish red of his glider's wings, seems to stop in the air for a moment, turns away, vanishing from Mazzini's sight and reemerging somewhat lower a few seconds later. The cliffs seem to attract the hang glider, then repulse it, but with a slow, steady downward force. Once the red sail and its booty float out of his field of vision, Josef Mazzini is alone with the mountain, which rises up just as it has for hundreds, thousands of years, its fissures, bluffs, and timberline unchanged. The last runs only eight or nine hundred feet above sea level, straggly low stands of trees, birches, mementos of forests, then juniper bushes, and above them lichens, bare stone, and moss. That's where Payer must have climbed, his barometer and other gear on a litter, Haller and the dogs behind him, the Laplander Dilkoa up ahead of them all. They are standing on top now, watching the black column of smoke that rises above Tromsø; the town is burning, and Weyprecht arrives from the harbor to help the local firemen; bells toll. And then the hang glider completes its loop and slides back into sight, dragging the present behind.

Mazzini follows it attentively up to where the gondolas of a funicular glitter against the cliffs of the Fragernes; no one need climb them on foot now, and if they do, it is merely for sport, an unnecessary exertion. The slender arches of a concrete bridge span the harbor entrance; two fish-processing ships, their large hulls covered with streaks of rust, lie at the dock. How the sailors of the *Tegetthoff* would have gaped—their bark a tidy pilot boat compared with those two colossuses, above them the thicket of antennas and the radar carousel. The harbor bridge serves as a track to guide his eyes to the church—no, he can't imagine Weyprecht in there listening to a mass being said before they sail. An ambitious piece of architecture, a vacationer from Hamburg had said of it over breakfast in the Hotel Royal, a successful building, modeled after the simple frames of the drying racks they hang their fish from here, with nets thrown over to protect against greedy birds. No, they did not kneel there. The architect from Hamburg is standing at the rail of some cutter in the fjord now, catching fish he won't eat, part of the program in an organized tour. Why didn't he just join up, the Hamburger said to Mazzini, one person more or less wouldn't make any difference, no big deal around here. Coppery hues, the mossy green and pink of the frame houses in the center of town, where things are quiet as in a village, the houses set a good distance apart as a precaution against a leaping spark—they still worry about fire here. Farther from the heart of town, the newer buildings are closer together and made of brick, glass, and concrete. The screech of gulls. A metal Amundsen towers ten or fifteen feet above a grassy plot, much bigger than real life, his vacant eyes directed to the gray sea.

I see Mazzini shoulder his sleeping bag and light pack and walk off down a sandy path, then a rocky one, violet slopes; it is a bright night and he has hiked twenty-five miles from Tromsø. Josef Mazzini is rehearsing being alone. Tall, restless columns of mosquitoes, millions of insects, rise to form a flickering parkway along the banks of a lake encircled by birches. He cannot lie down here to sleep. Ribbons of fog drift above the black water, stitching the land to the lake. On down to Skeivag, a deserted settlement on the Ullsfjord, ruins, a dilapidated hut covered with grass, blank windows. He has walked for twelve hours. He sets out while it is still night, and climbs high into the rocks, no path now. Far below him the Grøt Sound joins the Ullsfjord. Out beyond the cut there, the *Tegetthoff* steams toward open seas, but the water is empty now, quite empty, and then heavy fog descends. He still doesn't feel sure of himself with just a compass. By morning he is on a dirt road near Snarby, frame houses in the fog, he can see barely thirty feet ahead. He wanders back along Grøt Sound. Outside Vagnes a truck driver stops and offers him a ride; he hasn't realized how tired he is until now. The driver doesn't understand that the stranger is trying to say and sign that he has driven trucks as big as this and bigger, and just keeps shaking his head. People don't talk much on roads like these. The damp countryside hums by. A loud voice on the radio; static. The driver points at the sky and then at the down jacket beside him. A weather report. Turning cooler. Mazzini is back in town by evening. The architect from Hamburg has just returned from Vardø on a Twin Otter. He complains of a Vardø restaurant that required a tie. He has been to North Cape, too, a thousand-foot-high table jutting from the sea, the end of Europe, but with all the fog and rain it was a disappointment, unfortunately. And that tie! A tie, at the edge of the wilderness, in that one-horse town, idiotic. Mazzini thinks of the banquet at the home of Consul Aagaard. Was ice master Carlsen among the guests, too? Had he worn his white periwig, his Order of Olaf; was Payer in dress uniform? Dr. Kepes, a Hungarian, and the vainest of them all, was sure to have worn a fine frock coat. Are you listening to me at all, the architect asks. Your last evening here, right? Off to the Spitsbergens tomorrow? Well, cheers, we can make an occasion of that, too—the kid from Vienna won't say no this time. But Mazzini doesn't say yes, either. He walks behind the architect. He has just come from his small solitude, and Tromsø looks even newer now, more part of the present. Has he seen the bombed-out German destroyer, the wreck down by the cliffs? No, Josef Mazzini has had an eye out for a different ship. Rotten luck, German cannon fire burned old Tromsø to the ground in World War II.

Memories of a vanished town, of Payer's Tromsø perhaps, romantic views, lithographs—they hang framed under glass along the paneled walls of Fiskerogen & Peppermøllen, a seafood restaurant that looks like the inside of a sailing ship—hurricane lamps, wood, and lots of brass. Great bar, Mazzini says before the man from Hamburg can, and grins. The owner, an Austrian gourmet who has been here eleven years now, is proud of the fact that he can take the varieties of fish the locals along the Norwegian coast throw back into the sea as inedible and transform them into delicacies. Can he also transform pyrites into gold, Mazzini asks.

"What?"

"Pyrites into gold."

"Some notions you've got . . ." the owner says, turning to the next table, "but it'd be worth a try," haha, and he hopes they enjoy their evening. Monkfish *à la Norvégienne* for 118 kroner. Pyrites into gold, alchemy, the secret of great riches, the true adventure.

"You drink too fast," the architect says.

Mazzini needs more money for one week here than for a month in Vienna. He totals it up. But tomorrow he will be in arctic waters; this and everything else will change then. Tomorrow. A night flight.

"Well then, cheers," the Hamburger says. Looks like the kid from Vienna can't hold his liquor too well. The aquavit makes him so fuddled and clumsy that he cannot get his passcard to open the door to his hotel room. A drunken tourist. The receptionist helps him.

His last day on the continent of Europe is one of headaches and nausea. Even that evening, his baggage standing ready, Mazzini vomits bitter yellow froth. The cold wind at the airport does him good. The commercial plane under the glaring light surprises him. Another DC-9. He had figured it would be a Twin Otter or some other small propeller machine with a handful of passengers at most. Shortly after midnight he is above the clouds. A perfectly normal domestic flight—miners and engineers flying to their jobs in the coal mines of Longyearbyen, and a few tourists in garish anoraks on their way to a vacation with lots of wilderness, or so the travel brochure promised. About a third of the way into the flight, barely an hour out of Tromsø, the sky begins to glow; the sun rises deep red. The midnight sun will be visible above Longyearbyen for two more weeks. The strange light charges the tourists with expectant restlessness. They keep pointing out the burning cloudbank to one another. Most of the miners are sleeping. Even Mazzini's neighbor turns chatty—a Bulgarian, a musician, who plays in one of the many Bulgarian combos that grease the dance floors of Finnmark with oldies during the summer season. "Rock Around the Clock," "The White Rose of Athens," "Love Me Tender." The Bulgarian introduces himself, formally, as if presenting the members of his band to the audience after a particularly thrilling number: Slatyu Boyadshiev on bass. "Antonio Scarpa," Mazzini says, "sailor." And he is sorry right away. He has lied to a gullible, honest man. Now he has to ask interested questions and in repayment listen attentively to the Bulgarian, who would believe other lies with equal credulity. Slatyu Boyadshiev doesn't notice a thing. He has just played gigs in Hammerfest and Alta, and now, as every year, he'll be camping in a tent on the Spitsbergens for a week—even his boys tell him that it's just money thrown away. The boys don't understand, but he doesn't care. Why, of all people, should Bulgarians be the ones to satisfy the entertainment needs of Finnmark? The bass player doesn't rightly know. It just happened that way. Western musicians find the far north too boring and dreary maybe. Someday he'll ask for political asylum in Norway and then work in the mines at Longyearbyen for a year or so. Tax-free income, 10,000 kroner a month, plus fringe benefits, and then later his own bar maybe.

On the tarmac in Longyearbyen a piercing wind makes a leap for them. The Aeroflot plane for Murmansk rolls past. A group of Soviet coal miners is standing silently beside a barracks, waiting for a helicopter to take them to Barentsburg and the mines of the Trust Artikugol. The bass player yells something at him. The garishly clad tourists, including sky-blue Mazzini, pass their eyes over the Russians with a few embarrassed, almost shy glances: old-fashioned coats, suitcases tied up in twine. They are deep into adventure now.

10

The Leaden Flight of Time

They fight back. Striking in all directions. They hack at the floe with axes and picks, try to cut channels in the ice with long saws, bore holes in this damned frozen sea, fill them with gunpowder, firing charge after charge. The machinist Krisch takes an ice anchor and forges it into a powerful chisel that the sailors haul up onto a wooden frame and slam into the grasping ice, again and again. They will pound their way out of the ice, they will break free, they *have* to break free, so they can at least anchor in a winter-safe bay on the coast of Novaya Zemlya. But the archipelago sinks slowly from view. For days the mainsail and foresail are kept set so that no second may be lost when their island of ice finally cracks open and releases them. Dark streaks appear on the horizon, sky above water! They have to reach it, there must be a navigable trough there. But they are here. Here! Locked in. That dark streak of sky is not meant for them. In the cold the saws lose all flexibility and break. The cuts they have made freeze back up within a few minutes. The charges fling wild bouquets of ice crystals into the air, which fall as rattling hail. The *Tegetthoff* does not move, the rudder they sawed free yesterday is frozen solid again today. The craters gouged by the chisel are filled again with drifts from the northeast gale.

The snow turns glassy and hard. New ice, and the sails crack uselessly in the wind. Sometimes the sky races past overhead. The crags and rubble of their floe break off in the ice storm. The island shrinks, and cracks appear in it. Maybe now is the time. Every man to his post! But only even more mammoth masses of ice drift their way, binding with their floe to form a single numbing landscape.

The completion of our task proved a brief dream. We painfully came to realize our misfortune would continue, and we succeeded only partially in maintaining our composure. . . . The days grew ever shorter, each setting sun blazing more fiercely, encircled by red mists behind barriers of blue-black ice. And as it set, each twilight grew dimmer. . . . Only occasional gulls could be seen now to visit watering holes in the vicinity. With rapid strokes of their wings they would hover above the top of a mast, staring down on us, and then give a hoarse cry and shoot fast as arrows toward the south. The migration of the birds brought some melancholy with it; all creatures seemed intent on a hurried departure from the realm of long shadows awaiting us. . . . A dreary wasteland took us in, and we entered for we knew not how long nor at what distances. (*Julius Payer*)

The ship's tackle is so covered with ice that one reaches the crow's nest only with great difficulty and exertion. . . . The ice crystals attached to the tackle are quite peculiar, looking almost exactly like the loveliest feathers. (*Otto Krisch*)

And even if someone does climb up into the jingling iron frame and hacks free a spot in the crow's nest, he sees nothing now that he can shout down to the others. Those streaks of sky above water have scattered. The ice is endless. When Weyprecht orders the sails taken in, even has the topmasts removed, they know they have lost for this year. But perhaps some miracle will still occur. Perhaps the northern lights that have appeared now since the first weeks of September are heavenly tokens of some future liberation. When the first waves of light roll across their forlorn world, emerald green and then in all the splendid colors of the rainbow, Marola falls to his knees. The Madonna will help them. But Weyprecht tells them they should trust not in miracles, but in him.

More than anything else, it is the northern lights that fill the newcomer to these regions with amazement—an unsolved riddle that nature has written in fiery letters on the arctic skies.

Just as sheet lightning on a sultry summer night bears little resemblance to a thunderstorm at its fury, so the pale version of the northern lights visible in our regions is quite unlike their imposing natural spectacle in the far north. The entire firmament is on fire. From all sides thousands of bolts of light gather in massive clusters and shoot toward the point in the vault of heaven to which a compass needle turns. In a mad patchwork, intense flames of light rimmed with color flicker and flash, weave and lick about the central point. As if whipped by the wind, fiery waves of light chase one another, interlacing and tumbling from east to west and from west to east. In constant alternation red replaces white, green replaces red. Sheaves of thousands upon thousands of rays flash incessantly, coursing heavenward in an attempt to reach the point of their common desire, the magnetic zenith. It is as if the legend we know from old chronicles has come true, and the heavenly hosts are engaged in battle, hurling thunderbolts and fire at one another before the eyes of earth's inhabitants. All this occurs in profoundest silence, every sound is struck dumb. Nature seems to hold her very breath in motionless amazement at her own work. (*Carl Weyprecht*)

They have time to spare now, the leisure time of prisoners. They can do nothing more to free themselves. Just as the battle against ice barriers was an obsession, so now, too, is the battle against monotony. Against time. They sew coats and supply sacks from sailcloth, sole their boots, twice, three times, span a canvas roof over the deck, make the ship tight for winter—useful tasks are not enough, are completed too quickly. The sailors build structures of ice around the *Tegett-*

hoff, at first only a latrine, then walls, houses, towers!, and finally, almost in a rage of exertion, castles and palaces. They saw blocks of ice and use the shimmering bricks to build arches and gothic windows through which time is meant to fly. What a fine thing that their edifices and cities constantly crumble and sink with the shifting ice—although these are not yet the forces of compression that await them. This way they can begin all over again, make the newer version larger and more beautiful than the one before. Days of arduous labor are spent constructing streets and lanes through the walls of press ice. They smooth the stone-hard sea, pouring water over it. Then they buckle runners onto their felt boots and go skating. Krisch serves as the sailors' amused teacher. But the southerners are so talented and agile at this, too, that they master playing bocce on skates. Weyprecht is serious as always. Just as he has never shown any doubt or disappointment about the course the expedition has taken, so now, as they gradually make themselves at home in their prison, he takes no part in their lighthearted sport. He spends his nights sitting alone in an observation tent he has built out on the ice; he keeps meteorological, astronomical, and oceanographic journals, measures variations in the earth's magnetic force, records long columns of numbers, reckons the course of their drift, sounds the sea's depth, describes, calculates, establishes connections. He is all attention.

For someone to find excitement in nature he need not be a dry-as-dust academic for whom a flower's anthers are merely a feature to be used to classify it, insects merely an object for his microscope, a mountain merely its constituent stones—on the other hand one need not be a sentimental enthusiast, either, who is thrilled by twinkling stars and feels shallow amazement at a majestic bolt of lightning and perhaps knows nothing of the eternal laws by which nature orders all things. By examining the riddles with which nature surrounds us, we give fullest expression to thinking mankind's aspirations for progress. When Newton used a simple obser-

vation to formulate the immutable laws on which depend the movements of stars, the whole mechanism of the heavens, and the existence of the earth we inhabit, he was not merely enunciating simple formulas, he also pushed thinking mankind forward, raising its estimation of itself in its own eyes and showing it what human reason is capable of.

Whoever will truly admire nature should observe her in her extremes. In the tropics one finds nature in her fullest splendor and lushness, flaunting her Sunday clothes, but admiration all too easily leads one to overlook her heart. At the poles she is naked, allowing the grand internal structure to be revealed all the more clearly. In the tropics the eye loses itself in the multiplicity of details to be admired. But here lack of detail causes the eye to be directed at the overwhelming whole, at her productive powers in the absence of things produced. Here one's attention, freed of preoccupation and unmoved by particulars, can be concentrated on nature's powers. (*Carl Weyprecht*)

Life is confined and cramped aboard ship, encouraging an increasing intimacy among the lower ranks—Carlsen, who as a young man discovered Barents's winter camp on Novaya Zemlya; Klotz, who has climbed the highest mountains and can scramble up the rigging and brew medicinal teas; Pietro Fallesich, who helped build the Suez Canal and knows the most incredible stories about Egypt; boatswain Lusina, the chain-smoker; Marola, the harmonica player; and all the others, who tell each other their life stories in ever new and different versions. But not the commanders—they are unable to get close to anyone. They are becoming strangers to one another. Payer is unhappy about the time they are losing. He wants to discover new lands or sea routes, wants to travel unexplored regions with his dogsled; an observation tent is not enough for him. He wants to return home amid great celebration, bringing wonderful cosmographic news. For Weyprecht the unexplored sea through which they are drifting is itself new enough. There is so much to do yet. The data he is collecting are meant to serve the advancement of science, not the kind of national ambition that wants to conquer the North Pole at any price nowadays. The North Pole itself has no greater scientific value than any other given point in the far north. This international rush for new latitude records and the fame of discovery in the far north disgusts him, and he would rather return with solid results and a full crew than with some vague sketch of a glacier-covered land. New lands, fine. But not for mere glory, and not at any price. And Payer is willing to concede all that; but nevertheless, returning home with nothing to show, without a land; that would be more shameful than death. Just so, Weyprecht says. In his dreams Payer is obsessed with those gigantic icebergs that tower above this wasteland—those mountains cannot have been calved from the glaciers of Novaya Zemlya, they are too massive, too huge for its coastline. No, *those* icebergs must have drifted here from some other, unknown land, and he, Payer, *has* to find it.

The commander on land is preparing for his triumph. He rehearses his journey of discovery. Payer ventures out onto the floe again and again, chasing his dog team across the ice. The dogs are so savage and unpredictable that Krisch has to make muzzles for them out of leather and iron. Gillis, the big Newfoundland, rips apart the surviving cat from Tromsø, the one creature to which they could show some gentleness.

This was deeply regretted by the crew, for they all felt affection for the animal, especially the Tyrolean Klotz, who was very close to tears. (*Otto Krisch*)

Klotz—sensible, calm Alexander Klotz—flies into such a terrible rage that he turns on the dog, beats him like a madman until they have to pull him off. He sits staring at the plants he is growing in pots in the mess, pale yellow cress that no sunlight ever reaches, and talks with Haller in a dialect none of the others can understand.

When they finish whatever tasks they have assigned themselves, when they sit belowdecks, some with a book or magazine in front of them, and others, who cannot read, with only their hands, with nothing to confirm the passage of time except the chronometer, then, sometimes, a cry from the watch wrenches them from their torpor: *Un orso!* A bear! All brooding is cast aside and they scurry up on deck just as they are—often without their boots or furs. There is no greater consolation than the hunt. Each wants to be the first to take a shot. When they have the animal in notch and head-sight, there is no dejection and no leaden time.

On October 6th, the wind attacks from the southwest, driving snow before it. . . . In the afternoon I went on deck for a constitutional and to my great joy spotted a polar bear aft of the ship, I immediately advised the cabin of "a bear at close range" and everyone stormed the aft cabin, each man hurriedly grabbing a weapon. The bear walked alongside the ship at the aforementioned distance, sometimes rearing up and sniffing for the ship. Everyone was ready for a shot and hidden behind the planking, but the bear hid itself behind a floeberg and kept out of view. We waited for it to pass the berg, but in vain, straining our patience to the limit. I climbed the mainmast to have a lookout for the bear and saw it making ready to depart, which information I passed on, and it was decided to form a hunting party. We took to the ice, approaching the bear, but as we could not see it because of the intervening floeberg, we had no opportunity of coming closer. Herr Payer shot first, striking it in the back with an explosive bullet. The bear fell to the ice but was still capable of dragging itself forward, and as it neared the "wacke" that had formed near our stern, six more shots were fired, and it fell dead with its snout at the edge of the ice; . . . 8 men had had all they could to bring it on board, upon opening it we found not an atom of food in its stomach, the intestines were likewise quite flabby and empty, the poor animal must have been starving for some time. (*Otto Krisch*)

But they are seldom relieved by hunts now, and with increasing frequency driving snowstorms, in which they can breathe only with backs turned, force them belowdecks. And even when the storm abates and the only sound is the screech and rattle of ice fields bursting in the distance, the cold—a cold unlike any most of them have ever experienced—remains. It grows darker. Then the gentle glow of light is dimmed inside their shimmering theater of ice. But no curtain rises for some great event. The dramas of compressing ice, whose prologues trouble them now almost daily, will take place in darkness. They fear for their ship. They have carried emergency provisions and coal out onto the floe against the day that the *Tegetthoff* can no longer withstand the advancing ice. A necessary precaution, Weyprecht says, but the *Tegetthoff* will hold. On October 28 the sun sinks below the horizon for this year. But two days later the vanished sun suddenly reappears, a blurred ellipse—but no, that is not the sun, it is only its reflection, distorted and then multiplied above the horizon, a phantom of broken rays in veils of frost, an illusion. Only a reflection? What, then, is reality? They have seen land, too, mountains drifting across the sky and melting, mirages—no, that was not real land, oh yes it was, that was land, hovering there, whole worlds set in a frame of silver.

31 October, Thursday: Fine weather. The ice is fairly quiet near the ship. Continued working on a pair of felt boots for the first lieutenant. On October 30th saw the sun for the last time. On October 31st the last gull. The harpooner shot it. (*Johann Haller*)

By early November deep twilight surrounded us; a magical beauty transfigured our lonely wilderness, the frosty white of the ship's rigging traced in ghostly relief against the gray-blue sky. The ice, cracked a thousand times over beneath its blanket of snow, had the cold, pure look of alabaster, except for delicate shadings of aragonite. Only at noon, toward the south, could one still see a violet haze rising from evaporating ice. (*Julius Payer*)

Beauty here is more ephemeral than elsewhere, and the silence is only a pause, a moment. Gradually even the endlessness seems incapable of holding any more ice, this beautiful ice. In the next century it will be ascertained that the polar ice-cover varies between two and five million square miles. The polar cap is a pulsating amoeba and the *Tegetthoff* an annoying splinter in its plasma. The ice increases now. Everything increases. The darkness, the pressures on the *Tegetthoff*, the fear for their ship—they prefer not to fear for their own lives yet. Where yesterday a mountain had lifted, today there is a shimmering, frozen pond, and tomorrow a reef again. Their palaces gape wide. The town has ruptured. Perhaps their floe, their island, will protect them against the advancing icebergs, which appear to want the small space the *Tegetthoff* occupies as well. Still occupies. Now they nurse and bind up their island, their endangered asylum. When a crack opens in the ice, they sew it up with ropes and anchors, filling the open fractures with snow. But nothing heals.

This patchwork bursts open with each breath of the sea. . . . Like rabble in rebellion, all ice rose up against us now. Level areas became threatening mountains, soft groaning became a rattle, a growl, a roar, increasing to a thousand-voiced cry of rage. . . . The cracking and rumbling comes ever closer, like a thousand war chariots racing toward us across the sands of a battlefield. The pressure grows and grows; the ice beneath us begins to tremble, to lament in every conceivable voice, at first whistling like countless arrows, then screeching, raging, in highest soprano and lowest bass all at once—bellowing ever louder, it rises up, bursts in concentric circles around the ship, rolling up the broken pieces of the floe. The terrifying rhythm of a throbbing howl precedes the greatest tension. Then a loud crack follows, and several black lines scurry at random across the snow. These are new fissures very near us, that can open into abysses at any moment. . . . The rumbling scaffolds of ice rise, jerk, and collapse, like a foundering city. . . . New masses break off from the circumference of our small floe; the slabs sway vertically above the sea, an incalculable force raising them in arches and vaults, the fields literally lifting as bubbles, a grim reminder of the elasticity of ice. Crystalline hosts wage war on all sides, and between their flanks the surging water floods into the sunken basins; cliffs of ice plunge to ruin, and rivers of snow flow from their bursting slopes. . . . And amid this mad welter, a ship! It turns, sinks, and rises; but most terrifying of all is the force of compression. It flattens our "buffers," foot-thick oak beams, and the ship itself begins to rattle. . . . The men have long since halted their labors, the struggle for life is only in their minds now. They no longer sew the ice together with ropes; when it starts, they still run about helter-skelter, wandering among the cracks with lamps, until the bursting ice begins to throttle the ship itself. Here a face mirroring distress, there one of grim composure. The night hides them both. Words are lost, inaudible, only shouts can still be understood. . . . Where else on earth does such chaos reign? Oblivious to its terrors, nature's law holds sway. (*Julius Payer*)

The madness often lasts only a few minutes. Then calm returns and there is only the wind in the rigging. Then they sit wrapped in furs beside their emergency packs and wait for the next attack of the ice. They can do nothing except be ready for the moment when the ship bursts; then it's overboard, quickly overboard. But where to then? This new waiting is more agonizing than the old. Their sleep is light now, very light, frequently interrupted. "Move out!" If only the damned ship would finally burst. Then it would all be over. Shut your mouth, speak of the devil and . . . nothing will burst. The sailors throw bear skulls and the reindeer antlers they brought from Tromsø overboard. Harpooner Carlsen implores them: The skulls of dead animals are bad luck, nature will be appeased only if they give back what has been stolen from her. They do as he says. They offer a heathen sacrifice, for the power that threatens them cannot be a gracious God, but an alien deity, and they cast their trophies before him. Weyprecht lets them do as they like. Except that, as before, they must all gather on deck for Bible reading every Sunday; only those too ill to walk are excused. In these days of compressing ice, the commander reads from the Book of Job. With God's help, unhappy Job from the land of Uz overcame worse tribulations than this ice.

My days are past, my purposes are broken off, even the thoughts of my heart. They change the night into day: the light is short because of darkness. If I wait, the grave is mine house: I have made my bed in the darkness. I have said to corruption, Thou art my father: to the worm, Thou art my mother, and my sister. And where is now my hope? as for my hope, who shall see it? They shall go down to the bars of the pit, when our rest together is in the dust. . . . Behold, happy is the man whom God correcteth: therefore despise not thou the chastening of the Almighty: For he maketh sore, and bindeth up: he woundeth, and his hands make whole. He shall deliver thee in six troubles: yea, in seven there shall no evil touch thee.

Who can believe that? Are not Job's laments dearer to them than the happiness awaiting them after all these evils? This is not the land of Uz. They are standing on deck. They must stand very still.

9 November, Saturday: Wind and fog. For some time I have been suffering from "rheumatism." What am I to think of such an illness here in the far north? Three months of polar night . . . To live or die amid the rough and tumble of sailors. I am comforted by the hope I set in the doctor. He eased my pain at once, and within four days I could get up from my bed and soon started walking again.

10, Sunday: Wind and fog. I feel run-down.

11, Monday: Wind and driving snow. I feel run-down.

12, Tuesday: Wind and driving snow. Run-down.

13, Wednesday: Wind and driving snow. Run-down.

14, Thursday: Wind and driving snow. Run-down.

15, Friday: Windy weather. Feel run-down.

16, Saturday: Clear and windy. Feel run-down.

17, Sunday: A ruckus today close to the ship. Feel run-down.

18, Monday: Clear weather. A bear appeared close to the ship, but it could not be killed. The doctor has given me permission to go on deck, but only for a moment and right back again and to bed.

19, Tuesday: The pressure from the ice is threatening to crush the ship again. Poor comfort for me in my sick condition.

20, Wednesday: Clear weather. Temperature −29° R [−33° F]. The danger that the ship will be crushed continues. Feel run-down.

21, Thursday: Clear weather. Another powerful compression of ice. It threw up piles of ice big as houses near the ship.

22, Friday: Clear weather. The ice is fairly quiet near the ship. Some improvement in my illness.

23, Saturday: The ice is quiet. Took all my strength to resole a pair of felt boots.

24, Sunday: Clear weather. Church at 11 o'clock. I'm back to attending services. (Johann Haller)

December came, but with no change in our situation. Our life grew ever more lonely—there was no longer any visible progression of days, only a succession of dates and but one differentiation of time: that before and after dinner and that of sleep. . . . We sat there in the lonely cells of our camp, listening to the seconds ticking on the clock. Seventy-eight million ticks slowly crept by and became two and a half years; time's leaden flight passed without our mourning it, for it had no value for us. (Julius Payer)

They have achieved nothing, nothing! There is only the steady roar of the ice, of death. The temperature falls to −40°, −50°, −55° Fahrenheit and the world around them sinks beneath a darkness in which they can no longer see each other two, three paces apart. The cabin walls have long since frozen over with ice several inches thick, the moisture of their own bodies that condenses and freezes. Even in the mess, where they heat with their Meidinger coal ovens, the temperature at floor level no longer climbs above the freezing point. At the level of their heads it is hot. But the warmth does not reach their cabins. Little glaciers form beneath their bunks. Their woolen blankets freeze hard. They have given up the routine of washing in the bath every two weeks; the moisture only makes the ship's interior ice over that much more quickly. And several times men have had to spring naked from the lukewarm water when the compressing ice suddenly threatened their doom. Out into the cold, with just a fur thrown over them or stark naked—they did not see the beautiful wreath of colors of Payer's imaginings form around their bodies. But they gasp for breath now. No one undresses anymore. Krisch is coughing up blood. Hardly a day goes by but that some of them have to stay in their bunks with symptoms of scurvy. Their gums turn white and begin to fester, blood seeps from their pores, then someone writhes with stomach cramps—and their weariness is very great. They have too little fresh meat; it is a rare stroke of good fortune when they manage to kill a bear in this darkness. Their hundred bottles of lemon juice, the dried fruit, the canned vegetables and cloudberries are not enough to fight scurvy. When they have luck on a hunt, they drink bear's blood.

Three days before Christmas, harpooner Carlsen accidentally fires a shot while loading his rifle. The bullet hits the aft cabin, the ammunition depot—there are twenty thousand rounds on board. Cartridge boxes are starting to explode as Weyprecht and Krisch race to the aft cabin and pull out those that are still intact. The fire is a small one. They can extinguish it. Weyprecht says not a word about Carlsen's carelessness. But there are reproaches from the others, and the ice master grows even more taciturn. What next, Klotz says; Sundays are so holy to Mr. Harpooner that he won't hunt bears or skin them, but he's quite willing to blow up the ship on Saturdays.

The ice is no respecter of holidays, and on December 24 the *Tegetthoff*'s planks are again rattling under its pressure as the men open the crates of gifts provided by the navy and by Richers, their supplier in Hamburg: six bottles of cognac, two bottles of champagne, tobacco, a hundred cigars, cookies, playing cards, all wrapped in colorful paper from Munich—a picture of a Christmas tree and six porcelain maidens, ballet dancers raising their dainty arms and pirouetting, thighs glazed pink, mouths deep red, each maiden striking a different charming pose. Richers has also included a book in Plattdeutsch—*Swinegel.* About a man who lives like a pig.

Do they talk a lot about women? Or do they sometimes have a desire to lean against each other, to embrace? The world they come from severely punishes such love. But what laws are valid in the ice? Is it enough just to have the doctor or whoever is on nursing duty stroke their brows when they lie there with fever? I do not know.

If discipline is lost, Weyprecht tells them, then everything is lost.

Nowhere else on earth can exile be so complete as here, under this dreadful triumvirate: darkness, cold, and loneliness. Even angels surely feel some need for variety; how much more must such longing overcome men who have been wrenched from everything that arouses desire and that imagination can embellish. In the end, Lessing's dictum holds true: "We are too accustomed to an association with the other sex but that we would not feel a frightening emptiness were we to be totally deprived of its charms." (*Julius Payer*)

On New Year's Eve the ice is quiet; they light torches and walk around their ship—a procession of light. Then the sailors stand in formation on the ice and sing for the officers. Lorenzo Marola has the finest voice of them all, and Pietro Fallesich accompanies him on the harmonica.

> Solo e pensoso i più deserti campi
> vo mesurando a passi tardi e lenti,
> e gli occhi porto per fuggire intenti,
> ove vestigio uman l'arena stampi. . . .

But no, *what* they sang has not been passed down to us, nor what was in the photograph they placed in a tin can along with a couple of pieces of ship's zwieback and sank in the sea through a water hole. The tin can is the old year, it sinks to the sea floor—may all disappointments be forgotten—and they greet 1873 with three cheers. Payer has a bottle of champagne brought out, its contents frozen, has someone crack the bottle open, and a pale yellow splinter of ice chinks in every glass. And Elling Carlsen, who has spent so many winters in this wilderness, sits down to his log and deliberately, almost solemnly, completes the journal of their misfortunes thus far:

Vi önsker at Gud maa være med os i det nye aar, da kan intet være imod os. [*We wish God to be with us in the new year, then nothing can be against us.*]

II

Campi Deserti

But there are pine trees growing here.

There are no trees on the Spitsbergens, that's what it said. And there are no trees. It is just a solitary pine. Like a cloud of needles and thick branches, the wide crown engulfs the upper floor of the house. A snow-white house. A rarity in Longyearbyen, where the frame houses have the same mild colors he knows from Tromsø. Rusty brown. Rusty red. But this house is white. And the cloud, dark green. On the ground floor, as on a summer's day, the windows stand open.

But it is cold.

Everything is still. Except that curtains rustle in the draft and open a view to the outside. He gazes into the dark interior of the house, the windows at the back are open, too—foamy whitecaps on Adventfjord, a tongue of sea beating soundlessly against the rocks of Longyearbyen. No sound of surf. In the dark house someone starts to speak. Suddenly and loudly and in a monotone. A poem. An Italian poem! Here. You're the only Italian here, Kjetil Fyrand said, the only one.

> Solo e pensoso i più deserti campi
> vo mesurando a passi tardi e lenti,
> e gli occhi porto per fuggire intenti,
> ove vestigio uman l'arena stampi. . . .

Petrarch's sonnet! He had read the first stanza of the sonnet to Anna. But who would know it here? The voice keeps breaking off, and starts over again, falters, scrambles the words, the rhymes, breaks off, starts over again. The way you prepare for a school lesson, desperate repetitions. The curtains rustle, the surf. Three sonnets by Petrarch. By tomorrow. By heart. By heart, Mazzini. *Solo e pensoso i più deserti campi . . . a passi . . .*

> Alone and deep in thought I pass through desolate fields,
> my steps hesitant and slow,
> and thinking to flee cast my eyes about,
> taking notice of where human trace may be left in the sand. . . .

It is Anna's voice. Anna's voice! Not curtains, those are not curtains, but veils of snow trickling from the windowsills, veils of snow, and the crown of the pine is a green fist now, clutching the house, tight, ever tighter . . . *per fuggire intenti* . . . and the stucco is cracking now, the windowsills break off . . . *Oiiya Anore! . . . ove vestigio uman* . . . made of ice!, it is Anna's voice, the house is made of ice and the cloud rolls up into a chinking ball, splinters of ice fly from its branches. . . .

Oiiya Kingo! Anore! Yaaa!

He awakens with a piercing pain in the back of his neck. *Yaaa! Oiiya!*

The shouts through the closed window were loud enough to awaken him. Josef Mazzini almost loses his balance when he leaps up, and pain jerks him back. He takes a groping step to the window, where Kjetil Fyrand has brought his dog team to a halt. Two of the seven mud-caked Greenland dogs immediately begin to scuffle. Fyrand curses and pulls them apart. When Mazzini opens the window onto a cold August morning in Longyearbyen, the barking becomes a bedlam.

"Eh! Er du ikke stått opp enda, du?" Fyrand shouts to him, still having trouble with his dogs.

"Altro schermo non trovo che mi scampi!" Mazzini likewise sticks with his own language. What if he were to awaken from this dream now, too? What if the frame houses melted away and Fyrand disappeared and the stonemason's widow took his place: *Guten Morgen, Herr Josef*?

But the barren, bleak rocky landscape out there does not melt away or burst into pieces. *Campi deserti.* He really *is* awake.

"Eh?" Fyrand has not understood Mazzini's answer, and Mazzini has not understood what Fyrand asked him. For a moment each is all to himself. Each understandable only to himself. I won't claim they understood each other this way, either. But they both wave.

"See you!" *Oiiya!* The dogs leap up. Fyrand's vehicle jerks into motion again.

"See you!" Fyrand can no longer hear Mazzini; he sits on his vehicle—which is nothing more than the rolling floorboard of a small wagon with just a driver's seat and a high steering wheel screwed onto it—and lurches through the soggy morass of Longyearbyen's streets. The snow of the last few days has not stuck. After all, it is summer.

Without turning his gaze away, Mazzini backs away from the window. He tries to repress the thought of schnapps glasses, damp with moisture and filled to the brim—the source of his headache and dizziness. The thought is stubborn. But yesterday evening the glasses had been half full, they were all just half full; over and over, half full.

Boozing. On the *Admiral Tegetthoff* a bottle of rum was given to each sailor every eighteen days. And then they bartered and traded, because some of them drank their comfort away within a day or two. During the period of compressing ice there had been special rations.

Mazzini closes the window. Fyrand has shrunk to a small red figure, his dogs to bright leaping dots. Ubi, the lead dog, at their head, and behind him, like the six-spotter on a die—

Kingo, Avanga, Anore, Spitz, Imiag, and Suli. Fyrand is out exercising . . . after an evening like that. To prevent the sled dogs from losing their discipline during the snowless summer weeks, the oceanographer regularly harnesses the pack to his sled. *Yaaa!* And man and dogs dash through the mining town. But no one pays Fyrand any attention. Not here, where the conditions of the wilderness are noticeably more compelling than the standards of the civilized world, which lies deep below the horizon. Mazzini dresses slowly, clumsily. It is as hot as an incubator in the room he has lived in for a week now; the house belongs to the Store Norske, the coal company. The thermostats for the central heating seem to be reacting already to the coming winter cold. Wet snow is falling outside. And now almost vertical rain again. The mire in the streets between the frame houses is getting ever softer, deeper. It is August 10, 1981. His sailing day. The *Cradle* has been lying at the pier since yesterday evening: 1,300 gross registered tons, 197 feet long, a sea-blue hull and tall white superstructure—a small ship when compared to the icebreakers that ply the 1,100 miles of Northern Sea Route between Murmansk and the Bering Strait, the old Northeast Passage. But how dainty and fragile the *Tegetthoff* would have looked beside this trawler, which Fyrand says has only average fittings for the ice, good enough for a routine summer voyage, but not for heavy ice. . . .

. . . Weyprecht? Captain Kare Andreasen had asked, when Fyrand introduced Mazzini to him. Payer and Weyprecht? . . . Oh yes, sure, Franz Josef Land . . . Weyprecht! The names of so many navigators were linked with the Arctic Ocean, impossible to remember them all. . . . They had been standing at the counter in the bar that the Longyearbyen post office operated on its premises—Fyrand tall and loud, full-bearded, a forty-year-old in a bright yellow baseball jacket that made him look almost childish; the captain slight, hardly taller than Mazzini, and with no insignia of his captaincy. Andreasen had worn a heavy dark blue wool sweater and faded linen trousers; the only thing indicating he had something to say was the way it grew quiet all around him at the bar when he made a comment or asked a question.

The bar, the only one in Longyearbyen, had been packed; crowded around the counter were miners and engineers, scientific personnel, and crew members from the *Cradle* in their red overalls with the ship's name stitched in white. The loudest were three geologists; a project on Bear Island had been ruined by a violent shift in the weather, and they took turns making jokes about the presumed disappointment of an ambitious colleague who had been running it, aping his gestures, their pantomime constantly interrupted by applause and yowls from the others. It had been a long evening. Trudging back from the bar through the mire, Mazzini had been blinded by what was a very gentle ruby-red sun, its rays bringing on the headache with which he would wake up the next morning, awakened by Fyrand's commando shouts and the barking dogs.

It is late morning when Mazzini leaves his room. In the common room of the boardinghouse a television is blaring. Malcolm Flaherty is sitting alone in front of the screen, bathed in the blue light of a catastrophe. He watches as a camera pans restlessly, trying to document a rescue and firefighting operation. Cautiously, as if they are walking on clear fresh ice, men in asbestos suits move across a scene strewn with debris. Baggage and freight have burst open and lie strewn among the widely scattered sections of an airplane that has crashed; next to a mangled wing lies the incinerated body of a passenger. A babbling voice off camera, an eyewitness, describes the accident: an approach for landing, a flash of light, a V of smoke, the crash. The air in the common room is so warm and close that the smoke from a cigarette—Flaherty has wedged it in the notch of an ashtray and forgotten it—rises straight up; the thin column flows and rises, only later curling into a spiral. Flaherty begins most of his days off in front of the tube; but even the latest news is at least a week old before it reaches the mining town in the glacial valley of Adventfjord. People in Longyearbyen live without direct television connection to the mainland. The news from Norwegian television is recorded on videotape, and the cassettes are sent to the Spitsbergens and arrive after a calming delay that makes every event a mere memory. The tapes are then relayed by cable from the local station, Radio Svalbard, to all the frame houses. After such a long delay in delivery, even reports of catastrophes seem less dismaying, and the daily news is colorless.

"Funny," is Malcolm Flaherty's comment about this newsreel, "funny, funny." He reaches for his beer can, gets up with a yawn, lowers the volume, and turns to Mazzini. "Would the vacation boy like to play some pool, maybe?"

A tropical landscape appears on the screen now, then a map of Africa, across which white arrows move like vermin, military columns. Mazzini walks over to the pool table. He has grown accustomed to the tone of voice people appear to use with one another here. A language in which nothing is serious. A week in Longyearbyen has sufficed for him to become familiar with the simple arrangements and narrow confines of social life in the mining town. Boringly familiar. Only the privileged—mining engineers, scientists, and guests of the coal company—use common rooms like this one, where the clack of ivory balls now drowns out the dated news. Life becomes public only in the post office, which aside from the governor's office is the only stone building in Longyearbyen, the heart of the settlement. Relationships are tended there like plants in a greenhouse—connections with the mainland at the mail counter and local, casual friendships at the bar. In the lobby people get whatever material they need for another round of fantasies—at the kiosk hung with international newspapers and, most important, pornographic magazines. Sometimes they climb the stairs to the theater on the top floor, where a Hollywood film or, less often, a folklore show helps them forget that they live at the end of the world. Two days ago they showed Hitchcock's *The Birds*. The horror scenes of attacking swarms of birds, the staccato of their pecking beaks, were met with much laughter and applause by the audience. With the movie running, Flaherty bellowed into the darkness what he remembered about a radio technician who had been badly worked over by arctic terns last year. The man had been walking along the cliffs and gotten too close to the birds' nests.

The *Sterna paradisaea*, a marvelous, gull-like bird with white wings and black head, uses beak and talons in diving attacks—even on humans, when they seem likely to threaten its brood—quick, elegant attacks that leave lacerations and bruises on people's heads, wounds that customers in the bar then examine and have a laugh over. A handout from the Governor's Office recommends that newcomers wear heavy wool caps as protection against the terns. Jaor Hoel, the dentist, once had to sew stitches on the scalp of the radio technician.

Although the ivory balls from his last shot have not yet come to rest, Flaherty leaps at Mazzini, holding his cue like a foil in a feigned attack: "Come on, Weyprecht, it's your turn." Flaherty plays with speed and concentration. When he changes positions, he doesn't walk around the table, he runs, and in the next moment he freezes, poised in rapt attention. Flaherty seems to do everything with this strange amalgam of haste and devotion. Some years ago—he was living in Ny Ålesund, the northernmost settlement in the Spitsbergens—he lost a bet and set out in the middle of the night to construct a gondola on the anchor mast Amundsen and Nobile had used to tie down their dirigible. He spent the next thirty hours swaying in the air. As a result, Flaherty had four frozen toes and the little finger of his left hand amputated. And Governor Thorsen admonished him in the future to show more respect for the historical objects of the Spitsbergens. That at least was the story Kjetil Fyrand told yesterday evening.

But even a Malcolm Flaherty is no oddity in the little community of Longyearbyen, a place full of restless lives marked by abrupt changes. The mining town's frame houses are strung out along the glacial river of Adventfjord and may look like neat and tidy working-class homes, but among all the disparate life stories that Mazzini has heard during his first days on the Spitsbergens, there is none that has not shown at least *one* mark of eccentricity. What differentiated Flaherty from the other miners, however, was the fact that he had lived here for more than twelve years now. Most miners came here for only a few years to earn high, tax-free wages. But if they bore up under the hardships of arctic seclusion and work that was harder in the table mountains of Longyearbyen than elsewhere, then once their trials were over they had prospects of returning to a life a shade more comfortable. The work in mine shafts often as narrow as chimneys promised nothing more than these personal rewards—the value of the mined coal was poor in comparison with the expenses involved. Apparently the spreading maze of galleries was intended more as a palpable demonstration of Norwegian presence in this remote territory of the kingdom than as an example of the laws of the market. But what did laws of the market mean here, anyway? In this stony wilderness, what law would not become meaningless, or brittle at the very least. Nevertheless, sequestered from the world, the miners scratched away to find a better future and the state strove to assert its authority. But no one spoke about the beauty of the glacial landscape, or about nature in general or the fascination of solitude. Why should anyone? Any man who had to crawl on his belly through mountains for 10,000 kroner a month and a shitty life, Flaherty would say when the mines came up in conversation, either knew enough about Mother Earth already or didn't want to hear anything more about her.

Flaherty claimed he had come here for good. Forty-six years old now, the son of an English colonial officer, he had grown up in Kenya, studied mining in Poland, worked in mines in Canada and South Africa, been sentenced to prison for shooting and wounding his father, now a pensioner in Cardiff, and once he had served his time, lived as an unhappy husband and equally unhappy fertilizer salesman in the Shetlands. Twelve years ago Flaherty climbed into a seagoing rowboat and laid to the oars, alone with his rage. It took him three months for the journey across the North Sea—1,500 nautical miles from the Shetlands to the North Cape of Norway. The supreme effort of his life behind him, he smashed his boat in Hammerfest and then boarded a coal freighter for the Spitsbergens. Since then he has lived among the miners as a propulsion specialist and for five years now as the next-door neighbor of Kjetil Fyrand—who likewise had long ago given up plans of ever leaving the Arctic. Flaherty always wore white silk gloves, which he removed only when sitting down to the gold-lacquered harmonium that stood beneath a riot of potted plants in one corner of his room. With hands corroded by eczema he would cozy up to the keys and sing Welsh folk songs, Kjetil Fyrand sometimes accompanying him—as well as he could—on tenor sax.

"I quit." His attempted backspin shot goes nowhere, and Mazzini abruptly cuts the game short, ruining the formation of the balls with an angry sweep of his hand.

When a mud-caked Kjetil Fyrand enters the room—he has had to use brute force to get the dogs back in their kennel today—he finds Flaherty sitting and staring at a TV screen with nothing on it except a white, softly hissing flicker, and Mazzini bent down over a newspaper, both silent. Fyrand's entrance is crude and loud, as if he has not had time to change the tone of voice in which he has been shouting at his dogs. Fyrand is the first; behind him come the dentist Hoel; then Israel Boyle, a Canadian miner with a passion for hiking glaciers; Einar Guttormsgaard, in charge of explosives; and others who for Mazzini are nameless. It is noon. They exchange greetings, direct their usual brief questions to Mazzini, are content with his equally brief answers—it's going okay, sure, can't complain, his tub is sailing today, right, well then—and proceed to the table.

Josef Mazzini thinks he is an insider now; but they know what they are dealing with here—a journalist or writer or whatever, smitten with polar history. They could have passed right by this little Italian and forgotten him, if he had not always been at the side of Fyrand, Flaherty, or Boyle—he even showed up at the mine. Mighty curious he was, this little guy. Israel Boyle had taken him down into the galleries and let him crawl all the way to the working seams. They tell me some people have to dig for miles through mountains just so afterward they can write about how dark and narrow it was, right, Boyle? Governor Thorsen had even invited the little guy in for some schnapps, and now they were taking him along on the egghead boat, so he could have a proper look at ice for once; and Kjetil . . . hey, Kjetil, did you knit some wrist warmers for him, too, so he won't freeze when he's writing, huh? *Skål.* Ah well, there were plenty of busybodies out following the routes of earlier expeditions—draped with a mess of cameras and not the vaguest about how to use a compass.

Something, wasn't it? Nowadays every scurvy vacationer could fly over the fuckin' pole in a Boeing—yeah, wearing a coat and tie, eating steak from a plastic bag on his knees, and holding his Kodak to the porthole. And suddenly they're all hot again about a few loonies from back when heck was a pup, who froze their heads blue trying to get there in worm-eaten boats or on a sled or in a balloon. Crazy. They had heard the little guy wanted to take off now with Fyrand's dogs, too—just had to play a little mush-mush with his team; he must have got those mutts mixed up with ponies. Fine; who cares. *Skål.*

By late afternoon it is time to go on board. The snow shower has stopped. The rain, too. But the northeaster continues to blow as hard and cold as before, scuffing the fjord with whitecaps. The rust-eaten freight gondolas of an abandoned cable railway screech with each gust. A long procession of wooden supports leads up to the mouths of the shafts. No fog. The *Cradle* is to sail before midnight. Fyrand and Mazzini are standing at the counter in the bar, ready to travel. A Walkman hangs from the oceanographer's belt, where until now a large-caliber revolver has dangled during their brief hikes together along the Arctic coast or into the interior. Fyrand put on the earphones after his first beer, and from time to time suddenly he tries to sing along with snatches of lyrics he alone can hear—*Never put me in a job . . . Mama Rose . . . well, never, never again . . .*

In the last few days Fyrand has seldom been seen without his Walkman—just as always, whenever a shipment of new cassettes arrives at the Longyearbyen general store, a supermarket where you can buy everything from accessories for your arctic outfit to candied fruit and diapers. Fyrand could grapple with a melody for days, listening over and over to a piece—he ordered mostly saxophone tapes—going into raptures about the original and trying to play it on his own instrument. Then he would take the earphones off and cast it all aside and not play or sing another note for weeks. *Mama Rose!* Another beer, Eirik; but this one was definitely the last.

Kjetil Fyrand had first come here five years ago for a summer at the local branch of the Polar Institute and had stayed on because of Torill Holt, a teacher at the local school. But the teacher had married since then, was named Larsen now, lived with her husband in a house full of garish wallpaper—

photographs of Caribbean landscapes—and now saw the oceanographer only when he sat grumbling in the last rows of the theater at the shows her pupils put on. Fyrand was still here. He seldom left the Spitsbergens, and always only for a few days in Oslo to present to a small audience his hypotheses or work on plans for some research project in the high Arctic. He sometimes attended congresses, too, and always came home with an assortment of expensive tobaccos and liquors. Fyrand would often sit for nights on end in Guttormsgaard's office out at the end of the runway, where explosives were kept, maintaining radio contact with expeditions under way in the desolate wastes. And sometimes he would take his boat or sled and himself disappear for weeks, to tend his measuring stations and read data. He spent many of his free days together with Flaherty or Boyle on the glaciers, and during the winter months he made the most bizarre landscape mosaics out of little pieces of copper he enameled in a small kiln, or taught his sled dogs difficult tricks. When Fyrand gave the command, Ubi, the lead dog, would walk on its hind legs. No one in Longyearbyen had had to depend on dogsleds for a long time now; almost everyone here had a scooter for the winter, snowmobiles that turned the polar night into the noisiest time of the year, and once the snow had thawed, people plowed about in the morass of the few miles of roads with four-wheel-drive vehicles or, more frequently, used the taxis, muck-encrusted limousines that commuted between harbor, airstrip, and mines. Keeping a dog team was little more than an expensive hobby, even here, but an infallible sign, perhaps, of arctic manliness. Besides Fyrand and some others, the dentist Hoel kept four bearlike Greenland dogs in his kennel; he would stand upright on skis and have them pull him across the ice in the polar darkness. Members of the local dog training club considered them the most vicious dogs in the Spitsbergens.

Fyrand's most private but perhaps most passionate interest was devoted to something very remote from his research in the Arctic Ocean—the jellyfish of Mediterranean and tropical waters. The bookcases of his room were stacked with technical literature about hydrozoa; even the shade of his desk lamp was a precise milk-glass reproduction of a moon jellyfish. To him there was no stranger and more elegant sight, Fyrand told Mazzini, than a medusa floating through the submarine twilight—the fragile and tender tentacles hanging from bells, chalices, or domes. Each movement through the turquoise water was a gentle heartbeat. . . .

But this passion of the oceanographer's would also have had no importance in the life of Josef Mazzini, if years before Fyrand had not made a trip to Vienna primarily because of jellyfish, a trip that led to his stumbling into Anna Koreth's circle of friends. At a time when Mazzini was still having his troubles in the paperhanger's home in Trieste, Fyrand had gone to Vienna to study a wonderful model of a jellyfish made by a Bohemian glassblower, in the collection of the Museum of Natural History. He had become acquainted with Anna through a bibliophilic zoologist. The acquaintanceship ultimately exhausted itself in a long correspondence, often illustrated with a profusion of Fyrand's line drawings.

"That'll do it, Eirik, one last Glenfiddich for me, a quick one, and then call us a taxi. We're due at the pier." Fyrand has shoved the frame of his earphones down around his neck. . . . *Never put me in a job* . . . Mazzini shoulders his pack.

The harbor lies farther up the fjord. It is a short drive. The taxi windows are opaque with mud, and the countryside, bathed in red light, can be seen wending toward them only through the windshield, which someone has done a poor job of cleaning. Fyrand and Mazzini are the last to go on board. Handshakes. Then Fyrand puts his earphones back on, and he doesn't remove them in the mess for a brief speech given by Odmund Jansen, a meteorologist from Trondheim and the project director, to the ten assembled scientists, three guests, and twelve crew members: he is happy to be able to greet on board and so forth, especially the Polar Institute's guests . . . hopes they'll work well together . . . and so forth. They have all heard speeches like this before. The LED on Fyrand's Walkman glows red and obstinate; he grins at a blonde, the only woman on board . . . *Mama Rose!* . . . a glacier specialist from Massachusetts. Josef Mazzini understands only Jansen's greetings to his guests—the English portion of his speech.

The sailing of the *Cradle* is what it is, no different from the sailing of any ferry from any harbor—the standard start of an official voyage. The only echo of some muted solemnity is the long wail of the foghorn as it rolls back into Advent Valley, breaks on the rocks, and returns. With a force of 3,200 horsepower, the trawler steams out the fjord into the black turmoil of the Arctic Ocean.

I picture Josef Mazzini cozy in his cabin during those first hours on board, and I ask myself whether during his days in Longyearbyen he had not already begun gradually to detach his trip from memories of the voyage of the *Tegetthoff.* After all, nothing but the present lay over the Arctic, the imperative of a present that would not allow this barren land to dwindle to a mere backdrop for a memory. Conjuring up scenes of a fading past cannot have been an easier task for Mazzini in the mining town than it had been in the reading room of the naval archives in Vienna, where he had paged through the log of the *Tegetthoff,* paged through it again and again. But I have no records that would confirm my guesses beyond a doubt. Mazzini's diary entries from the Spitsbergens are as spare as the journals of Haller the hunter or Krisch the machinist—a brief notation of what has occurred, sometimes in unintelligible catchwords and with hardly a thought beyond the present moment. And so I shall hold fast to my picture of Josef Mazzini's feeling something close to relief when, for instance, Malcolm Flaherty mocked him a little by calling him "Weyprecht," showing him in an offhanded way that there is probably no fantasy, no idea, from which one cannot free oneself with a little laughter.

12

Terra Nuova

January. The sea of ice is truly the land of Uz. And everyone here is Job.

Hunter Klotz is ill with melancholy and consumption;
Able seaman Fallesich with scurvy;
Hunter Haller with rheumatism;
Able seaman Scarpa with scurvy and cramps;
Machinist Krisch with consumption. . . .

There is no one who does not show some sign of disease and weakness; for every man who rises again from his sick-bed, another lies down. And so things continue.

Hope for the end of polar night, for the redemptive return of the sun, could not be greater aboard the *Admiral Tegetthoff* during January 1873 if the ship were the wooden temple of a cult of light honoring sunrise as the return of a divinity. The sick will regain their strength, the walls of ice will tumble and drift away on the waves like melting ruins, and the wind will be favorable—if only the sun will climb above the horizon again.

But the darkness is still great.

On clear, starry days, the pale image of some future dawn can be seen now at the edge of their sky—a dull arc of light that quickly seeps away in a violet dusk. They stand at the rail then and praise this light; it really is a hint brighter and stronger today than yesterday; today they can almost make out a line of print that had been quite unreadable only a few days before, can even recognize a face at four paces without a hurricane lamp.

But the compression of the ice continues. The sea appears to be buried for all eternity under rigid bulwarks of ice. Weyprecht's observation tent and a portion of their stock-piled coal disappear in a fissure that suddenly opens up. Bop, one of their sled dogs, is torn into the deep. Broken only by a few slight rises in temperature, the cold of January turns gin into glassy clumps, and mercury left out in the open becomes so hard that when they load a rifle with it, the bullet pierces an inch-thick board.

Even if life has not become gentler, nor their fear less acute in the horrible hours of alarm as they await catastrophe, the glowing arc of light on the horizon gives them courage to summon energies against the chaos out there. Weyprecht tells them that above all else it is order that keeps them alive; the most ordinary daily chores—meteorological measurements, the routine of changing the watch, even kitchen duty, or the officers' inspection tour of the crew's quarters every Sunday—are beacons to the fact that human order dare not lose a whit of its value, not even in this wilderness. Maintenance of law and discipline is, in fact, simply an expression of humanity and the only way to survive in this desolation.

Ice master and harpooner Carlsen serves as an example. The old man, who has spent so many years of his life in arctic seas, always wears his white periwig when invited to the officers' table; on feast days of martyrs whom he holds in special honor, he pins his Order of Olaf to his furs. (But when the waves and veils of the northern lights flare up in the sky, Elling Carlsen removes everything metallic from his body, even his belt buckle, in order to prevent any disruption in the harmony of their flowing figures and to ensure that the ire of the lights is not directed toward him.)

In the last weeks of January, Weyprecht has a school set up. None of them has ever spent a winter so close to the North Pole or experienced the unremitting threat of this screeching wasteland, but that was no reason why *every man on board* should not learn to read and write. To counter the endlessness of time and their own melancholy, let them put the ship's library to use—four hundred volumes, including the plays of Lessing and Shakespeare, Milton's *Paradise Lost*, and yellowed editions of the Vienna *Neue Freie Presse*. They shall have poetry! and thoughts that carry them beyond the woes of the present. Weyprecht and the officers Brosch and Orel teach the Italians and Slavs; Payer instructs his Tyroleans. They sit in the main cabin wrapped in furs, their beards white with frost—some copying the alphabet, some learning the principles of physics and mathematics.

When an exercise was to be checked, students had to hold their breath so that the teacher, speaking from a cloud of frost, could make out what was on their slates. Or in the middle of a division problem they would suddenly have to stop and rub their hands with snow. Is it any wonder, then, that school was not popular? (*Julius Payer*)

Often an alarm breaks off the daily lesson and forces them to their lifeboats. At last the cold becomes so intense that their lesson degenerates into an irregular series of instructions and homework. What's the point, Klotz says, are we supposed to read Holy Writ to the bears? Build rafts made from our lesson books? Toward the end of January—with dawn shedding some light during the late hours of morning now—their Newfoundland Matochkin is mauled by a polar bear. Payer's team is now barely able to pull a large sled. Does the commander on land still believe in journeys of discovery now? Undaunted, Payer forces his dogs into their harness, sometimes beating them so hard that Haller must nurse them after the exercise. Payer's excursions become more frequent—and more furious. If there is another no-man's-land here in the far north, then he will harry his dogs to find it.

I do not know whether the occasional dissension between Weyprecht, the earnest, reassuring scholar, and Payer, the enthusiastic discoverer, began to take on dramatic forms in the first months of 1873. The diaries from this period contain no entries about it. I do know, however, that Carl Weyprecht was commanding officer; he was *the* authority—the judge when arguments, and fights, arose among the sailors, the comforter and prophet when the issue was the fragile hope of returning home, and the final arbiter in all questions. And Payer, the commander on land, was still quite without land. The following year, as they make their agonizing retreat across the ice back to the inhabited world, Weyprecht will make mention in his diary of an argument of which there is no record in their journals of that first polar night.

Payer is starting in again with his old jealousies. He is once again so charged with rage that I am prepared for some serious collision at any moment. In front of the men he made offensive remarks to me about some trivial matter (a sack of bread; he claimed he was being made to carry too much), which I could not let pass without reprimand. I told him that in the future he should be careful not to use such expressions, otherwise I would have to censure him in public. He then went into one of his rages, said that he still remembered quite clearly how I had threatened him with a revolver a year ago, assuring me he would steal the march on me next time and declaring outright that he would try to kill me the moment he saw he might not make it home. (*Carl Weyprecht*)

I have difficulty imagining the deliberate Weyprecht confronting his comrade and former friend with a revolver, or for that matter imagining Payer, the poet and painter, uttering murder threats—but worse metamorphoses have occurred in arctic seas, and later, after the triumphant return that seems so unattainable in January 1873, their hate will recede into polite phrases. *I begin the work at hand*—so Julius Payer will one day open his report on the expedition—*with unreserved acknowledgment of the splendid services rendered by my colleague, Lieutenant Commander Weyprecht, measured against which any success I may have achieved is of little importance. . . .*

But if the event did occur as Weyprecht records it in his diary—its closely written pages are slowly fading now in the files of the Austrian naval archives—then it was probably during these days of internal and external twilight as they waited so expectantly for the sun's return.

The lighter it became, the more horrifying were the scenes of destruction revealed. Mountainous cliffs of ice rose all about us. . . . Even at a short distance from the ship, one could see nothing but its masts; all the rest lay hidden behind a high wall of ice. The ship itself had been lifted seven feet above sea level and was resting on a bubble of ice, this removal from its natural element lending it a most wretched appearance. The bubble had formed from a floe cracked by numerous fissures that had opened and frozen to again. This most amazing vault was the result both of ice pushing up beneath and of the recent violence of lateral compression. . . . The eager expectation with which we awaited the returning sun also gave us cause to regard one another more closely, and we were surprised at the changes our external appearance had undergone in the long period of night. Our faces were hollow and the pallor was stark. Most of us bore the marks of convalescence, protruding noses and sunken eyes. . . . (*Julius Payer*)

I am in considerable pain, particularly when taking in breath, and am confined to bed. I have lost much flesh and look very poor, was quite alarmed at seeing my emaciated body in the bath, but hope nonetheless that my regimen of whale oil will set me in order again. (*Otto Krisch*)

11 February 1873, Tuesday: Wind and snowfall. The ice shifting near the ship. A channel has opened of late. Dogsledding and lessons.

12, Wednesday: Clear weather. The ice shifting near the ship. Dogsledding and lessons.

13, Thursday: Wind and fog. Cleaned the doctor's cabin, and lessons.

14, Friday: Dogsledding. In the afternoon, post in bottles was sent on its way, to the north, south, east, and west. The post was placed in the bottles, the bottles corked and sealed and then given over to the ice. The bottles contained news of our expedition and are intended to give tidings of us in case we should perish and none of us four-and-twenty ever be seen again. (Johann Haller)

Austrian Bark, "Admiral Tegetthoff," Expedition to Siberian Arctic Seas. Frozen in Pack Ice, 14 February 1873

On August 21st, 1872, near the coast of Novaya Zemlya, at 76° 22' north and 62° 3' east of Greenwich, trapped in the ice and frozen fast. Since then, drifting with the pack ice depending on prevailing winds, and throughout the winter endangered by constant movements of the ice. The ship has been raised several feet and rests among ice of the heaviest sort, yet is in perfectly sound condition. All are well on board, no particular cases of illness. Intend to press on to ESE once the ice opens, in order to reach the Siberian coast near the Taymyr Peninsula, and then to proceed eastward along its coast as far as conditions permit. In the summer of 1874 we shall begin our return voyage through the Kara Sea. Our farthest northern latitude thus far was 78° 50' north by 71° 4' east of Greenwich, with no sighting of new land. Until the middle of October 1872 the coasts of Novaya Zemlya were enclosed in thick ice in all directions, we later lost sight of them. Should the ship be crushed by ice, we intend to return to our supply depot on the coast of Novaya Zemlya. (Payer m.p.) (Weyprecht m.p.)

It will be forty-eight years before a Norwegian sealer will find the first of the bottles that the expedition set out, again and again and at different latitudes along the west coast of Novaya Zemlya. By that time the addressees of the document—the Naval Department, Vienna, and the Imperial

Royal Consulate—will have disappeared, the monarchy will be dissolved, the expeditionary commanders long dead. News that the bottle-post has been found will appear in the news supplement of the Vienna *Neue Freie Presse,* and upon reading it the former first officer of the *Tegetthoff,* the aged Gustav Brosch, Vice-Admiral, Retired, will add precise memories of his own and the wish *that this bold voyage of exploration may never be consigned to the past. . . .* But enough. The expedition's post still lies somewhere within a two-nautical-mile radius of the bark, and the crew has gathered as if for a celebration. It is February 19, 1873. Two days ago they saw a distorted phantom of the sun above the horizon, a reflection—but today they await the sun itself, golden-red reality.

There, for a moment, a wave of light rolled through the wide space, a herald, and then the sun, enveloped in purple, rose above the icy platform. No one spoke; who could have put words to the feeling of redemption shining now in every face and unconsciously revealed in the soft, artless cry of a simple man: ''Benedetto giorno!'' Hesitantly showing only half its disk, the sun rose above the bleak rim of ice as if this world were not worthy of its light. . . . Bleak and dreamlike, ruined colossi of ice, like countless sphinxes, towered into the radiant sea of light. The cliffs and ramparts stared out from encircling fissures and cast long shadows across the expanse of snow sparkling with diamonds. (*Julius Payer*)

Klotz is so enraptured by the sight of the half-sun that for hours afterward his eyes see leaping mirages—turquoise, pale green, and white balls. How often have they seen morning arrive, glowing and great—on freighters, in the mountains above the Passeiertal, or on the battlefields of the Imperial Army. But what are all the daybreaks of their former life compared with this single incomplete sunrise. And although they are not released from darkness, or from the sea of ice, or from their imprisonment and the rigors of illness, for this one day they nevertheless try to be released from it *all.* They set a sign. They celebrate Carnival.

The officers promise a special ration of rum to anyone who appears in Mardi Gras costume. And so the sailors cut crowns, helmets, and bishop's mitres from empty tin cans, sew academic gowns from rags, make flippers and paws from felt, pour alcohol down Zumbu, the dog bought in Lapland, and with the magic of a few bits of felt transform him into a staggering dragon. And towing the dragon behind them, they dance amid the crags of ice to the music of a harmonica and Marola's songs. For this one day, Job shall be a Carnival fool. And when the unsuccessful pursuit of a bear leaves both Haller and Klotz with frostbitten legs, Antonio Catarinich presents them with crutches wrapped in garlands.

21 February, Friday: Clear weather. Klotz and I feeling seedy with our frozen feet. Terrible pain.

22, Saturday: Clear weather. Klotz and I seedy. Early in the morning another bear approaches the ship. Because no one was up yet except the officer on watch and one sailor, the bear is killed with no ruckus.

23, Sunday: Services at 11 o'clock. Klotz and I seedy, so that neither could attend church.

24, Monday: Klotz and I both seedy with bad feet.

25, Tuesday: Bright weather. Klotz and I seedy. Gifts are given to the crew as prizes. I won a bottle of raspberry juice. (*Johann Haller*)

For two long weeks in March they must fear for the doctor's life. It now looks as if medical officer Kepes, who has helped them so often with a ready ear for all their pain, will himself perish in feverish convulsions. He lies there hallucinating, batting away medicine and food like a madman. What happens if the doctor dies? Who will advise them then, when they are wounded and sick? Only a few sailors trust Alexander Klotz's medical skills. And so they take turns sitting by the doctor's bed, helpless except to stare at him and talk to him.

Commander Weyprecht does not leave his side and makes every effort to succor him; in the brief periods when the doctor is rational, he tells him dosages of appropriate medicines, which the commander then prepares himself; . . . but the doctor's condition has not improved but grown worse, he screams, weeps, and moans incessantly day and night. (*Otto Krisch*)

I kept watch over the doctor. He is unconscious now, and his howls are dreadful in the small cabin. (*Johann Haller*)

On March 28th, wind at 1–3 out of NNW, temperature of −26° R [−27° F]. The doctor's condition changed significantly during the night of the 27th to the 28th, the convulsions have ceased, but to all appearances he is now out of his mind. He babbled all night, seeing all sorts of ghosts, and has been delirious all day. (*Otto Krisch*)

Demons. The men nursing him know this evil. When Klotz and Haller are alone with Kepes for an hour, they pour alcohol over the doctor's left arm, the "heart arm," and set the hallucinating man afire. The medics roar with laughter and joy when Kepes screams in terror and for a brief moment awakens to consciousness—then sinks back into a peaceful sleep with no feverish dreams.

When a few days later Kepes takes his first walk on deck, Klotz says that the powers of fire freed the Hungarian of his demons, pulling him out of his madness and back into the world. But perhaps it was not such a good turn they had done him, for what sort of world is this world.

Their spring is stormy and sometimes so radiantly white that they have to wear their snow goggles in order to search the wastes for favorable signs, for channels and fissures. Out of ice blocks they build a sun deck where convalescents can spend the afternoon out of the wind. Sometimes within a few hours the temperature rises from −40° F to above the freezing point, and every tear of thawing water wept by the rigging is an event. They can see themselves under sail now. A day of good omen—the first arctic petrels alight on the yards. Their imprisonment will soon be at an end.

The snow, till now like sandy gravel, begins to grow moist, can be packed, and the unaccustomed temperatures feel unpleasantly sultry, like the sirocco winds of our own country. The thick furs, which only a short time ago provided inadequate protection against the intense cold, are uncomfortable. A heavy fog covers the sky, smothering every trace of light whether at noon or midnight. The snow falls now not in fine needles but in enormous masses of large flakes borne by the wind and burying everything in their path.—The warmth holds sway for only a brief time in those regions. Usually within 48 hours the wind abates and turns slowly to the north, the dark clouds open here and there to reveal the flashing northern lights and stars, the skies clear, and the thermometer begins to fall.—There is a pause in the battle between the contending powers of the air. But only a brief one! As if in rage at this brash intruder before which it fled, a chilling snowstorm breaks from the north with redoubled strength, the scourge of all arctic travelers. . . . The air is so filled with snow that a man can breathe only with his back turned, and will meet certain death should he expose himself unprotected to the storm.

It is impossible to determine if the sky is clouded over or not, for everything is a single restless mass of driving snow whipped onward by the wind. . . . This mass of snow races across the icy plain, building great walls wherever it meets a barrier, leveling all rough places, and pressing everything together so firmly that the new blanket is firm beneath the foot.

In summer the heralds of such a snowstorm are usually mock suns, in winter mock moons.

Their rays fractured by invisible ice crystals hovering in the air, a complete system of suns and moons appears, always set at certain prescribed angles. Usually it is only a circle of light surrounding the sun at a distance of 23°; on both sides and directly above it, 3 of these mock suns are arranged inside the circle. If the phenomenon is more intense, a second circle of light forms at the same distance from the first, in which 3 more mock suns appear. Light from the real sun then builds clusters that radiate vertically and horizontally as far as the first circle, forming a large cross. It can happen that another inverted arc of light forms above the vertical shaft and tangent to the outside circle, and that yet two more suns appear, one on each side, but at a greater distance. The phenomenon is one of imposing beauty. (*Carl Weyprecht*)

With each new day the hour of liberation for which we so passionately yearned seemed more imminent. Once we were free again it was well within the realm of possibility that we would reach, if not legendary Gilies Island, then at least the uninhabited arctic coasts of Siberia. Thus Siberia had become the rosiest of our hopes. Even as we drifted, however, someone indulging in especially wild expectations still counted perhaps on discovering new lands. In point of fact, however, our wishes were so modest that even the smallest rock would have satisfied our pride as discoverers. (*Julius Payer*)

They have once again taken up the difficult task of dealing with the ice. For eight and a half hours every day they hammer, blast, saw, and dig at their floe; they club the ice from the rigging and split open the glaze of armor enclosing the hull. They suspend kettles above fires and boil the stench of winter from their clothes, use lye to scrub the soot of their petroleum and whale-oil lamps from the cabin walls. Krisch scrapes the rust from the boiler, fits the copper tubing, the inlet cock, and the skimming tap with new oakum seals, polishes the pistons and expansion valves, and oils the bearings—the engine is like new, ready for a head of steam. The hull is tarred and the sails are aired, lying at the ready. But they are still frozen fast. When, after Bible readings on the Lord's Day, they look at what has been accomplished, it seems as if no time at all had passed between their renewed labors and the futile efforts of last year, as if they must repeat the year like some exam they have failed to pass. All is unchanged. All in vain. Every hand's turn is the labor of Sisyphus, Payer says. Sisyphus? they ask. He went through what we're going through, Payer says.

The masses of ice that winter has pressed in under their ship lie thirty feet thick in some places, the water holes are as deep as wells, and all attempts to bring the bark back to sea level end with the *Tegetthoff* so askew that moving on deck is like crossing a mountain slope, and Orasch, their Austrian cook, says he can't keep a pot on the stove. The *Tegetthoff* lies like a wreck on a dry dock of ice; they have to prop up the hull with beams to keep it from capsizing. And the guest perched in the crow's nest burns his eyes on the sparkling distance.

On May 1 the bitch Zemlya whelps four puppies, only one of which survives—Torossy, a male, the first creature on board with no memory of green landscapes, trees, and fields, of anything that is *home.* Y'see, Haller says, trying to comfort his friend Klotz, who is tormented by homesickness, that pup ain't never seen no medders 'nd it's the friskiest of us all.

Bear skeletons, the bones gnawed clean, rim the puddles of thawing water, but Torossy jumps around among them as if this were a beautiful reed-edged pond in the Passeiertal. He rummages in the dung and ashes, in the craters of garbage that encircle the *Tegetthoff* and are slowly sinking into the ice beneath the warming sun—it is his field, his meadow, his garden. The sailors spoil the puppy and watch over him as over some sacred animal, and even Jubinal, the lead dog—who normally allows no one near him and is said to have been brought from the Urals by a Siberian Israelite who was unable to tame his savage energies—allows Torossy to tug food from his jaws.

The days of the puppy's youth are the months of their continued captivity. Their diaries grow more hopeless and monotone, the entries a record of work that never changes. Even the smallest event is a sensation for them now. They celebrate royal holidays—Church holidays, too—with silk flags, ceremonies, and improvised banquets. Midshipman

Orel bakes special cakes. Bear hunts are orgies; celestial phenomena, operas.

On May 26th there was to be a partial eclipse of the sun in these latitudes; by mistake we gathered to await the start of the eclipse 2½ hours too early. Everyone on board who owned a telescope set it up and we watched expectantly for the moon to enter the solar disk. But when our wait proved in vain, we realized our error as to the time, but remained in position beside our telescopes so as not to detract from the dignity of the observation for the crew. (*Julius Payer*)

But is it dignified and proper for Payer, the commander on land and geographer to the Kaiser, to set his crew to helping him build an artificial track three nautical miles across the ice? A track that leads over viaducts and through tunnels along the shores of thawing lakes that bear Austrian names, and past post offices, temples, statues, and taverns made of ice? True, Payer needs the track to exercise his team of dogs. But temples, post offices, taverns—an entire playground resembling a Japanese garden? For the crew, this job is as dignified as any other. The temples are more splendid, their towers higher, than Payer has ordered. They aren't obeying, they are *playing*. One Sunday in June, able seaman Vincenzo Palmich dresses up as a mountain lass and takes his place on the tower balcony of Snow Castle, while Lorenzo Marola stands at the portcullis below. Joined by his squire Pietro Fallesich, whose face is disfigured by open chilblains, he serenades Palmich. But then there is cry of *Open water!* from the crow's nest, and they are hurled from their fairy tale into reality.

23 June 1873, Monday: Clear weather and north wind. Temperature 0° [*32° F*]. *All of us, officers and crew, are working with hacks and saws to open a canal and move the ship into it. It is hard work and a struggle to free the ship, but to no purpose and there is no chance that we will move it from here. A canal with open water is visible in the distance only from the top of the mainmast. Our ship remains locked in the ice.*

24, Tuesday: Clear weather and north wind. Temperature +1° [34° F]. Helped the doctor to make wine. A bear approaches the ship. The first lieutenant saw him coming and called to me: "A bear!" We moved toward it under cover and killed it at a fair range. Toward evening a second bear approaches the ship, still at some distance. Lieutenant Brosch was on the mast and spotted the bear. He calls out: "A bear!" Commander Weyprecht runs straight for the bear, some 500 paces from the ship. The first lieutenant and I follow at double time under cover. The bear is now only ten paces from Commander Weyprecht. He shoots, and misses the bear. Weyprecht had only one cartridge with him. The bear was about to make a leap for Weyprecht. At that moment, however, the first lieutenant put a bullet into the bear's chest and Commander Weyprecht was saved. The bear fled wounded. I hit him a second time with an exploding shot, but the bear kept going. I gave him a second and a third hit; he lay there for a moment, but then got up again and fled on, until I could shoot him through the heart from up close, and he finally lay there dead.

25, Wednesday: Clear weather and north wind. Temperature +2° [36° F]. Cleaned a bearskin.

26, Thursday: Cloudy weather and north wind. Temperature −2° [28° F]. Cleaned a bearskin.

27, Friday: Cloudy weather and north wind. Temperature −1° [30° F]. Spent the day waiting table.

28, Saturday: Cloudy weather and east wind. Temperature −1° [30° F]. Hacked ice.

29, Sunday: Sts. Peter and Paul. My birthday. At about 1:30 in the morning a bear approached the ship. The officer on watch and a sailor killed him. Then I was awakened to skin the bear. At the same time I turn thirty, I am skinning a polar bear. What a fine birthday present. (Johann Haller)

Whatever they do now—they have done it once before.

The days repeat themselves. Time is a circle. Things return that they thought had sunk from sight long ago. One morning the cadaver of Bop, the Newfoundland that had been swallowed by the winter's ice, is lying there in the snow again—stiff and hard and not rotted at all, as if he had died yesterday. They tie a stone from Payer's geological collection around his neck, dig a well down to sea level, and sink the carcass. Everything, including every hope, must be buried here twice, three times, again and again. And because everything that happens is only a repetition of itself, their conversations stray further and further into the past. The officers talk about the naval battle of Lissa as if it still lay ahead of them and quarrel over political issues that have long since been decided. July seems a single, endless day, and then it is August and they begin to realize that the ice will never release their ship, that they are the plaything of winds and currents, drifting toward a second winter.

In the middle of August their floe drifts to within four nautical miles of a massive, rubble-covered iceberg. Even if it is only a floating waste dump, at least they have discovered stones!, the crumbs and splinters of a coastline. The commander on land is at the head of a detachment of seven sailors hurrying toward the mountain.

There were two moraines across its broad back. These were the first stones and boulders we had seen in a long time, limestone and argillaceous schist, and so great was our joy at these messengers from some land or other that we rummaged in the rubble as eagerly as if we stood among the treasures of India. The men found what they took to be gold (pyrites), and their one concern was whether they would ever be able to return to Dalmatia with it. (Julius Payer)

Although Payer explains to the sailors that their find is totally worthless, they make aprons of their furs and carry the pyrites back to the ship. Perhaps they would have desisted if Weyprecht, too, had confirmed the sterility of their stones;

but Weyprecht says nothing. And so they pile the stones in their cabins, run back to the berg, and return with another heavy load. And then, slowly and powerfully, the iceberg drifts from view and three foggy days later it has vanished. They mourn it as a paradise lost. No upheaval breaks the sharp edge of the horizon now, and they sink back into uneventful time.

I have given much thought to the chaotic moment they will later claim to be the greatest and most thrilling of their arctic voyage—and I have come to the conclusion that I have no right to describe it: the moment when someone on board—who it was is not recorded—suddenly cries *Land!* LAND!

It is August 30, 1873, at 79° 43′ north latitude and 59° 33′ east longitude. The morning is cloudy, scraps of fog drift above the ice; it clears off in the afternoon. The wind blows from the north-northeast in the morning but then falls. The high temperature for the day is measured at 30° F, which sinks to 26° toward evening; the sounding at noon measures the depth of the sea at 692 feet, muddy bottom: a day on which Pietro Lusina will conclude his log entry with *Terra nuova scoperta*—New land discovered—the first record that the Old World is now free of one of its last white spots.

It was around noon, we were leaning over the side staring into the desultory fog, through which sunlight broke now and again, when a passing wall of mist suddenly revealed a rugged line of rocks far to the northwest. Within a few minutes a radiant alpine landscape came into view! In the first few moments we all stood there incredulous, bewitched; then, overcome with irrefutable evidence that our good fortune was genuine, we broke into boisterous cheers: ''Land, land, land at last!'' No one on board was sick now; everyone hurried on deck to convince himself with his own eyes that we had before us an achievement of the expedition that could never be taken from us. Granted, not because of anything we had done, but because of a chance whim of our floe. We had achieved it as if in a dream. . . .

Millennia had come and gone without bearing the tidings of the existence of this land to mankind. And now its discovery had fallen into the lap of a paltry band of men almost given up for lost—as the reward for tenacious hope and perseverance in overcoming all their sufferings. And this paltry band, who were now counted among the missing in their homeland, were so overjoyed to be able to show their distant monarch some sign of their homage that they gave this newly discovered land the name

Kaiser Franz Josef Land

(*Julius Payer*)

It appears to be a fairly large land, for you can follow it far to the north and west. At its christening everyone raised a glass of wine and gave three cheers, then bearings were taken of the best-defined mountains and promontories. It was indeed a joyful event to see land again after 11 months, and all the more joyful for us as it was undiscovered land and our expedition had thus achieved its goal. (*Otto Krisch*)

Knowledge of our globe is a matter of self-evident interest to every educated individual; but inasmuch as those latitudes that are uninhabited and uninhabitable because of prevailing conditions are of purely scientific importance, descriptive geography is of value only to the extent that the topography influences the meteorological, physical, and hydrographic phenomena of earth; a sketch of broad outlines suffices. A detailed geography of the Arctic is in most cases of secondary importance; but if, as is often the case, it relegates the true purpose of expeditions—i.e., scientific research—to the background, stifling that purpose, as it were, then it is absolutely reprehensible. . . .

It is unnecessary for us to extend our field of observation to the highest latitudes in order to achieve scientific results of major importance.

If, however, principles pursued thus far remain unchallenged, if arctic research is not conducted systematically and on a sound scientific basis, if geographic discovery continues to be the goal to which men aspire and to which all their labor and effort are dedicated, then new expeditions will continue to be sent out whose success is little more than a piece of land buried in the ice or a few miles wrested from the ice at infinite pain—all of which is of practically no value in comparison with the larger scientific problems, solutions to which will ever be the concern of the human intellect. (*Carl Weyprecht*)

27 August 1873, Wednesday: Rain, snow, north wind. Temperature −1° [*30° F*]. *I am steward again. This damn waiting table.*

28, Thursday: Rain, snow, and strong north wind. Temperature −2° [*28° F*]. *Spent the day waiting table.*

29, Friday: Rain, snow, and strong north wind. Temperature 0° [*32° F*]. *Spent the day waiting table.*

30, Saturday: Clear weather. Temperature +2° [*36° F*]. *We have discovered a new land. We made an attempt to get closer, but came upon a channel and could get no farther. For five quarter-hours we gazed from on board at the land in the distance. It gave us all great joy. We have given the land the name "Kaiser Franz Josef Land."*

31, Sunday: Clear weather. Church services at 11. Spent the day waiting table. (*Johann Haller*)

During the first days of September they surrender and give up their effort to free the *Tegetthoff*. All of their attentions and cares are directed now at the land, their land!, which appears at varying distances of ten to fifteen miles, sometimes disappearing in the fogbanks, only to reemerge more beautiful than ever—their land, spinning before them in the slow dance of their drift and displaying its ridges, palisades, and cliffs like a beguiling, massive lady. *Terra nuova*. No hoax, no mirage. They have really discovered a new land. Again and again they make a run for its coasts. And again and again a labyrinth of channels and ice barriers forces them to turn back out of fear that colliding ice may cut off their retreat. They sense their own impotence, rage, and despondency as never before when the land melts into fog and vanishes from view for seven days. Is the sight of those coasts in the distance to be all, a single fleeting image in their long, inexorable drift? During this period they swarm from the ship, bewildered, undisciplined, without marching orders or caution—not even Weyprecht can hold them back. Nor can he calm them when, exhausted and disappointed, they return out of the wall of white. But this time the arctic winter is merciful. Their floe freezes fast to the belt of ice surrounding the archipelago. Their drift begins to solidify into a slow movement up and down the coast. The land itself is now their anchor. And even though their year will grow dark again and the pressures of winter ice and all the terrors of darkness will threaten anew, the land will remain with them, changing its form only hesitantly now, often lying stretched out before them, silent and tamed, a familiar friend.

On the morning of November 1st the land lay in the dusk to the northwest; the clarity of detail in the rocks told us for the first time that it must be possible to reach it without having to remain away from the ship so long as to endanger our return. All our scruples vanished; wild and impetuous with excitement we scrambled and leapt across the towering waves of ice toward the north . . . toward land, and when we surmounted its icy pedestal and actually set foot upon it, we did not see that only snow, rocks, and frozen debris surrounded us and that there could be no more dreary land on earth than the island upon which we stood. For us it was a paradise, and for that reason it was given the name Wilczek Island. So great was our joy finally to have reached this land that we gave its features the kind of attention they otherwise would not have deserved. We gazed into every cranny, touched every boulder; we were delighted by every form and contour that its thousands of fissures offered on all sides. . . .

The vegetation was indescribably scant, reduced it seemed to a few lichens; nowhere did we find the driftwood we had anticipated. We had also expected traces of reindeer or foxes; but all our searches proved in vain, the land appeared to be devoid of any living creature. . . . There is something sublime about the solitude of a land upon which man has never trod, although that feeling results only from the imagination and the appeal of novelty, and the polar lands of snow can in fact have nothing more poetic about them than Jutland. We were, however, most receptive to new impressions, and the golden vapors that rose from some invisible ''wacke'' on the southern horizon and spread like a billowing curtain against heaven's noonday glow had for us the same magic as some landscape in Ceylon. (Julius Payer)

On November 2 they again march in formation toward Wilczek Island, the nearest one in the archipelago. Payer precedes them all again this time. Finally! he is in command, and Weyprecht walks with the crew, carrying the furled silk flag. And they solemnly take possession of their discovery in the Kaiser's name, raise the double eagle among dark green columns of dolerite, erect a stone pyramid, and deposit within it a document that identifies His Apostolic Majesty Franz Josef I, Emperor of Austria and King of Hungary, as the first sovereign of these glacier-covered wastes of crystalline stone. It concludes with laconic mention of their own future:

We now lie three to four nautical miles SSE from the point at which this document has been deposited. Our further fate depends entirely upon the winds that drive the ice. . . . (Payer m.p.) (Weyprecht m.p.)

13

Whatever Will Be, Will Be—A Log

Friday, August 14, 1981

The ice is pale blue in the night. On the fourth day after sailing from Adventfjord, at 80° 05′ 98″ north latitude and 14° 28′ 19″ east longitude, the first ice floes bang against the ship—an endless field of drift ice rent by mirror-smooth channels, seas, and ponds. Hardly a barrier. The *Cradle* does fifteen knots an hour, shoving the smaller floes to one side like annoying splinters and riding up onto the larger flards. Without slackening speed it hesitates on a slant above the ice for a moment, then breaks through with a roll of thunder and has open water under its keel again. This is how you travel the Arctic Ocean in 1981.

This sunny night Josef Mazzini is standing at the far front of the bow surrounded by the noise of their progress. He grips the railing and watches the hundredweight fragments of ice below him swish up out of the water like shining insects.

Saturday, August 15

"Day" and "night" are empty names for the flow of time here. There are no nights. There are only changing hues and intensities of brightness, only a sun that circumnavigates the ship without ever sinking below the horizon, only time told by a clock, only the date.

A map of the Arctic hangs under glass in the mess; at the push of a button fluorescent lights blaze up behind the blue shadings of the Arctic Ocean's depths. The band at the bottom of the map bears both the legend and a table with data relating the length of the polar night and the periods of midnight sun to each degree of increasing latitude. Josef Mazzini interrupts his daily tour of the ship and sees himself mirrored in the glass of the map. The jagged white line denoting the extent of drift ice in summer runs diagonally across his face, on his shoulders he bears peninsulas and islands, above his head is the fluorescent halo of unnavigable ice. The table of sunrise and sunset is pinned to his chest like a prisoner's ID.

TABLE 1

	Midnight Sun			*Polar Night*		
Latitude north	*First night*	*Last night*	*Number of nights*	*First day*	*Last day*	*Number of days*
...	...	...	...	...	...	...
76°	Apr. 27	Aug. 15	111	Nov. 3	Feb. 8	98
77°	Apr. 24	Aug. 18	117	Oct. 31	Feb. 11	104
78°	Apr. 21	Aug. 21	123	Oct. 28	Feb. 14	110
79°	Apr. 18	Aug. 24	129	Oct. 25	Feb. 17	116
80°	Apr. 15	Aug. 27	135	Oct. 22	Feb. 20	122
81°	Apr. 12	Aug. 30	141	Oct. 19	Feb. 23	128
...	...	...	...	...	...	...

"We're about right here." Einar Hellskog—a painter of stamps, who is sketching arctic landscapes for the Norwegian post office and who, after Mazzini and the glaciologist from Massachusetts, is the third guest on board—has stepped up to the map and is pointing at a spot in the blue northeast of Moffen Island; the outline of the island touches the black 80° mark like a cipher cleanly set atop a line.

Sunday, August 16

Cloudbanks and south wind; snow. The *Cradle* moves through thick drift ice, a twisting, seething channel in its wake. The engine burns twelve tons of diesel oil a day, says Seip, the ship's engineer; a normal amount. The engine noise, a rumble that rises and falls with the thickness of the ice, can be heard everywhere. Only way up in the crow's nest is it more peaceful. Enveloped in the play of light from the armatures, the mainmast guest can sit in a climatized glass turret and observe what radioed satellite pictures have long since confirmed: The ice is growing.

When Captain Andreasen orders the engines stopped—and he does this often now—it is so quiet you can hear the ringing in your head. Then arms of cranes swing out and data buoys and hose levels are lowered onto the ice to measure the surface curvature of the Arctic Ocean. Zoologists shoot seals and birds to prove that industrial toxins from the south have traveled long food chains to enter the blood of polar fauna. The geologists never seem to weary of taking samples from the floor of the arctic waters, but they have difficulty disguising their interest in possible oil reserves behind a mask of pure science. Worms and starfish wriggle in the dragnet. These events are routine. Time is a murky pond in which bubbles of the past are rising.

Was it two days ago or three that the *Cradle* lay in Kongsfjorden below Ny Ålesund? They walked for hours on land and received a noisy welcome in the little settlement; they drank pure alcohol mixed with juice out of plastic canisters; a cassette recorder was blaring and the woman from Massachusetts decided to go for a walk in the muck rather than dance with Fyrand, who was drunk. They had thought

Fyrand had gone to fetch her when he, too, went outside. But he came back from the kennel with a yowling Greenland dog, beat it on the hind flanks, pressed the animal to him, danced with it, and spat schnapps between its lips once he was no longer able to hold onto the uncooperative dog. It was Odmund Jansen, the commander on land and the highest authority on board next to Captain Andreasen, who broke it up, ordered them to move out, and had to put up with Fyrand's drunken curses.

Two or three days ago, long ago, Josef Mazzini had stood before the 120-foot mast in Ny Ålesund, an obelisk of metal struts that Amundsen and Nobile had used to tie down their dirigibles, the *Norge* and the *Italia*, and that still towered as high as ever into the arctic skies. Mazzini had seen Malcom Flaherty swaying in his seat up on that mast, but he had also seen the *Italia* rise tragic and powerful, had heard "Free the lines!" and the voice of Lucia, the painter of miniatures, who had told him about the gold-embroidered epaulets of handsome General Umberto Nobile. No, Josef Mazzini had not remembered. He had relived it all. Here at this anchor mast—at four A.M. on May 23, 1928, at four below zero Fahrenheit—disaster had begun for Nobile, Lucia Mazzini's gentle, shining hero. "Free the lines!"

This time, too—just as two years before on his joint polar flight with Roald Amundsen and Lincoln Ellsworth—Nobile reached the North Pole twenty hours after leaving Ny Ålesund, hovered there in ecstasy above the icy barren wasteland, and dropped the flag of Italy and a wooden cross blessed by the pope. But on his return flight a coating of ice crystals weighed the *Italia* down, bringing it inexorably lower, till it finally crashed on a floe. The general and his eight companions were flung from their triumph out onto the pack ice. He lay there wounded and bleeding. The dirigible, relieved of half its load, rose again into the snowy skies, vanishing forever with the rest of the crew.

Nobile's true downfall, however—which sent him plummeting through all the spheres of adoration to the depths of contempt—would first be sealed by a rescue attempt that cost many lives, including those of Amundsen and five companions, who died while searching for him in a plane. Because after the crash Umberto Nobile violated the code of honor that governs how one is to meet one's doom. And the world did not forgive him that.

First the stranded general allowed two of his captains, Mariano and Zappi, along with the Swedish oceanographer Finn Malmgreen, to leave behind the other castaways, some of whom could not walk, and attempt to reach the Spitsbergens on their own.

Weeks passed.

When a Swedish pilot named Lundborg finally managed to bring his pontoon plane down onto Nobile's drifting floe, it was the general, however, who allowed himself to be rescued first. His pet fox terrier Titina in his arms, he climbed aboard the plane, which had room for only one passenger, and was soon safe aboard the Italian auxiliary ship *Città di Milano*. A commander who let himself be saved before all the others! Even Lucia's voice had not been silent about that. But the litany of her exculpations was long.

It took weeks until the other men under the general's command were rescued from their desperate situation, for Lundborg was forced to make a crash landing on his second rescue flight and became a casualty himself. More than fifteen hundred people were en route to the drifting floe with sixteen ships, twenty-one airplanes, and eleven sled teams. Seventeen rescuers met their death. Seventy-four days after the crash of the *Italia*, the Soviet icebreaker *Krassin* at last found a way through the heavy pack ice and reached the exhausted castaways. What then became public turned a voyage dedicated to the greatness of Italy into an ugly scandal. The sailors of the *Krassin* had also found the breakaway captains wandering confused and far from their path. Mariano was bewildered, dressed in tatters, and near starvation, whereas Zappi still had astounding strength, was almost well nourished, and was wrapped in Mariano's and Malmgreen's furs. Malmgreen was missing. Mariano had no comment or only babbled. But Zappi repeated, swore over and over, that the Swedish oceanographer had been left behind at some point; Malmgreen had demanded that they go on without him, giving them his now useless equipment, and he, Zappi, had merely accepted the offer of Malmgreen's fur and food.

His account struck horror in the audience to this tragedy. Reporters were quick to forge the chain of clues and corroborate the suspicion that the well-fed Zappi had either harried the oceanographer from Uppsala to his death or killed him outright and then eaten his corpse. Zappi denied it, as did Mariano when he later came to his senses. This did not alter the suspicion. Had not Mariano's first coherent statement to the man who kept the log on the *Krassin* been: "I gave Captain Zappi permission to eat me after my death"? It was a good thing the truth lay buried forever in the ice. Heroes who ate one another! That could not be true, that must be a rumor fabricated by Italy's enemies.

And then Lucia's voice had fallen silent. And Josef Mazzini was again looking through the struts of the anchor mast, at the houses of Ny Ålesund, and at Fyrand, who had dragged the sled dog back to its kennel and was coming clumsily toward him screaming, "Admiral Odmund Jansen has called us to evening vespers on board! Dogs on their leashes! Idiots to their posts! Discipline, sir! But of course, sir! *Skål*, sir!" Fyrand came to a halt a few paces from the anchor mast and stopped screaming. "*Signore Mazzini! Cavaliere!* Did you notice the correct method for dealing with a genuine descendant of Roald Amundsen's sled-dog team? You dance a foxtrot with it to the tune of the weather report from Radio Svalbard."

Monday, August 17

Phippsøya, Martensøya, Parryøya—bleak massifs in the ocean, tongues of snow in their clefts. Black coasts. The *Cradle* cruises along the northernmost islands of Svalbard. The guest in the crow's nest searches this landscape of icy debris for a passage. By afternoon the ice is so thick that Andreasen's attempts to batter the barriers prove useless. No crack follows the thunder. No passage. The captain's laconic voice is heard over loudspeakers on every deck. They will bring the ship to, course southwest, then southeast, retreating below a latitude of 80°, reaching open sea again through the Hinlopen Strait, and after sailing around Northeast Land resume their course to the north. Thanks.

The card game in the mess is interrupted for the duration of the message.

Tuesday, August 18

No wind. The Hinlopen Strait between West Spitsbergen and Northeast Land is midnight blue and calm. Clear weather. Not much ice. The geologists are arguing with the zoologists about the best place to anchor to "conduct research." Their course, the zoologists complain, is always the one these oil prospectors want; probes of mud are apparently more important than flocks of birds and their nesting places. Odmund Jansen tries to mediate.

On this day, the Kaiser's birthday, the *Admiral Tegetthoff* had raised its flags and given three cheers for His Distant Majesty. "Well, do like those guys did," Fyrand says, when Mazzini tells him about it. "Have Hellskog draw a double eagle on your hankie for you and stand up on the bridge with it."

Wednesday, August 19

The Kaiser is one day old, a bawling, pudgy baby. And there is already a new land for him in the Arctic Ocean. The

Cradle is proceeding slowly. The coast of West Spitsbergen to starboard; the coast of Northeast Land to port. Depth soundings. Bottom probes. Bird hunts.

Around noon Kjetil Fyrand brings Mazzini on deck and shows him a menacing mountain on the coast of West Spitsbergen. "Before you, *Signore,* lies Cape Payer . . . my gift to you."

He had visited this Austrian cape last summer, together with his friend, the miner Israel Boyle—Fyrand tells him this as they lean on the railing. On foot. A hike of almost 120 miles from Longyearbyen, across the Negri, Sonklar, and Hann glaciers: a first-class rough-go. Under some circumstances hiking glaciers is comparable in risk to surfing on avalanches or hang gliding in the Himalayas. After every snowfall a hiker who crosses a fissured glacier with all its cracks and chasms is like a ball in a pinball machine or a pool game—any moment he can unexpectedly vanish under a snowdrift and plunge into an abyss. All the same, it was a comforting thought: To outlast the centuries as the deep-frozen victim of the ice, down there in some crevasse shimmering with turquoise and silver-blue. And to be *the* sensation of the year 2300: Well-preserved Hiker Found.

"How long did it take you?"

"Nine days."

"Both ways?"

"Nineteen days, both ways."

"Carrying your own packs?"

"The dogs pulled all that."

Thursday, August 20

The precipices of glaciers tower 130 feet, 160 feet above the breaking surf—overhanging walls of radiant turquoise ice. The thaw water emerges from crevices. Falls leap the glaciers' edge, many of them blown away as misty veils before they reach the sea. Rainbows appear and fade above the cascades, and flocks of birds flutter in and out of the splendor. Hellskog, the stamp designer, sits and stares and draws and stares. If that glacier were to calve now it would create a wave as high as a cathedral, and the iceberg would turn in the raging waters—slow and glistening and new.

But nothing of the sort happens this Thursday.

And if it were not for the surf and the noise of the engines, they would surely be able to hear the groans of the glacier shoving its huge mass toward the ocean, inch by inch.

But there is nothing to be heard this Thursday except the familiar racket of sea and motors.

That evening a videotape of *The Barefoot Contessa* is shown in the mess. It features Humphrey Bogart as the aging, chain-smoking, worldly-wise director, and Ava Gardner as the dancer from Madrid, whom he pulls out of poverty into the film studios and glamour of Hollywood. The dancer works her way up to become a tragic-sweet star and finds no happiness. So she finally marries an Italian count, who has been emasculated by a bomb in the Second World War (the girl from Madrid learns this only after their marriage; laughter in the mess). One rainy night she is shot and killed by her handicapped husband. The count then has the family motto, not exactly a clever one, as he notes, chiseled into his wife's gravestone: *Che sarà, sarà.*

That Thursday Josef Mazzini includes among his journal entries—barely readable stanzas of catchphrases dedicated to the beauties of the Bråsvell glacier—the count's family motto: *What will be, will be.* The maxims on the mossy stones in widow Soucek's backyard were no better.

Friday, August 21

Course northeast. Strong gusts in the morning. Then calm and drift ice. After protracted maneuvering in the heavy ice, the *Cradle* again crosses 80° north latitude. Northeast Land is still close by. The anchor chains rattle off Cape Laura.

Saturday, August 22

The day for radio calls. A Japanese ornithologist has had enough. He has spent six weeks in a tent on Kvitøya and wants to be picked up. They'll take care of it, Captain Andreasen radios. They must touch at Kvitøya in any case.

Course east. Fogbanks and towering icebergs. Up on the bridge, they are watching the radar screens intently. That evening an inflatable boat with a five-man crew, Fyrand and Mazzini among them, is set out among the floes off Kvitøya. Soaked by spray, Josef Mazzini arrives at a dreary beach—pebbles and driftwood, lichens and the massive skeletal remains of a whale, flocks of birds among cliffs smeared with droppings. Naomi Uemura, the ornithologist, is standing there amid the flotsam and his own equipment. He bows.

Alone? Six weeks alone in this godforsaken place? Mazzini asks the Japanese man. Not always, Uemura says, not the whole time. A Swedish film team was here. Jan Troell, the director, a quite pleasant fellow, was filming an epic about the polar flight of the balloon pilot Salomon Andrée. Mr. Troell had been very careful not to disturb the birds.

After they have serviced the automatic weather station—hardly an hour's work for the team—spray is once again drenching the inflatable boat. The ornithologist from Nagoya talks on and on, about battles for territory, nesting places, and migration routes. Kvitøya falls back into the fog.

The crew of the Norwegian sealer *Bratvaag* found the corpses of Salomon Andrée and his companions, Strindberg and Fraenkel, on this same island in August 1930. The three pilots had been listed as missing for thirty-three years. Andrée's diaries, even exposed photographic plates (showing the doomed men beside their wrecked balloon), were unharmed, and the wool clothing the Swedish engineer had worn—not serviceable arctic wear—was still encrusted with his vomit when they found him.

"I don't understand you," Josef Mazzini interrupts, as the

ornithologist climbs the gangway of the *Cradle,* still talking about wing strokes and glides, "I don't understand you. Be quiet."

People had warned Andrée, had implored him to give up his flight to the North Pole, so long in planning and so many times delayed. Under arctic conditions the pressure in his balloon would quickly fall, the silk envelope would ice over, and the whole mad enterprise would end in the pack ice. But no, something *had* to flutter at the North Pole, had to crack and whip in the wind of its total solitude—a flag! And be it ever so small, the Swedish flag had to decorate the pole! For centuries to come, the history books would drone on and on: Salomon Andrée, Swedish engineer. Salomon Andrée, the conqueror of the North Pole. Salomon Andrée, the first.

On July 11, 1897, Salomon Andrée and his gullible, devoted companions climbed into a balloon sewn in Paris and rose above the lowlands of the Spitsbergens on their flight to the pole. That same evening two homing pigeons fluttered from the basket with confident messages—and arrived nowhere. And on the fourth day after their ascent, the last of the evil prophecies came true and the balloon, over which they had long since lost control, fell to the pack ice just beyond 83° north latitude—but far, infinitely far from the pole, and from other human beings.

After seven hopeless days of misfortune, all of it captured on their own photographic plates, the castaways decided to set out for the nearest land; their goal was the most desolate place on earth—Kaiser Franz Josef Land.

The balloonists harnessed themselves like dogs to the emergency sleds they had brought and toiled in agony across the towering, numbing ice. They used a canvas boat to cross "wackes" and channels, and although often collapsing with exhaustion, they dragged their burdens onward—to Nowhere. For the drift of the ice threw them off course. After a month of torture they were in fact closer to Svalbard than to

Franz Josef Land; they changed the direction of march and labored on toward the Spitsbergens, and reached Kvitøya by late autumn. But only death awaited them there. Strindberg died. Then Fraenkel, who had been maimed by a polar bear, and finally—Salomon Andrée. Salomon Andrée, the last. Examination of his soiled clothing thirty-three years later suggested that he died of eating tainted bear meat. "It is truly strange to hover here above the polar seas," the heirs of his literary estate would read in his diary. "We are the first to float here in a balloon. When will others emulate us? Will people think us mad or follow our example? I cannot deny that all three of us are filled with a sense of pride. ~~We~~I feel we can die confident that we have achieved something."

A fleeting, grand moment in which he could discriminate between reality and madness may have led Salomon Andrée to strike "We" and replace it with "*I*." And it was good so.

After the ascent and disappearance of the Swedish engineer, the North Pole remained untrodden for more than a decade—a decade in which a whole series of polar explorers followed the engineer into the ice, in the name of science or some fatherland or other, and disappeared . . . the companions of Prince Luigi Amedeo, Duke of the Abruzzi, for instance, whose First Italian Arctic Expedition, after wintering on Franz Josef Land, reached an unprecedented 86° 34′ north latitude in March 1900, surpassing Fridtjof Nansen's previous record by twenty-two miles. A third of the ducal team died in the ice storms of this sublime latitude. The duke, his indomitable captain, Cagni, and the rest of the crew returned to Italy in August 1900—with their record and a list of the dead and missing.

When finally, on April 21, 1908, after months of forced marches and dogsledding, Frederick Albert Cook, a physician from New York, and on April 6, 1909, his rival, Robert Edwin Peary, a career navy officer from Pennsylvania, finally reached the ice of the North Pole (or what they assumed was the North Pole), not much more was achieved than that the pole began to lose its importance as a vanishing point of vanities. The far north was "conquered." And its conquering was followed by embarrassment, by an angry row concerning the honor of first rights.

Cook, who shared his triumph with his companions Avelah and Etukishuk, two Eskimos from Greenland, had been carried westward on his retreat from the pole by a drifting floe and returned from the wilderness only after a yearlong odyssey in the ice. In the meantime Peary, four Eskimos, and his black servant, Matthew Henson, had set up camp in the pack-ice wasteland at a spot that must have been in the immediate neighborhood of the pole—or so their calculations indicated. Peary had allowed no white men to accompany him on his dash to the pole, which would have meant his having to share his victory with an "equal." He had good luck with the drift ice on his retreat and was able to present the world with his victory at about the same time as Frederick Cook—and the brawl for the honor began.

Robert Edwin Peary moved heaven and earth to claim the glory for himself alone; he wrote vehement columns in *The New York Times*, calling Cook a wretched impostor who had simply holed up in the wilderness for a year only to return with his incredible lie. Cook was a charlatan, a swindler, a madman—all of this and more, but not a conqueror of the pole.

Frederick Albert Cook rejected all such accusations as irrational splutterings and set out his own position in the *New York Herald*. He would not budge from his claim of having been at the farthest point north one year before Peary. Peary was a bad loser, a fanatic, a calumniator. . . . And so it went. Commissions and parties of sympathizers took up positions as to who truly deserved the credit of being the first. Learned men were at loggerheads, enemies were made, and the newspapers kept the battle going for years. No matter how many times the credibility of one of the two conquerors might successfully pass all the stages of verification, the issue remained unresolved. Encyclopedists and chroniclers were as confused as ever. Depending on the employer or party represented, the victory was awarded now to Peary and now to Cook, the one never mentioned without nasty remarks about the other. The two foes became the Siamese twins of cosmography.

When Josef Mazzini enters the mess late that evening, there is Naomi Uemura—clean-shaven, smiling, and with fresh pomade in his hair—sitting at the "science table," which is separated from that of Andreasen and his crew by a philodendron climbing a bamboo scaffold. Odmund Jansen is standing between the tables beside this green line, his glass raised—a signal that he is about to make a toast to the health of the ornithologist in the name of the crew. By his lonely work on Kvitøya, Uemura deserved equal honors with a gentleman of the same name who, like Peary, Cook, and all the others before him, had made it to the North Pole on his own in 1978. He, Jansen, disliked such rigors, but wished his Japanese colleague the recognition due him from his peers and drank to him as the unwavering friend of the birds of Kvitøya.

Applause on both sides of the philodendron.

Sunday, August 23

Course east-northeast. Thick drift ice. Another hundred nautical miles to Franz Josef Land. Clear water and north wind. A barrier of pack ice in the afternoon. No passage. Course southwest. An encircling horizon. No land. Josef Mazzini spends the slow afternoon hours reading the copy he has made of Johann Haller's diary.

23 August 1872, Friday: Snow and wind. Frozen fast. Shoveled snow on deck.

23 August 1873, Saturday: Fog and westwind. Temperature 0° [32° *F*]. *Pounded a sugar loaf.*

23 August 1874, Sunday: Clear weather and wind. We have left Matochkin Strait and are sailing down along the coast in our little boats. A small storm burst upon us in the night. We have lost sight of one another. My boat sailed on until morning, then we beached it and went on land. We found driftwood for a big fire, prepared breakfast, and dried our clothes.

Monday, August 24

Back at Kvitøya. The fifteenth day on board. Visiting day. For the first time since they sailed from Longyearbyen, Kåre Andreasen is wearing his captain's uniform. At two p.m. the governor's helicopter lands on the *Cradle*'s helipad. Governor Ivar Thorsen and Ole Fagerlien, who has come from Oslo, review the crew in casual parade formation. Shoulders are pounded and hands shaken.

"And how about you?" Ole Fagerlien says to Mazzini. "Getting on with your work?"

"The ice is too thick," Mazzini replies.

"What did you expect?" Fagerlien says as he moves on.

That evening, small talk and a banquet in the mess. Big-band music from the stereo in the background. Protests when Fyrand follows a Glenn Miller number with Archie Shepp's "Mama Rose" and turns up the volume. Fyrand curses the protesters, calls them assholes, and then puts on a tape of marching music. Late that night, two short speeches and more toasts.

Tuesday, August 25

Bear hunt. Three zoologists climb aboard the governor's helicopter, which swings in low flight above the ice. Over the course of the morning their tranquilizer darts bring down four polar bears fleeing in panic. The zoologists break a tooth from each of the sedated animals, clamp metal markers in the flesh of their ears, and spray large marks of red paint on their cream-colored pelts. Then they record the gradual awakening on videotape: the bears' clumsy attempts to rise from their stupefaction; their wobbling and tottering; the gradual, almost imperceptible return of energy and elegance to their movements; and finally their beauty, splotched with red. The large bloodstains on the floes fade quickly under the eddies of ice crystals whipped up by the rotor blades.

For the bear hunt the *Cradle* is able to break out of the ice only three nautical miles to the northeast. An accident occurs at the end of the third: the lurch of mounting an ice barrier flings the unprepared stamp designer against the railing with such force that he ends up lying on deck with an open head wound. Holt, the medico, urges he be taken to the hospital in Longyearbyen. The hunters return at one o'clock; Governor Thorsen and Ole Fagerlien say good-bye. Assisted by Fyrand and Holt, his face drained of blood and hidden under bandages, the stamp designer climbs aboard the helicopter, which rises gently, its rotors beating their way through the snowy sky for a while; then the black humming dot vanishes. Awkward silence in the mess. Andreasen has taken off his uniform and is back at the bridge in jeans and a freshly ironed flannel shirt. Course northeast. Slow, very slow sailing.

Wednesday, August 26

Measurements on the ice. The *Cradle* is at anchor. Josef Mazzini spends the morning in the stamp designer's chair, which has been roped fast to the railing; his snow goggles protect him from the glare of the wide distances. Hellskog had spent entire days in this chair, his numb fingers sketching the contours of desolation. Mazzini misses him; he had shown the painter photocopies of sketches done by Julius Payer, sketches drawn at twenty to thirty below zero—and Hellskog had expressed admiration for their delicate line. At zero, he had said, he would be thinking of anything but drawing.

Thursday, August 27

Silence. No sound from the engine, no rattle from the anchor. Their drift is barely perceptible.

After hours of lying in ambush in an inflatable boat camouflaged by white tarps, the zoologists manage to kill two ring seals—*Phocae hispidae*—both from a good distance. Josef Mazzini, a guest on this day's hunt, stands on a floe, gazing at the carcasses. Entrails burst like jewels from the animals' torn bellies. The rich colors spread steaming out onto the ice and are soon covered by formations of crystals. As the colors fade, Josef Mazzini thinks it is nausea he feels rising within him. But it is only the dampness and a cold that pierces everything, that grabs and shakes him. Then the blood-covered carcasses, including the entrails, are put into plastic bags—material for labs in Oslo. An extended, loud conversation in the mess follows. The men talk about perfect shots that have saved lives, about attacking bears, about stalking prey in winter.

Friday, August 28

Course east and northeast. Gloomy weather. Fyrand stands under the arm of a crane, swearing, apparently trying to curse into position a buoy dangling from a rope. The buoy bangs the hull like a battering ram several times.

Saturday, August 29

A day in a sea of ice, very close to 81° north latitude. A day when nothing happens. Now, after more than four months, the sun is again sinking below the horizon, but that seems to concern hardly anyone. Josef Mazzini experiences the sunset—the sun merely vanishes into a cloudbank, nothing special, no shimmering halo or arcs of purple—as the restarting of a celestial mechanism that he has missed for a long time now. At last the alternation of day and night has begun again. But no, this is no night, only a silvery dusk that no darkness follows.

Sunday, August 30

Calm and fog. Heavy ice. It is the anniversary of the discovery of Franz Josef Land. A white sun in the haze. Nothing happens.

It was around noon, we were leaning over the side staring into the desultory fog, through which sunlight broke now and again, when a passing wall of mist suddenly revealed a rugged line of rocks far to the northwest. Within a few minutes a radiant alpine landscape came into view!

Josef Mazzini celebrates a memory. Hell yes, Fyrand says, you can drink to anything in this boring place. No, that was *not* what his protégé meant. But then they are both standing at the bow with a bottle of aquavit. They bellow three cheers into the cold; the sound of their exultation sounds thin amid the screech of bursting floes under the keel. Then the noise of the ship's motion is swept away by the wail of the foghorn—one of Andreasen's jokes, this one intended for the two figures there at the bow. Even a few paces away all anyone might notice was their open mouths and not a hint of hurrah. But they have already fallen silent.

Hours later Josef Mazzini is again sitting all bundled up at the railing in Hellskog's chair. He does not know how long he has sat there, growing more and more sleepy, immersed in watching the emptiness, only to start up wide awake when slowly—endlessly slowly, and black as a wave of pitch crowned with glaciers and firn snow—land rises above the horizon. His land. The ridges and spines of mountains melt and flutter, but always regroup again—columns of basalt and bouldered slopes. *Its valleys are adorned with meadows and alive with reindeer undisturbed in the enjoyment of their asylum, far from all enemies.* The land turns, sinks back into the clouds, reappears, but no waves batter its rocks; the ocean is smooth as a mirror reflecting the image of the ragged coastline. There is no ice.

But on board the *Cradle* everything is silent. No one shouts

Land! No one in the crow's nest, no one among the crew gives a cry of triumph. There is only the rumble of their progress. A man has discovered a land that belongs to him alone.

Monday, August 31

Driving snow and wind from the southeast. Toward noon, nine minutes past 81° north latitude, the pack ice closes to form a barrier running from west to east—the endless ice that the wall map in the mess calls unnavigable. Endless now.

Josef Mazzini has fallen asleep reading and rolls over startled when Fyrand knocks at his cabin door. Without waiting for an answer Fyrand flings the door open and from the threshold repeats what Jansen and the captain have decided: "We're turning back. We can't get through. You won't get to see your Franz Josef Land. Shit. Did you hear me? We're turning back!"

Then the maneuvering to turn around—a procedure void of any ceremony, or regrets for that matter. What could be measured has been measured; what work was to be done is done. No passage to the north or northeast. That was to be expected. So, then, their course is to the south. Toward Longyearbyen.

South. Southwest. South. A perfect monotony. I close the log. The days of the return voyage are meaningless. The *Cradle* passes through the Eriksen Strait, the coastal waters of Kong Karls Land, and Freeman Sound between Barentsøya and Edgeøya, and following a fan of south headings, falls back five degrees of latitude. At one point South Cape in the Spitsbergens appears to the starboard, then disappears—the course is again northwest. On September 3 the *Cradle* enters Adventfjord. It is early morning. Josef Mazzini is now one of those who have circumnavigated the Spitsbergens. Elling Carlsen, ice master and harpooner, was honored with the Order of Olaf for just such a journey. But how ridiculous to imagine that a medal on a velvet cushion might be waiting for him in the harbor of Longyearbyen. Ridiculous, as well, to imagine cheers breaking forth on the dock. Cables slap against the landing pier. Then the engine noise stops. Someone on the pier raises a hand. It is Hellskog. This is what the end of a working voyage looks like.

It remains to be said that Josef Mazzini was seldom seen at the railing on the trip back. Like someone preparing for release from prison, preparing for his great freedom, he sat in the mess and in his cabin reading the books on polar history he found in the ship's small library, constantly copying passages from them at random. A secretary of memory. Was he writing to combat boredom? Did he want to collect *all* the images of the north and by copying them make them his own? The thin notebook bound in blue that he filled with his scribbles now lies before me. Kjetil Fyrand sent it to Anna Koreth along with the other writings and possessions of the missing man. To be sure, it is not Josef Mazzini's hand that set the title on the cover of this hopelessly confused collection: *The Great Nail*—which is what the Eskimos of Greenland called the North Pole. It is not Josef Mazzini's handwriting. I wrote it. I did. I have given Mazzini's other notebooks names as well. *Campi deserti. Terra nuova.* I treated his writings the way every discoverer treats his land, its nameless bays, capes, and sounds—I baptized them. Nothing should be without a name.

14

Third Digression
The Great Nail—Fragments of Myth and Enlightenment

Have you entered the storehouses of the snow, or have you seen the storehouses of the hail, which I have reserved for the time of trouble, for the day of battle and war? What is the way to the place where the light is distributed, or where the east wind is scattered upon the earth?

Have you entered into the springs of the sea, or walked in the recesses of the deep? Have the gates of death been revealed to you, or have you seen the gates of deep darkness? Have you comprehended the expanse of the earth? Declare, if you know all this.

Surely there is a mine for silver, and a place for gold, which they refine. Iron is taken out of the earth, and copper is smelted from the ore. Men put an end to darkness, and search out to the farthest bound the ore in gloom and deep darkness. They open shafts in a valley away from where men live; they are forgotten by travelers, they hang afar from men, they swing to and fro. As for the earth, its stones are the place of sapphires, and it has dust of gold. That path no bird of prey knows, and the lion has not passed over it.

Man puts his hand to the flinty rock and overturns mountains by the roots. He cuts channels in the rocks, and his eye sees every precious thing. He binds up the streams so that they do not trickle, and the thing that is hid he brings forth to light. But where shall wisdom be found? And where is the place of understanding?

Man does not know the way of it, and it is not found in the land of the living. The deep says, "It is not in me," and the sea says, "It is not with me." (Book of Job)

If the vast expanse of the Atlantic Sea did not make it impossible, we could sail the distance from Iberia to India along the same degree of latitude. (Eratosthenes, third century B.C.)

The day will come, however, in latter years when the ocean will loose the chains with which it binds all things, when the immeasurable earth will lie open, when the sailor will discover new worlds, and then Thule will no longer be the farthest land. (Lucius Annaeus Seneca, first century A.D.)

Winters in the north are an ordeal, a punishment, a plague. The air is stiff with cold and causes faces to wither, eyes to weep, noses to run, and skin to crack. The earth there is like shining glass and the wind like stinging wasps. He who is driven to the north and its painful cold longs to enter the fires of hell. (Kazvini, twelfth century)

The north is full of peoples of terrible strangeness and without human culture. (Saxo Grammaticus, twelfth century)

On this great sea one does not sail in respect to the magnet. (Legend on a compass map of polar seas, fifteenth century)

Light conditions in summer must be uncommonly favorable to a voyage in arctic seas, which, by common assumption, are very dangerous and heavy, or, rather, quite impassable; for when one has once passed that small portion of the journey which is proclaimed so dangerous, which is to say, a distance of perhaps two or three nautical miles before reaching the pole, and an equal distance when the pole has been passed, the climate of the seas and lands there must be as temperate as that of the regions in which we reside. (Robert Thorne, sixteenth century)

The Northern Ocean is a broad field upon which Russia's glory, together with unprecedented profit, can be enlarged. . . . In the summer months the ocean along the Siberian coast for distances of five to seven hundred versts is free of such masses of ice as hinder navigation and expose sailors to the danger of being locked within it. Concern for men, however, is always a matter of much greater weight than concern for the means employed—therefore, let us make a comparison in terms of the profit and glory for our fatherland. Whereas nations are willing to further their ambitions by sending thousands, indeed whole armies, to their death for a small piece of land, we have the fate of but approximately a hundred men to bemoan in arctic seas, where we are dealing with the acquisition of whole nations in those regions, the increase of navigation, of commerce and of power, all to the greater glory of our nation. (Mikhail Vasilyevich Lomonosov, eighteenth century)

But on the basis of my own experience and, in addition, information gathered by Dutch captains, one can assume with certainty that a Northeast Passage through the polar seas is impossible. (Vasily Jakovlevich Chichagov, eighteenth century)

Some wished to make no attempt, believing it pointless and navigation impossible; others remained in their prejudice that a voyage in the Northwest were preferable; and yet a third party was pleased to accept my design—to sail north between the Spitsbergens and Novaya Zemlya—and that opinion was at last given preference by the Royal Society, to the end that His Royal Majesty be petitioned for two ships to sail toward the North Pole. For if, as is my opinion, one may there find more or less ice-free waters, then all difficulties must vanish, and there were no further need to delay voyages through those straits and on toward Japan, etc. If, however, the sea be iced over, the voyage need not prove to be without profit, for it would have its uses in astronomical, physical, and other observations. (Samuel Engel, eighteenth century)

I concurred in the opinion of many learned naturalists that the seas of the North Pole could not be frozen, but that within the zone of ice, which as is well-known encircles it, there must be an open area of varying dimension, of which I wished to offer further proof. . . . Previous experience led me to conclude that I would be able to push my vessel into the encircling ice to about the 80th parallel north latitude, and from there take a boat across the ice to the open seas I hoped to find. Should I be so fortunate as to reach open water, I intended to launch my boat and sail northward into the sea. For the transport across the ice I put my trust primarily in the dog of the Eskimo. (Isaac Israel Hayes, nineteenth century)

Mr. Hayes, you could just as easily sail across the roofs of New York City. (Henry Dodge, nineteenth century)

Our hope of finding a broad expanse of smooth, unbroken

ice limited only by the horizon was never fulfilled. (William Edward Parry, nineteenth century)

In our minds, however, we steered our boats northward, crossing parallel after parallel and making world-shaking discoveries. (Emil Israel Bessels, nineteenth century)

We reached 83° 24′ 3″, a higher latitude than any mortal had ever reached before, and saw a land of which no one knew. We unfurled the star-spangled banner in the cold northwind. (David Legge Brainard, nineteenth century)

To be sure, it is amusing to sit by the fire at home and read of spending a winter in the pack-ice, but actually to do it is a test that can age a man before his time. (George Washington De Long, nineteenth century)

The North Pole cannot be reached! (George Stronge Nares, nineteenth century)

"Thus far and no further" has been said by many a polar voyager, and his successor has then calmly sailed across the walls of ice his forerunner had declared "built for all eternity." The pole is neither absolutely practicable, nor absolutely impracticable. There will always be wide stretches of the polar region which are one or the other depending on the conditions of the ice in a given year or season. . . .

As a scientific goal, however, the pole itself is of perfect indifference. To have approached it serves at most the gratification of vanity. . . .

In light of the increasingly lively interest in arctic research and the readiness of governments and private persons to provide funds for new expeditions, it is desirable that principles be enunciated under which those expeditions are sent out, so that their value to science may correspond to the great sacrifices they demand and that we may discourage that adventurous character, which though it may excite public interest, can only prejudice science. (*Carl Weyprecht, nineteenth century*)

We discovered (*after our return from the north*) *that we were honored far beyond our due and had achieved the highest honor earth can offer: the recognition of our fellow citizens. . . . As to the discovery of a land unknown before, I personally place no value in it today.* (*Julius Payer, nineteenth century*)

We certainly did not set out in search of the mathematical point that forms the northern end of the earth's axis—for to reach that point is in and of itself of little value—but rather to investigate those large, unknown regions of the earth surrounding the pole. Such investigations will be of equal scientific importance whether the journey lead across the mathematical pole itself or pass some distance from it. . . . One must reach the pole, however, so that this obsession may cease. (Fridtjof Nansen, turn of the century)

The strangers seek the Great Nail that was once driven into the ice of the north but has been lost. Whoever follows those who seek the Great Nail and finds it will have iron for his spears and axes. (Eskimos of Annotoak, twentieth century)

When they hear the word "discovery" most people think of "adventure." I wish to differentiate between the two terms from the standpoint of the discoverer. For him an adventure is only an unwelcome interruption of serious work. He seeks no thrills, but facts unknown till now. Voyages of discovery are often no more than a race against time in the hope of escaping starvation. For him adventure is but an error in calculation revealed by "testing" the facts, or disastrous proof that no one can allow for every eventuality. . . . Every discoverer has his adventures. They excite him and he enjoys thinking back on them. But he never seeks them out. (Roald Amundsen, twentieth century)

Frozen and bleeding cheeks and ears are minor discomforts that are part of a great adventure. Pain and discomfort are unavoidable, but seen as part of the whole, they are hardly important. (Robert Edwin Peary, twentieth century)

Life in the ice? I doubt that men have ever felt as lonely and forsaken as we. I am incapable of describing the emptiness of our existence. (Frederick Albert Cook, twentieth century)

The geographic North Pole is the mathematical point pierced by the imaginary axis about which the earth rotates. It is where all meridians join, where the only direction is south, where the wind comes only from the south and blows only to the south, where a magnetic compass always points south, where earth's centrifugal force is zero, and where celestial bodies neither rise nor set. (Geographical definition, circa 1980)

15

Sketches from the Land of Uz

Klotz is getting quieter and quieter. No one can console him now. He wants to go home. He has to go home.

But the land! They have discovered a land, beautiful mountains! They have their new land now.

Land? Ah, that land. But its mountains have no forests of fir, no pine, no scrub spruce, nothing. And its valleys are full of ice. He wants to go home, Klotz does. Home.

On a dark, achingly cold December afternoon in 1873, the hunter Alexander Klotz—who has just returned with Payer and Haller from one of their joint excursions to the coast—casts aside his ice-covered fur coat, his gloves, his fur hood, his leather face-mask, casts aside everything, and dons his summer clothes. He doesn't need heavy furs where he is going now. The winters in Sankt Leonhard, the winters in the Passeiertal, are mild, with plenty of snow.

Klotz empties out his bunk but then simply leaves behind the linen sack full of belongings. He takes only the most precious items—the pocket watch he won at his last shooting match held in honor of His Majesty's birthday, the paper money Payer has slipped him whenever he has done some special service for the first lieutenant, and finally, a wooden rosary. Tall and serious, Klotz then steps up to his comrades and shakes each man's hand: "G'bless."

"Klotz! You crazy?" Haller asks.

"G'bless, Haller," Klotz says, and goes up on deck. Those who follow see him standing at the railing, his gun on his shoulder. He stands there like a painted picture and answers no one, and gazes into the gloom, gazes out over the ice.

Maybe they should just let him alone, this Klotz. He'll come to his senses on his own. You just have to let him be.

"He's loaded," says the stoker Pospischill, "just loaded, that's all; he drank up his whole rum ration."

It's okay. Just let him be. He'll come back below deck on his own. Let him be.

But when Commander Weyprecht returns from the officers' mess two hours later—the gentlemen were conferring about the future of the expedition and have not been aware of Klotz's craziness—and orders both hunters brought to him, Johann Haller obediently appears on deck, but Klotz is no longer at the railing. The Tyrolean has disappeared. That wasn't craziness. He wasn't drunk, either. That was a farewell. Alexander Klotz, hunter and dog-team driver, has gone home.

Time races now as never before. Now, when not a minute dare be lost, time suddenly flies. And they run after it, run after Klotz, who will be frozen in a few hours if they don't find him. The damned Tyrolean! Going out in this cold in summer clothes! They hurry off in four squads, each to one of the four points of the compass. The air cuts at their throats like a knife. Don't stand still! Faster! Klooootz! Let the bastard freeze. He wants to freeze to death. He's done for. He has to be dead by now.

But they find him, and not dead. At last, after five hours, they find him. Bareheaded, his face almost totally iced over, Alexander Klotz strides with slow dignity toward the south.

They stop him; they speak to him; they scream at him. But

he says not a word. They lead him back to the ship, lead him away. He lets them do as they like. They thaw out their fugitive in the mess—break his clothes from him, immerse his frozen feet and hands in water and a little muriatic acid, rub him down with snow hard as glass dust, pour schnapps down him, and curse their own helplessness. Klotz lets them do as they like and remains mute. Then they lay him on his bunk, cover him up, and keep watch. There he lies, staring, no longer taking part in their life, holding his own against every look—just lies there and stares. Now they have a lunatic on board.

Weeks will pass, but Alexander Klotz remains petrified. At times when the compression of winter's ice ravages them, when the men sick with scurvy lie weeping in fever and an ice storm reminds them of the end of all time, they will envy the hunter, lost in himself and apparently unaware of their reality. But all the same, this winter is less fierce and cruel than the previous one. Here, close to land and protected by it, the compression of the ice is less violent, the emptiness is not as immense, and they have hope of being able to explore the land next spring and then returning home at last—even if they must cross the ice on foot to do it. Even if nineteen of them now show symptoms of scurvy, they shall return home. It is a good thing the machinist Krisch knows nothing of what medical officer Kepes has told the officers' staff: Even though the machinist shows a fair amount of strength and is able to do his duties now and again, there is in fact no hope for him; his lungs have been eaten away beyond any cure. Krisch is closer to death than anyone on board.

And what, someone asks after a period of silence around the table, what if Krisch is so ill he is unable to walk and they have to abandon the *Tegetthoff* and make their retreat to Europe on foot? On foot across this ice! What do they do with Krisch then? "Then," Weyprecht says, "we will carry him."

Krisch tries. Krisch fights on; he will be well again by

spring, able to bear any burden. Payer has to promise him he will take him along on sled rides once spring arrives. Krisch wants to walk in firn snow across land no man has ever trodden before. Payer promises. A discoverer who served his fatherland and science will later tell how every day Krisch carefully recorded the temperature, the strength and direction of the wind—even then. But by December death begins to take him by the hand and his diary becomes more and more a protocol of agony.

On December 15th calm wind, temperature between −28.6° R and −31.2° R [−39° F], beautiful clear weather, the mercury is frozen solid, the crew is building a snow palace, countless northern lights in the southern sky. I still have much pain and have started to have trouble sleeping, so that I can sleep only 2 to 3 hours daily without interruption, I am getting weaker from day to day.

On December 21st wind from the SSW . . . At 11 a.m. reading of H. Scripture, inspection of the crew's quarters; worked in the magnetic-observation hut, temperature rising. My illness has gotten worse again, I have terrible pains in the right side of my chest. On December 23rd wind from WSW . . . cloudy, light snowfall, the crew is decorating the snow palace, magnetic observations . . . besides pain I now have fever that has taken my appetite and I can eat only soup, I feel very weak, my feet can hardly bear me any more. (*Otto Krisch*)

On December 24 they put a Christmas tree made of planks in their snow palace and decorate it with whale-oil lamps, but this time Midshipman Eduard Orel has to read from scripture, because Weyprecht is feverish and has difficulty speaking. But the commandant stands among them, propped up by his first officer, and listens to the tidings of joy.

And lo, the angel of the Lord came upon them, and the glory of the Lord shone round about them: and they were sore afraid. And the angel said unto them, Fear not: for, behold, I bring you good tidings of great joy, which shall be to all people. For unto you is born this day in the city of David a Saviour, which is Christ the

Lord. And this shall be a sign unto you; Ye shall find the babe wrapped in swaddling clothes, lying in a manger. And suddenly there was with the angel a multitude of the heavenly host praising God, and saying, Glory to God in the highest, and on earth peace, good will toward men.

They are reassured when on the next day, Christmas, Weyprecht takes the Bible in hand himself and reads to them. That morning able seaman Lettis had spread word in the crew's quarters that he had seen the commander cough and wipe blood from his mouth. That isn't true, they had told Lettis, hold your tongue, you're lying.

The truth is simply that the commandant reads more slowly today than usual, that when he pauses you can hear him breathing.

On December 26th wind from NE, then calm . . . beautiful clear weather, arcs of northern lights in the east—shifting ice audible from a good distance in all directions . . . Adding to my ills Doctor Kepes has diagnosed something much more dangerous, symptoms of scurvy, my gums are swollen and streaked with blood, red spots visible on my hands and feet, pain in my knees and wrists, plus constant fever.

On December 27th calm, beautiful clear weather . . . lovely twilight, my health hasn't changed, violent pains in my extremities; observations in the magnetic hut continue.

On December 28th calm . . . moonrise at 10 in the morning, 11 o'clock reading from H. Scripture, then inspection of crew's quarters, about midnight a steady distant rumble of ice in the SE. My health has not changed.

On December 29th wind from the south, then calm . . . light clouds, large pale ring around the moon, toward evening dusty snow falls . . . violent pains in my feet.

On December 30th wind from ESE, then calm . . . misty light snowfall at times, bright mock moons on both sides and pale semicircle at the zenith . . . My health is still unchanged.

On December 31st wind from the east 3–4 and ENE 2–3 . . .

misty light drifting snow, foggy gray ring around the moon with cross and traces of mock moons. Today we celebrate New Year's Eve and welcome in 1874, I remain at the table until 10 p.m., then go to bed.

On January 1st, 1874, wind from the south 6–7 and SSE 5 . . . cloudy, snowfall and steady drifting snow. Little comfort at midday meal, everyone asleep except I have a light head from drinking wine for my fever yesterday, herring and sardines meet with approval. Temperature rising from hour to hour.

On January 2nd wind from SSW 5–6 . . . cloudy, snowfall and driving snow . . . the moon is dull behind a veil of mist my health remains unchanged, in addition to violent pain in my knees, daily attacks of fever.

On January 3rd wind from SE 2–3 and SSE 5–6 . . . cloudy with occasional swiftly moving fog mixed with fine watery snow . . . boats freed of drifts . . . today marks 540 days at sea, or better, in ice.

Because of violent pains I've had to spend the day in bed.

On January 9th calm . . . minimum −31.1° R [−39° F], fairly clear, several pale northern lights visible . . . The fever lasted all night and I never closed an eye.

On January 11th wind from NNW and north . . . minimum −35.1° R [−31° F], very bright stars moon in last quarter rises at 3 o'clock, northern lights in pale green colors in quadrants III and IV pale, dawn on the southern horizon . . . My health has improved a little with only a very light attack of fever.

On January 12th wind from WNW . . . minimum −35.6° R [−48° F], clear bright weather, severe cold, northern lights above the zenith . . . I can feel nothing but severe pain in my feet and a nameless weakness. (*Otto Krisch*)

On January 15, 1874, two months before his death, the machinist writes only numbers in his diary—temperature and wind measurements, but not another word about his condition, about what he feels, not another word about clouds and northern lights. It is his last entry. Krisch will make only one attempt—in February, when his illness relaxes its grip for a few hours—to fill in the lost days, pasting a scrap of paper into his journal, the fragment of an order Weyprecht has issued in case it should prove necessary to "abandon ship." The order says that if the *Tegetthoff* is abandoned, Otto Krisch will be part of the crew of the third lifeboat, along with Brosch, Zaninovich, Stiglich, Sussich, Pospischill, Lukinovich, and Marola. Otto Krisch is to return home in the third lifeboat. But after this pasted-in order there are only empty pages. It is the time of empty pages.

While the machinist wastes away in his battle against death, sinking repeatedly into unconsciousness and hallucinations, something happens that no one believed possible: Klotz returns from his petrified state. No, not slowly and bit by bit, but abruptly, as if he were someone waking from workaday sleep, who sheds his dreams, gets up, and goes to work as on every other day. One morning in early February, Alexander Klotz rises from his bunk—the arc of dawn is already big and bright above the horizon—dresses, while his fellow crew members watch in speechless amazement, reaches for his gun, stands at attention for the commander, and reports for deck watch. Klotz, who for so long has lain in his cabin as mute as if he were his own monument, wishes to return to his duties; he has spent the winter in Sankt Leonhard; now he has returned from the Passeiertal.

Alexander Klotz is his old self. Not as merry, but his old self. They also see ice master Carlsen burst into laughter for the first time: "Look at him, old Klotz. Just look at him! Standing there like Saint Olaf; he's just like Saint Olaf!" Norway's patron saint had found his way back into the world after long periods of brooding and silence, had brought his foes to bloody justice and continued his work of conversion. And he, Carlsen, believes he knows why Klotz has returned a whole man: Krisch's soul has been leaving its mortal shell more and more frequently of late, scouting out the path to eternity; on one of these scouting trips it must have met the hunter's soul and urged it to return. And so the hunter had been freed from his numbed state.

On February 24, after 125 days of darkness, the sun rises again. I shall not say anything about the celebration. More important is the fact that Weyprecht uses that cloudless Tuesday to have his decision concerning the expedition's future read to the crew. The commander orders all hands on deck and Orel reads them a document signed by the officers: *The members of the Austro-Hungarian North Pole Expedition intend to leave their ship at the end of May and return to Europe. But whereas that event shall be preceded by one or perhaps two sled trips to explore Kaiser Franz Josef Land, the necessity arises to clothe the latter project and its concomitant expectations in certain forms which shall render so daring an undertaking as untroubling as possible for both those who participate in it and those who remain behind. Those forms are: the men traveling by sled will have to rely on emergency supplies left behind to supplement what they carry with them; further, they will have to rely on having these supplies stored on land by the first day of their first trip. The trips will begin in March and last for six to seven weeks, commencing sometime between the 10th and 20th of March and if possible proceeding in several directions: one detachment along the coast toward the north, one to the west, and one to the interior. Each operation shall conclude with the scaling of a dominating mountain.*

The length and sequence of these trips cannot be determined at present—nor even at the moment of departure—such matters being reserved for decisions made on the spot. This has been mentioned both to allay unnecessary worries and to forestall any misguided searches. If upon their final return, those traveling by sled should not find the ship here, they will at once attempt to return to Europe on their own, and only under the most compelling circumstances will they attempt a third wintering, for which purpose the surplus supplies to be deposited on land are in part intended. It goes without saying that these trips should not be extended to a point which would preclude a needed rest for the entire crew prior to the return home to Europe and that they must be completed before the beginning of May.

The return home to Europe. They talk about the approaching retreat as if it were a trip from Vienna to Budapest, as if the return home were signed and sealed and not contingent on months of torturous marching through an icy wasteland. Between them and the inhabited world lie thousands of square miles of drift and pack ice—but they talk as if they did not know that most of their predecessors have perished on such retreats, have frozen to death, starved, died of exhaustion and scurvy. But they probably have to talk this way. And of course all of their attention and pains are now directed to preparing for another, less threatening task: to walk and measure their land, which has been close to them throughout the polar night. And despite the agonies of scurvy, more sailors than Payer can use volunteer to accompany their commander on the first sled trip. They stop by the officers' table, describe their stamina and strength and minimize their illnesses. The man who lay in bed with fever yesterday wants to pull hundreds of pounds of sled through broken ice today. No, not just for the honor, what can honor mean after two polar nights? But with every passing day the monotony of life on board is harder to bear. And bonuses have been promised as well.

Early in March, Payer decides to take able seamen Lukinovich, Catarinich, and Lettis, the stoker Pospischill, and the hunters Haller and Klotz. Yes, Klotz will be coming, too. They could have no more experienced guide than Klotz for mountains and glaciers. The seven of them—plus the three strongest dogs, Torossy, Zumbu, and Gilies—will pull a large sled to the north and measure and baptize the glaciers, capes, and mountain chains. By March 9 they are ready. They will get under way the next morning.

"The machinist is dying," Haller says. "Can we leave when one of us is dying?" But the commander on land has already flagged his sled. Nothing will hold him back now.

On March 9th, Krisch lay on his lonely sickbed, in agony yet not moving. Lukinovich was on watch, and believing that Krisch was about to die, he began to open the eternal gates for the unconscious man, calling out for a good hour in the loud, fanatical fashion of his southern homeland: "Gesù, Giuseppe, Maria, vi dono il cuor e l'anima mia!" At the time we were busy at work in our cabins and did not dare interrupt an act whose intent was pious enough but whose effect was ghastly. . . . On the morning of March 10th we left the ship. . . . I was so moved by this "at last" after a year of waiting that I was unable to sleep the night before; both those departing and those left behind were filled with excitement, as if we were about to conquer Peru or Ophir and not cold snow-covered lands. With indescribable joy we began the hard mechanical work of pulling the sled. (*Julius Payer*)

11 March, Tuesday: Cloudy and windy. Temperature −19° R [−13° F]. Traveling with the sled is sad work. (*Johann Haller*)

Their sled weighs seven hundred pounds. Their task is not to pull, but to tug and tear at the burden, exhausting practice for the torture awaiting them on the retreat to Europe. Again and again they have to unload the vehicle—stove, tent, kegs of kerosene, food, all of it removed piece by piece—to maneuver the empty sled over the hummocks of ice. Sometimes they prepare their way with pickax and shovel. The ice is like stone. Whenever their midday rest—spent crouching behind a crag of ice or rock—has ended and someone wants to fall back and just lie there, Payer threatens to leave him behind alone. And then fear is greater than exhaustion. This first sled trip is supposed to last only six days, and in those six days they must follow every path that can be followed, climb every mountain that can be climbed, and do everything that discoverers and surveyors are supposed to do—without dying in the attempt. They bury themselves in the ice by night and stretch their tent over the pit. These quarters are then covered by falling snow. They lie pressed tightly together in a communal sleeping bag made of buffalo hide, cursing and complaining until Payer snaps at them. When they rise in the morning they feel as if they will shatter. The buffalo hide is as hard as a board, and their tent is a cave shimmering with the icy condensation of their breath.

Whenever we broke up camp, every object that fell into the snow was buried at once under its drifts. There is in general no more difficult test of stamina on an arctic journey than dealing with such driving snow and continuing one's march in the accompanying low temperatures. Several of my companions were not accustomed to the dreadful inclemency of such weather, and their fingers froze at once when they unwisely tried to button up their wind screens and nose protectors or fasten their coats after leaving the tent. Our canvas boots were hard as stone; everyone stomped his feet trying to prevent frostbite. . . . Frosted with snow and crouched tight, men and dogs moved on, the dogs with lowered heads and tucked tails, stiff with snow, only their eyes still free. . . . Walking against the wind, which is the hardest way to make progress, left almost everyone with a frostbitten nose. . . . A small band of men exposed to such low temperatures is a curious sight. If they are marching forward, misty vapors stream from their mouths, enveloping them in a cloak of fine-needled ice and rendering them almost invisible; the snow over which they pass likewise steams with warmth received from the sea below. Countless crystals of ice fill the air, turning a clear day into a steamy yellow-gray dusk and giving off a continuous hissing sound; the fine dust of snow falling from them or the cloud of hovering moist frost they create is also the reason one feels such dampness, which is all the more noticeable the greater the cold and is constantly replenished by currents of water vapor rising from the open places in the sea. . . .

Even when the wind is calm, one's eyelids ice over, and to keep them from freezing shut one must frequently free them of ice. But one's beard is less ice covered than usual, because the vapors one breathes out instantly fall again as snow. . . . But one feels the vise of cold worst in the soles of one's feet after a period of immobility, presumably because of the abundance of nerve endings there. Nervous lassitude, apathy, and narcolepsy result, and this explains the well-known correlation between resting and freezing. Indeed the first proviso for a traveling party that must accomplish great physical labor in very cold temperatures is to stand still as little as possible, and the principal reason why afternoon marches particularly tax one's moral energies is to be found in the intense chilling of the soles of the feet during the midday rest. Intense cold affects bodily secretions as well, just as it thickens the blood and increases the loss of carbon dioxide, resulting in a greater need for nourishment. The secretion of sweat ceases entirely; mucus from the nose and the conjunctiva steadily increases, urine assumes an almost bright red color, the urge to urinate increases as well. At first constipation occurs, lasting five and sometimes even eight days, and this is followed by diarrhea. Another interesting phenomenon is that one's beard bleaches out under such conditions. (*Julius Payer*)

The first lieutenant's traveling companions sense something uncanny about him now. He suffers the same hardships, is exposed to the same severe cold and frostbite, knows the same painful thawing of numb limbs—but he does not weary of surveying and baptizing the land. This is *Cape Tegetthoff,* that is *Nordenskiöld Fjord,* that *Tyrol Fjord,* there is *Hall Island* and there *McClintock,* and in the distance the *Wüllerstorff Mountains* and the *Sonklar glacier. . . .* Payer forces his hunters to climb cliffs with him when the others are resting; he sketches and writes, his fingers frozen blue, when the others are lying apathetic in the tent; he examines his broken skin, the ravages on his own body, as if they were the damage caused by cold to a machine. He is the subject of an experiment who feels nothing, nothing except enthusiasm. The commander on land drives his companions on—angrily, fanatically, drives them ever onward. And yet in these few days they get no farther than the southernmost islands and coasts of the archipelago. The land resists with a roar; all Payer's anger and enthusiasm can do nothing against these storms.

Towers of basalt, fractured ice, dead mountains, ravines, ridges, slopes, cliffs—and no moss, no shrubs. Just stones and ice. And the constant roar. The storms. Lord Jesus Christ! If this is paradise, what must hell be.

Franz Josef Land displayed the full rigors of nature in the far north; particularly at the beginning of spring it seemed devoid of all life. Monstrous glaciers stared down on all sides from the high mountain wilderness rising boldly in steep conical masses. Everything was wrapped in blinding white. The columned rows of symmetrical stratified mountains looked as if they were covered by an icy glaze.

None outrivaling the others, the mountains of each region tower to an average height of 2–3,000 feet, toward the southwest to perhaps 5,000 feet. . . . A crystalline igneous rock predominates everywhere; the Swedes call it hypersthenite, but it is identical with the dolerite of Greenland. The dolerite of Franz Josef Land is medium-grained, dark leek-green in color, and consists of plagioclase, augite, olivine, titaniferous iron, and iron chlorite. The bulk of it is plagioclase, although this exceeds the augite by only a little. The crystals of plagioclase are usually a millimeter, sometimes up to three millimeters long. They consist now of thinner, now of thicker laminae whose few inclusions reveal nothing striking. The augite is greenish gray, shows no crystal structure, but instead forms grains, often a millimeter in length and of equal width. It has frequent inclusions consisting of the other minerals, as well as small attenuated steam pores. The olivine forms grains smaller than those of the augite but seldom reveals a crystal structure. These grains are often covered with a thick yellow-brown layer of minerals (iron chlorite); they also often show jagged cracks filled with the same brown material. The olivine has very few inclusions. The titaniferous iron occurs in longish plates or fills cracks in the other minerals.

This dolerite reveals similarities in all respects with some of the dolerites of the Spitsbergens . . . which as good as proves geological correspondence between the new lands and the Spitsbergens. . . . Nature in the far north cannot adorn itself with the colors of vegetation; it can impress only by its inflexibility and the unbroken light of summer, and just as there are lands smothered with the glut of nature's blessing to the point of being uncivilizable, so here the other extreme lay before us—total neglect, uninhabitable exiguity. (*Julius Payer*)

On the fourth day of the sled trip—March 13, 1874, a Friday—the temperature falls to −49° F. The rum Payer has doled out to comfort them is as viscous as whale oil and so cold that they feel as if their teeth will break when they drink it. Pospischill can no longer pull the sled, both his hands are frozen and he is spitting blood. Lettis and Haller have Klotz cut their canvas boots from their swollen feet; they limp about now with feet wrapped in reindeer hide. Lukinovich shits his pants when he tries to pull, and Catarinich is snow-blind. The hollows of his eyes are weeping wounds; exertion forces blood from his pores, which freezes to a black crust on his skin. Payer's face is disfigured by a festering rash. They have had enough. They must go back. Pospischill's sufferings are the worst; he groans in pain and is afraid the doctor will amputate his frozen hands. On the morning of the fifteenth, Payer gives the stoker a compass and orders him to go back to the ship ahead of them. Maybe Kepes can save the stoker's hands.

When Pospischill reaches the *Tegetthoff* that evening, he can no longer speak; only babbling and blood come from his mouth. Weyprecht questions him, shakes him, questions him. The stoker only stammers. Weyprecht takes hold of his arm, of the whole man, as if trying to set up a signpost, turns the semiconscious man in the direction from which he has come, and shouts over and over: *Where?* At some point the arm points out into the frosty haze to the northwest. Weyprecht doesn't even take a gun with him. He runs off without his furs. Officers Brosch and Orel and eight sailors race after him. But they cannot catch up. They see him stand still in the distance sometimes and hear him call for Payer, but they cannot catch up. Almost three hours must pass before Weyprecht receives an answer: *Carl! Here!* It is the first time in their years of ice that the commander has been called by his first name. It will not happen again.

It is a stumbling, dreary procession that returns to the ship. They have to help Catarinich walk, and Lettis must be pulled on the sled. But there is no comfort aboard the *Tegetthoff*. As they climb the ice stairway, a frivolity from days past, they hear Pospischill's screams of pain, and then the doctor, too, who keeps shouting, "Do you hear me? You'll keep your hands, keep them! Do you hear me?" But then the stoker's pain suddenly becomes meaningless, and they can hear no one but the machinist. That a dying man can scream like that. The whole night and all the next day Otto Krisch moans and screams his waning twenty-nine years to an end.

What a silence, when late in the afternoon the noise of his dying abruptly ceases.

16 March 1874, Monday: Clear weather and windy. Temperature −29° R [−33° F]. *Made ready for the second sled trip. At 4:30 this afternoon our machinist Otto Krisch died! God grant him eternal rest!* (*Johann Haller*)

In the 847 days that must elapse between the Austro-Hungarian North Pole Expedition's departure from and return to Vienna, Johann Haller uses an exclamation mark only twice in his journal entries: both times on the day of the machinist's death. The punctuation of mourning or horror—I do not presume to judge. I have simply preserved these marks and passed them on, so delicate and so natural, as fossils of an unrepeatable emotion.

Space inside the ship is too cramped for them to keep a corpse for the prescribed period of lying in state. Krisch must be brought on deck. But he shall not lie there naked, unprotected. In the hour of his death, Antonio Vecerina—although bent with scurvy, rheumatism, and fever—begins the work of making a pine coffin. He saws, hammers, suffers. The others hold a wake. The crew, the officers, even those ill in bed, gather around the machinist's bunk, pressing in around the distorted face, and Weyprecht prays the prayer for the dead, in Latin as befits the dignity of the moment.

Libera me, Domine, de morte aeterna in die illa tremenda, quando caeli movendi sunt et terra, dum veneris judicare saeculum per ignem—Preserve me, O Lord, from eternal death on the terrible day when heaven and earth shall tremble, for Thou hast come through fire to judge mankind. . . . Requiem aeternam dona ei, Domine, et lux perpetua luceat ei—O Lord, give him eternal peace and let Thy eternal light shine upon him. They pray like this for more than an hour—Italian, German, and Croatian appeals to the Almighty. Then Klotz and Haller wash the machinist's body and clothe it. Krisch shall be interred with all due dignity and care on the coast of their new land, and not be given to the sea like a common sailor. Able seaman Antonio Lukinovich donates a funeral shirt; it is a linen shirt, starched and embroidered, the one he wanted to wear on the day he returned to his hometown of Brazza, and into its hem he sews a relic, an eyetooth that a dealer in religious articles in Trieste had claimed was taken from the mouth of St. Stephen and had the power to assist a poor soul to enter paradise. Boatswain Lusina gives him an alabaster rosary, which Lorenzo Marola, who is so good at decorating, then lays in the machinist's blue hands. Marola has always been in charge of decorating the Christmas tree and the banquet tables at New Year's and Easter. They prepare a funeral—a solemn rite, not a perfunctory one. Alexander Klotz sits late into the night painting a rude inscription on the wooden sign he wants to nail to the cross above Krisch's grave:

Man being in honor
abideth not
he is like the beasts that perish

"Klotz, y' can't put that on his grave," Haller says, interrupting his comrade's careful work only toward the end.

" 'nd why not? It's from Holy Scripture."

"Y' can read it there, but y' dassn't write it."

For two days the coffin containing the machinist's decorated body lies on its catafalque on deck. Despite the protective planks that cover the aft deck, bizarre fragile formations of ice crystals grow on the bier, their shapes changing unexpectedly, bursting, and then returning. On both days of the lying in state, ice master Carlsen appears again and again beside the catafalque, loses himself as he watches these ice crystals, trying to read from the play of their transformations what awaits the machinist's soul on its way out of time. Ice flowers, Carlsen says, are omens of purgatory and the delay of blessedness; only shimmering ice as clear as glass is a sign and token of redemption. On March 19 they break the ice covering the coffin and bear Otto Krisch from the ship.

A sad parade left the ship, in its midst the coffin, decorated with flags and a cross and resting on a sled, which we intended to pull to the nearest rise on the beach of Wilczek Island. Silently battling the violent driving snow, we moved out across the desolate fields of ice, reaching the rise of Wilczek Island after an hour and a half of walking. Here a crevice between two columns of basalt received his earthly remains, above which we set a simple wooden cross—a sad place of eternal rest amid all these symbols of death and isolation, far from all mankind, inaccessible to earthly pieties and yet rendered more worthy than a sarcophagus by inviolable solitude. We knelt in a circle around the grave, painstakingly covering it with stones we had broken loose. Wind wrapped it in snow. We spoke our prayer for the departed aloud. . . . And then we were con-

fronted with the question: Would we be permitted to return to our homeland, or would the arctic seas also be the inaccessible site of our own demise? (*Julius Payer*)

With their own end so immediately present, they dare not lose another day in mourning, despondency, or anxious projections of the future. Every hour must now be devoted to preparations for the second sled trip, the great journey to the farthest north of their land. This is what Payer wants. And Weyprecht agrees with him. Even if they all perish and no homeland and no academy ever learns of their discovery, at least they must ascertain for themselves the size and cosmographic importance of Kaiser Franz Josef Land. This is what Payer wants. And Weyprecht agrees with him.

This time they lash sixteen hundred pounds of equipment and supplies to their pack sled; they will be under way for a month. The Tyrolean hunters and Lukinovich go along for a second time. Sussich, Zaninovich, and Midshipman Orel are new. Payer has promised his companions 1,000 guldens in silver if they reach 81° north latitude, another 2,500 if they reach 82°. For the commander on land, the numerous islands of the archipelago are apparently no longer sufficient recompense for years of hardship; Payer now wants to set a new latitude record. The rumor spreads in the crew's mess that the first lieutenant not only wants to cross the 82nd parallel but in fact also hopes to conquer the North Pole.

Our departure occurred on March 26th, a morning of driving snow and temperatures of 17° R below zero [−6° *F*]. . . . *No more than a thousand paces from the ship, the driving snow became so bad that one could not see one's closest neighbor, and we began to walk in circles. It was impossible to continue the journey with any success until the storm abated, and a return to the ship would have been our simplest expedient. Nevertheless we decided to set up our tent, hidden from the ship behind an ice formation, and spend the next twenty-four hours inside it. . . . On March 27th the snow was blowing more gently and we resumed our journey, and made such good progress that we were confident we could conceal yesterday's defeat from the men on board ship. As we reached the southern tip of Wilczek Island and the ship disappeared from view, the temperature fell and the driving snow once again grew so violent that both of Sussich's hands froze and we were forced to rub them with snow for an hour. When we moved out a second time, walking into the violent wind, we were all at risk of freezing our faces. Pulling the heavily laden sled required such exertion that for the first time we were bathed in sweat.* (Julius Payer)

And so the surveyors move painfully ahead again, repeating all the hardships of their first sled trip. They drag their burden along the coastlines of more new islands, cross frozen straits, climb mountains, map the land—and everything that happens happens in a world of icy, snow-blown lifelessness broken only by roving bears. Arc second by arc second, the surveyors toil on toward the farthest north. They measure and baptize and suffer. Only Payer appears to bear these renewed tortures with enthusiasm.

There can be hardly anything more exciting than the discovery of new lands. One's powers of deduction are constantly engaged by the visible configurations, and one's imagination is endlessly busy filling in gaps where one cannot see. However often one's next step destroys erroneous assumptions, one's imagination is ready at once to create new ones. . . . The excitement is diminished only by days on which one must journey across snowy wastes whose far shores lie at such distances that they do not change quickly enough to allow the traveler's imagination room in which to play. (Julius Payer)

But whatever games the commander plays and whatever it is he experiences, his subordinates experience something else. After all, it is Payer alone who has the freedom to slip out of the ropes at any time, to point into the haze of some cape lying in the distance, declare it their next meeting point, and then walk on across the land, alone and free of all burdens. Who can say how beautiful and exciting this land might have been for an underling freed of the drudgery of pulling the sled, who would be able to wander it, moreover, protected by the light, warm down shirt that the first lieutenant wears under his furs. But if anyone should speak of this journey, of this ordeal, in the years ahead, he will most certainly not speak of "Zaninovich, the discoverer," or "Giacomo Sussich, the famous sledder"—that much any man knows who has sworn to obey and bear the burdens. They will speak only of *Payer*, of Payer and Weyprecht. What underling ever hoped that his name might be preserved in history books or that he might leave some trace of himself on a map of the world? Giacomo Sussich, for example, would certainly never have thought of baptizing a plateau in this new land "Monte Volosca" simply because his gentle, republican mother had brought him into this world in Volosca. Or Zaninovich—would he have christened a nameless cape "Lesina" because his girlfriend was waiting for him in Lesina? The first lieutenant can, of course, go about naming and baptizing quite differently—as a gentleman, as the consummate discoverer. Because the commander on land had been trained as a lieutenant in the infantry at the military academy in Vienna Neustadt, a whole island, which lies like a vast mussel in Austria Sound, is now called Vienna Neustadt Island. Payer strews names across the archipelago as if they were charms. He probes his memory and constantly finds new cities and friends to immortalize in the ice, at the same time never forgetting to render tribute to the royal house, to the arts and sciences. Cape Grillparzer, he says to one chaotic tower of rocks, Cape Kremsmünster to a second. The litany of lovely names grows longer with each day—Klagenfurt Island, Crown Prince Rudolf Land, Archduke Rainer Land, Cape Fiume, Cape Trieste, Cape Budapest, Cape Tyrol, and so on. But Payer's companions grow weaker each day. The underlings cannot follow the Baptist with the same energies he gives to his mission.

After only one week of dragging the sled, Antonio Lukinovich is convinced beyond any doubt that this is his last journey. He prays much and loudly. Until Payer reprimands him: If the sailor simply must pray while pulling the sled, then he is to do so silently and to himself, thereby saving his energies.

On April 3, Good Friday, Lukinovich grows obstinate. On this day, he says, the heavens turned dark above Jerusalem and the Savior gave up his ghost on the cross; on this day all work must be laid aside and our thoughts turned solely to the martyrdom of our Redeemer; no pulling of sleds, no forced marches.

Forward, Payer says, we dare not lose a single day. Sin, says Lukinovich, sacrilege. The bonus for marching on this day are the wages of Judas.

Shut your mouth, Payer says.

Holy Saturday, April 4

Heavy driving snow, which finally becomes a blizzard, forces the surveyors to spend the morning in their tent. A sign, Lukinovich says, that we must keep our day of rest after all. They wait, huddled together. At some point the sled dog Zumbu leaps up and bounds off after invisible prey, bounds into the howling whiteness and vanishes in it forever. A sign, Lukinovich says, God help us.

Easter Sunday, April 5

The raging storm grows weaker. At last they can go on. No one dares ask the commander for holiday rest. They have no holidays now. Their salvation lies solely in marching northward. Eduard Orel must, as per Payer's orders, use every opportunity to determine their position—and at last the midshipman's calculations supply the long-overdue results: They have crossed 81° north latitude. Payer orders the sled flagged. They kill two bears on this Sunday; they cannot possibly carry them over such terrain on the sled. They leave behind a cache of meat to be used on their retreat to the ship.

Bear meat now became our preferred food; we enjoyed it raw or cooked. Poorly cooked meat, particularly of older bears, tasted worse than raw, more a diet for gulls, hardly fit for devils on fast days in hell. Nor will gourmets find other satisfactions in polar regions; with few exceptions the products available to humans for their meals are coarse and oily. The approbation with which they are nevertheless greeted stems solely from necessity. For indeed the desolate meadows of the Arctic are the true home of hunger. (*Julius Payer*)

Easter Monday, April 6

The day is dim and so hung with fog that the surveyors begin to argue about a silver-white dome lying some distance ahead of them. The sun shining on a cloudbank, says one; a promontory, says another. It is steam from the frost; no, the roiling of a snowstorm, or maybe the most monstrous iceberg of all their years here. They head for it. And then it is only just an island. Another island.

Then we climbed up onto its ice-covered spine; full of high expectation we stood on its summit. To the north lay an indescribable wasteland, more desolate than any I ever met in all the Arctic. (*Julius Payer*)

Wednesday, April 8

We dragged the sled forward with great effort; here and there we had to dig a pathway free, and we were often in danger of breaking the sled. We moved constantly in a maze of zigzags, as a result of both the tangled, chaotic state of the ice and the scant value of the compass in such high latitudes. (*Julius Payer*)

Friday, April 10

The exhausted surveyors make their camp at the foot of a pinnacle on an island Payer has named Hohenlohe. There is still no end to the archipelago. To the north, on the far side of a strait visible from their refuge, rises the massive wall of a glacier. How large must the island be that can bear such glaciers. That's where we must go, Payer says. Perhaps they could go on like this forever, onward into all eternity, and they would always see a new coastline, another island, more mountains—except Sussich and Lukinovich can go no farther. But nothing, no one can bring the first lieutenant to turn back now. The first lieutenant wants to measure this land to its end, he wants to see it all, he has to see it all, and he wants to cross 82° north latitude, too. And maybe 83°, and the next one. He has no use for limping, feverish, despondent sailors.

The first lieutenant decided to proceed farther north with only a portion of the sledding company. The others, somewhat weakened by the hardships met thus far, were to remain on Hohenlohe Island near Cape Schrötter, and the first lieutenant put me in command of this detachment. The sled and the tent were both cut in two and the provisions divided. I packed the items, and the first lieutenant departed. I shall wait here until he returns, which should be in about seven days. A dreadful separation . . . (*Johann Haller*)

Seven days of waiting!

Johann Haller does not even write down a second, even more worrisome order that Payer has given. Emergency procedures: If the first lieutenant, Klotz, Orel, and Zaninovich do not return from the north within fifteen days, the men waiting on Hohenlohe Island are on no account to look for the missing party but are to begin their retreat alone to the *Admiral Tegetthoff* at once. Perhaps Haller suppresses these orders in his journal because he knows as well as Payer and the others that none of them will find their way out of the labyrinth of ice and back to the ship without Orel, their navigation officer.

Naturally, Payer will note a few days later, *the sailors were quite conversant with compasses commonly used at sea. The mariner's compass that I gave them, however, was very small, and they were confused by the declination. . . . When I asked them what direction they needed to take to return to the ship, to my horror they pointed toward Rawlinson Sound instead of Austria Sound.*

The track is good that day. Once they have rested for four hours and said farewell to the two unhappy sailors and their guard Haller, they quickly leave Hohenlohe Island behind. As always—as if they fear that the solid sheet of frozen sea is a trick—the dogs strain every muscle to pull toward the nearest coastline, the glacial wall to the north. The blood from their torn paws leaves a red pattern behind on the ice, which is then sliced by the sled's runners. Red splatterings and dark parallel lines of sled tracks: on this April day the route of these northern travelers is like a carpet unrolling toward infinity. The track is good.

But as we approached the lowlands of Crown Prince Rudolf Land, we found ourselves among countless icebergs, each a hundred to two hundred feet high, and in bright sunlight a constant cracking and snapping came from deep within their bowels. The vast walls of the Middendorff glacier extended beyond our sight to the north. Deep fields of snow and chinks of open sea produced by their calving and upending filled the spaces between them. We kept breaking through, and our canvas boots and clothes were soaked with seawater. But the view down passes between gigantic colossuses of glacial fragments was nevertheless so enthralling that we turned our attention almost exclusively to the tall figures shimmering above us, and wandered lost but cheerful among the pyramids, tables, and cliffs. Only after I sent Klotz on ahead to climb one of the icebergs and direct us by leaving footprints leading to some scalable portion of the Middendorff glacier did we find our way into a more open region. With all of us in harness and using snow bridges to cross the crevasses, we conquered the heights of the Middendorff glacier. Its lower portion opened in broad rifts. . . . But farther up, the glacier seemed to have no fissures, despite an inclination of several degrees, so that by setting our united energies to the sled we were able to pass to the north without great exertion. (*Julius Payer*)

But now it is Klotz who can go no farther. The Tyrolean long ago gave up wearing boots and has only wrapped hides for shoes—and now he pulls off the rags and shows the first lieutenant his bloody, ulcerated feet. Where toenails once grew, there is only raw, decaying flesh. With feet like these, Klotz says, his own weight is pain enough—any other burden, however, even pulling the sled, is unbearable.

Payer is furious. Why hadn't he owned up to these wounds before they left Hohenlohe Island, he snaps at Klotz; there would still have been time to exchange duties with Haller. He hadn't wanted to annoy the lieutenant, Klotz says, and everything had been arranged with Haller. Haller hadn't been as afraid to be left alone on the island as he had; what with his sore feet and two sick Italian sailors, Klotz hadn't placed much hope in the island.

You're going back to them, Payer says.

Back? Klotz asks. Back? Alone?

But Payer . . . Orel tries to object.

I don't want to hear it, Payer says.

But Klotz has nothing more to say anyway.

Burdened only by his sack and revolver, he set out. Soon he had vanished in the labyrinth of icebergs below.

We ourselves had repacked the sled, harnessed the dogs, and wrapped our ropes around us. But at almost the same moment as we set in motion, the snow under our sled opened up, and Zaninovich, the dogs, and the sled plunged soundlessly downward—from some unknown depth came the wails of man and dogs. Such were my impressions in the brief moment before I myself, as the first man on the rope, was wrenched back. Stumbling backward and staring at the black abyss before me, I did not doubt for a second that I, too, would soon plummet down into it. But a wonderful providence caught the sled between ice formations about thirty feet down the crevasse. . . . The sled was wedged tight, and there I lay, motionless on my stomach, held by the taut rope cutting deep in the snow . . . but when I called down to Zaninovich that I was going to cut the rope, he implored me not to do it, because otherwise the sled would continue its fall and he would surely be killed. For a while I simply lay there and considered what to do next, although my head was swimming. I recalled how Pinggera, my guide in Lombardy, and I had plunged down over an eight-hundred-foot wall of ice in the Ortler Mountains, and had escaped unharmed, which gave me the needed confidence to risk a desperate rescue under these conditions . . . by cutting the rope wrapped around my chest. The sled below lurched slightly, and then wedged itself tight again. I got up, pulled off my canvas boots, and leapt about ten feet back across the crevasse. As I did I spotted Zaninovich and the dogs. I called down to him that I would race back to Hohenlohe Island and bring men and ropes to rescue him, that this would work if he could manage not to freeze to death in the four hours it would take. I could hear his answer: ''Fate, signore, fate pure!''—Do it, sir, do it! (*Julius Payer*)

Payer races off. Orel has difficulty keeping up, falls farther and farther back, finally loses the runner from view. His eyes fixed on this morning's sled tracks, half erased now by drifts, Payer runs on. He can no longer see Orel. Zaninovich is trapped in the depths. And Klotz is somewhere out there. Each of them is alone now.

The vanguard of the Austro-Hungarian North Pole Expedition is a panicky ragtag band, scattered by the terrors of this land like a roof ripped away by a storm wind. And the worst damage has been done to the commander on land himself.

My personal affection for Zaninovich aside, I reproached myself for having undertaken an unconsidered crossing of a glacier despite my own ample experience in high mountains, and I found no peace of mind. . . . My body glowing and bathed in sweat, I pulled off my down shirt and cast it, my boots, gloves, and shawl aside, and ran on in my stocking feet. (*Julius Payer*)

Zaninovich in the crevasse—if only *he* now had the down shirt his commander had thrown aside, and not just his tattered fur, maybe then he would have more than three, four hours until he froze to death. . . . I have asked myself how Weyprecht might have dealt with this disaster and how the day would have turned out under his command. Would Haller and the exhausted sailors have been left behind on some island or other on his orders? Would he have moved up onto this fissured glacier just to gain a few minutes of northern latitude? And would Klotz now be wandering the ice after such a reprimand, alone and humiliated? This report is also an ongoing tribunal held in judgment of the past—I weigh, consider, imagine, and play with the possibilities of reality. Because the grandeur and tragedy and absurdity of what has been can be measured against what might have been. But as to some other possible course of events on the day of this disaster, I have decided to forgo all guesses. I will not project what Weyprecht would have done in Payer's place.

And so I return to imagining Zaninovich, pressing against the dogs in the blue darkness of the crevasse and expecting only his death. I see Payer and Orel racing on, but miles apart and both without weapons—they were left on the sled and are inside the glacier now, along with all the other things they need for survival. And then I see Klotz; he is approaching Hohenlohe Island, but in such pain and moving so slowly that Payer catches up with him. Klotz stops and stares at the breathless man but asks no questions. Gasping and wrapped in the white vapors of his exertions, Payer reports, with long pauses, how things stand. Klotz does not seem to understand the lieutenant as he fights for air. He just stands and stares at the man, who looks as if he were clad only in frosty mist. Then suddenly Klotz sinks to his knees and weeps.

For in his simplicity he laid the blame for what had happened on himself. He was so distraught that I made him promise not to do harm to himself, and leaving him there in his silence I ran ahead to the island. (*Julius Payer*)

Extant documents give no further clue as to what Alexander Klotz felt, but I assume that even years after he had returned from the ice, the hunter was convinced that on that day he survived the worst loneliness of his life.

When Klotz finally reaches the camp on Hohenlohe Island, it is empty. Haller, Payer, and Orel and even the two sailors have long since started back to the glacier to help Zaninovich.

Ten hours, twelve, fourteen—Klotz waits in the lee of the cape, sits in the tent, paces it despite his pain, three hundred times and more, stamps his feet to ward off the cold, stares in the direction from which they must return at some point, and finally comes to believe that no one will find his way back here, that he is alone forever. Perhaps the Tyrolean has already begun to die, to prepare himself for another world, when the canvas, stiff with ice and heavy as a door, is suddenly flung back and someone says, "Klotz, Klotz. You asleep?"

Haller has found the way even in driving snow; he has returned with the two sailors. They have come to get him; have come to get him out of this fearful ice.

No, Haller says, we're not here to get you; we were sent back here ourselves; we have to stay here and wait. Zaninovich has been rescued, Haller says, but after the rescue the lieutenant didn't want to waste any more time and headed north again right away. He told the three Hohenlohers to go back to their island.

It is cold in the tent, and dark, as if they were deep under the earth. Now Haller is their leader; he is in charge of what is to be done. They light whale-oil lamps and warm their hands by them.

Haller keeps going over the day's events with the others, as in a school lesson. He can't stop worrying about what has happened. The lieutenant made a mistake. The lieutenant made a mistake on a glacier and then lost his head.

When Haller records the events of this day in his journal, however, he sees that despite the commander things have taken their normal course and have come together again; only then does he realize how tired he is.

The first lieutenant led his group onto a glacier. A short distance up, able seaman Zaninovich along with the dogs and the sled fell into a crevasse. The only way the first lieutenant could save himself was by cutting the line. I was ordered to hurry back to the crevasse with the first lieutenant and my own company, to bring my glacier rope along and help rescue Zaninovich.

I was lowered into the crevasse, where I found the sailor and the dogs still alive. I tied them to the rope, one after the other, and had them pulled up. The sled was in one piece and it was pulled up, too. Finally I retied myself to the rope and was pulled out of the crevasse. And so things ended well and with no damage. The first lieutenant could continue his journey, and I returned with my company to land, there anxiously to await the first lieutenant's return. (*Johann Haller*)

Sunday, April 12

Around noon Payer's dream is fulfilled: Orel's calculation of their position appears to confirm the fact that they now have 82° north latitude behind them. They have passed the 82nd parallel. And they go on. They go on and on. But by evening land abruptly comes to an end. Far below them lies the sea again, a black strip of open coastal water. The horizon is empty at last.

But no, Payer says, that dark, jagged band in the north, that is no cloudbank, that must be a rim of alpine blue, mountains.

Fine, it's a rim of alpine blue, some tongue of land, whole continents—they don't care. For whatever that dark image in the north may mean, land or mirage, it lies at an inaccessible distance beyond open water; they have no boat. So now they must finally turn back, and even their commander can do nothing more than hurl names at the phantom: Petermann Land, Cape Vienna, and so on. Even the commander no longer knows whether he is baptizing rocks or clouds.

More than a decade will pass before Fridtjof Nansen and his companion Hjalmar Johansen will realize that what Payer saw as alps was only a void, that the image in the north was a mirage, a fogbank, a reflection, a hallucination—all of the above, but not land.

But what does a truth mean if it still lies in the future?

With proud excitement we planted the flag of Austria-Hungary for the first time in the far north; we were conscious of having brought it as far as our strength permitted us. We were cruelly aware of our inability to walk upon the lands we saw before us. . . . We placed the following document in a bottle and deposited it in the cleft of a rock:

The participants of the Austro-Hungarian North Pole Expedition here reached their northernmost point, 82° 5′, after a march of seventeen days from 79° 51′, where their ship lies trapped in the ice. They saw a small stretch of open water along the coast. It was bordered by ice extending to the north-northwest, as far as land masses that lay at an average distance of 60 to 70 miles but whose form and structure could not be determined. Immediately after our recovery from the return to the ship, the entire crew will abandon said vessel and return to Austria-Hungary. We are compelled to do so by the irremediable position of the ship, and illness.

Cape Fligely, 12 April 1874
Antonio Zaninovich, able seaman
Eduard Orel, midshipman
Julius Payer, Commander

That very evening, April 12, 1874, the vanguard of the Austro-Hungarian North Pole Expedition turns back. What lies ahead are hardships to be endured. Between them and the *Admiral Tegetthoff* lie some 180 miles—of fear. The coastal ice in the south may already have broken and their retreat to the ship be cut off. Twelve days will hover above that fear. The first station of their forced march is the camp on Hohenlohe Island.

We hardly recognized the men we had left behind. Blackened by soot from whale oil, faint, suffering from diarrhea and boredom, they crept from their blackened tent looking equally joyful and unkempt. (*Julius Payer*)

The days are often cloudless now, filled with long hours of cloudlessness. The land is garishly bright, as if refusing to accept a single ray, as if to cast the sun's image back, ray by ray, into skies already dazzling. To think that light can hurt like this. Orel suffers the worst from snow-blindness and can walk only with his eyes closed. He stumbles frequently.

The snow is deep and sometimes bottomless. Where a few days before there had been a path of hard pack, they now sink up to their belts; then someone breaks through and flails about in a water hole. But they dare not rest or waste time drying wet clothes; their furs petrify in the wind. Their commander decided late, too late perhaps, to turn back. However rigorous the days may be, six hours of sleep, sometimes only four, will have to suffice. They have to rise and move on before the path breaks open and turns to water beneath their feet.

But when on April 19 they reach the southern shore of the archipelago, all they see stretching before them is what they have feared. Three weeks before, everything lay frozen fast and the eye lost itself in towering edifices of ice; now there is only the black, raging sea. The coast is open water.

Walls of ice had been thrust up and now encircled the water, rolling in high crested waves and driven by a violent wind that sprayed the surf thirty paces up onto shore. . . . Pieces of ice tossed and tumbled about as if playing some carefree game for our amusement, as if nothing had changed in the least for this small band of men, who in reality found themselves before an impassable abyss. (*Julius Payer*)

Out there, somewhere out there and most certainly still trapped in ice towering as high as ever beyond the open water, must lie the *Tegetthoff*. But the horizon is empty, a wall broken only by jagged splinters of what looks like glass. No ship.

For three days they search for a bridge of ice crossing from their land to the distant point where they assume their ship is. The Tyroleans always walk ahead along the beach and over glaciers. No, they do not walk, they drag themselves along, they creep. But the path, which they first check with their long alpenstocks before waving for the others to follow, is safer than the commander's. As they move among fissured glaciers and floes covered with drifted snow, Klotz and Haller find a tortuous, firm path.

We were forced to rest frequently. Lukinovich and even unflinching Zaninovich were overcome with fainting spells as a result of the inordinate exertions. (*Julius Payer*)

On the night between April 22 and 23—a cloudless, deep-red night—the commander on land goes scouting and climbs a rocky peak, from which at last he once again sees a shimmering plain before him. At last, the huge, unbroken blanket of ice stretches across the ocean from the coast to infinity, and in it, far away and tiny as an insect, the ship, its masts like fine hairs. The ship.

No celebration follows the vanguard's return. Too great is the wordless exhaustion of the men who were believed lost—ragged figures who climb aboard like living prophecies of what awaits them all.

Weyprecht has had them preparing for their retreat to Europe for weeks now, ordering them to make a sharp separation between what is essential and nonessential: all personal possessions, indeed every object whose value for the common good cannot be proved, must remain behind in the north. Anyone who until now secretly believed that the lieutenant commander would find some other way out for them after all . . . or that perhaps the Holy Virgin would part the pack ice at the last minute and create open seas in place of these lakes, straits, and ponds, these unnavigable scraps of ocean seething at the coasts of their new land—anyone, that is, who had hoped for a miracle—was now forced by Weyprecht's orders concerning departure preparations to realize that only one way out was still left to them: the march across the ice. They have been talking about it for so long now, and yet it is a strange and frightening thought that they really will have to leave the *Admiral Tegetthoff*, their home, their protection, their asylum, and surrender themselves to their doom. A third winter, Weyprecht says, will kill us. The commander on water and ice calculates the strength of his crew, the weight of their provisions, and the pathless route, prudently checking and rechecking the variables. But all the equipment and supplies that these twenty-three men can drag with them, in addition to their three heavy lifeboats, cannot ensure their survival beyond three months. In those three months they will have to haul their boats across hundreds of miles of obstructing boulders of ice, big as houses, to find open sea, and then they must sail or row until they reach Novaya Zemlya. And even if they succeed in making the coast of that uninhabited archipelago, their only hope is that they will be taken aboard some seal schooner or whaling ship that has not yet fled before the oncoming winter. Because they can never reach Europe on their own; the Russian coast—maybe. But no, even that coast is unattainable; even a three-master would have trouble battling the storms of the White Sea. No, lifeboats wouldn't save your life on the White Sea.

In conversations at the officers' table and in the mess these last weeks before departure, they try over and over to talk their way around one fact: Their chances of escaping the Arctic on foot are slim, very slim. No crew has ever survived such a retreat without loss of life. All the same, they are almost relieved to turn away from the Kaiser's cold lands and give all their attention to preparations. Only Payer finds the separation from their discovery difficult. Barely one week has passed since the second sled trip (unable to perform his duties, Lukinovich still has to be nursed in his cabin) when the first lieutenant insists on one last overland trip—this time to the western mountains. On April 29, Payer departs on his third sled trip, accompanied this time only by Haller and First Officer Brosch. By the third day Brosch cannot go on; then neither can Haller. The commander on land climbs his last mountain alone. They turn back; on May 3 they are again on the *Tegetthoff.* Payer calculates that he has covered more than 450 miles of Franz Josef Land. That is enough, says Weyprecht, commander on water and ice, no more explorations. And the commander on land yields.

Our cares were over; we could return with honor, for the observations and discoveries we had made could not be taken from us, and the return trip awaiting us could bring with it no greater evil than death. (*Julius Payer*)

On May 15, five days before departure, astronomical, meteorological, and oceanographic observations are terminated and the scientific notebooks, the log as well, are closed. Weyprecht has the most important records soldered inside tin boxes and distributed among the three lifeboats. The sailors have a name for this cargo that must be watched and transported with the same care as their provisions: *frutti.*

Reluctant but obedient, Johann Haller leads the dogs Zemlya and Gilies out onto the ice and shoots them—Zemlya because she has become too weak to pull the sled and Gilies because the harness has turned him into a beast.

When Weyprecht orders the crew to fall in for a last visit to the grave of the machinist Krisch, Elling Carlsen is missing. The ice master has gotten so drunk on the spirit alcohol intended for their zoological collection—worthless ballast now—that he is lying in bed like a dead man. The sailors take the framed pictures of their families and girlfriends along and nail them to a rock. This portrait gallery has decorated the mess in their years on board; and when the abandoned *Tegetthoff* is at last crushed by the ice and sinks, and if their retreat, too, should lead them nowhere but the bottom of the sea, then this rock of pictures shall symbolize that they saved what was to be saved.

16

The Time of Empty Pages

There are no records or reports by witnesses about how Josef Mazzini spent the morning hours of September 6, 1981, but perhaps he stood on one of the piers in Longyearbyen harbor and watched the *Cradle* cast off—the hawsers falling away, the seething water under the keel, and then the brief drama of disappearance. Within a few minutes the ship melts into the watery whirlwinds of an early-winter snowstorm. And the wake? Was the wake dotted with white? Shards of drift ice already, here in the fjord?

According to the meteorological records of West Spitsbergen, the skies cleared early in the afternoon that September 6. Wind from the north and northeast. The *Cradle* must have covered some distance by then. I know that Hellskog, the stamp designer, had reboarded in Longyearbyen, and I imagine him taking his place in the tied-down chair at the railing and resuming the task of transferring the proportions of the polar landscape to the page. What colors did he use? Indigo and ivory black for coastal palisades, ramparts? Zinc white for tattered fields of snow? But what shade did he use for the tiers of primal rock?

There are no more colors now. Only images. No guesses. The fact is that the *Cradle* lay at anchor in Adventfjord for two weeks after ending its mission in the high Arctic, then departed for the coast of northern Norway, leaving the Spitsbergen archipelago behind for this year. And above all, the fact is that Josef Mazzini stayed behind in the mining town and pestered the oceanographer Kjetil Fyrand to teach him how to handle the dog team.

For months after Mazzini's disappearance, the people who gathered at Anna Koreth's soirees would make equally improbable and disinterested surmises (it was only a ritual question-and-answer game out of respect for their hostess) about why, once his cruise was over, Josef had made no arrangements whatever to return to Vienna before the arctic winter was unleashed, but instead had stayed on in the Spitsbergens, obsessed with the idea of driving a dogsled. Although I still visit these soirees in Rauhensteingasse, I no longer participate in the table talk about the missing man's probable plans and intentions. Whatever guesses may be made in that circle, they will always be impossible to prove, and open to argument. Because on the very day he returned from the pack ice aboard the *Cradle* and took up quarters in Longyearbyen, Josef Mazzini stopped making entries in his journal. *The Great Nail*—the notebook he had scribbled full on board ship—was to be his last record. The quotations are followed only by a few sums—calculations about the cost of room and board at the mining company's guest house—columns of numbers, and then empty pages. I say: A man who has found his place keeps no more travel diaries. It was the middle of September, the days were breaking apart quickly, and after a heavy snowfall the angry wail of snowmobiles, the sound of winter, had suddenly begun. That day Fyrand took his pupil Mazzini to the kennel for his first lesson. The path to the kennel was covered with knee-deep wet snow. Fyrand carried the tangled knot of the dog harness over his shoulder, Mazzini had a steamy sack of warm meat scraps from the canteen kitchen.

The instructions on how to handle the dog team were easy to understand and difficult to carry out. In his first lesson Josef Mazzini learned that the primary task was to excite the dogs.

Sled dogs always have a goal—if they are running across an open plain it is the nearest rise of land, a line of boulders, a hill, sometimes only a slowly ascending column of smoke; if they are running over sea ice the goal is always the coast; in the dark of night it is the moon, and if there is no moon then the teams race toward a star. A dogsled driver, Mazzini learned, must either use all these goals for his own purposes or divert the dogs from them—but only with calls and rhythmic shouts, never with bit and whip—turning the team into a barking, onrushing extension of his own will. But on this first day of lessons, when Mazzini tried to slip the leather harness over Ubi, Fyrand's lead dog, the animal suddenly pulled back into a crouch as if ready to leap, bared its teeth, and growled with such menace at his shaky tamer that Mazzini froze in his bent-over position and did not move until Fyrand smacked the dog across the eyes with his glove and so brought the lesson to an end.

The perseverance, the doggedness if you will, with which Josef Mazzini tried to win mastery over the team in the following weeks was one of the few things people in the mining town appear to have noticed about the Italian's presence. Whatever else I later learned about Mazzini's last weeks, if people talked about this period, they never failed to refer to his diligent practice with the dog team. Even Governor Thorsen and indifferent witnesses like Jaor Hoel, Longyearbyen's dentist, recalled dog-training scenes. True, his time was not exclusively devoted to the dogs. In my records reconstructing his days there are also reports about trips Mazzini took up fjords and his daylong hikes across glaciers. There is the crossing of Isfjorden in Malcolm Flaherty's boat—seven hours in heavy seas, hardly any protection against the spray, the danger of capsizing, and probably fear as well; then two days of waiting for a gentler sea and the whitecaps of the return trip. There is the recollection of an appointment Mazzini had with Krister Røsholm, the surveyor of mines: There was no job for him in the coal company office, Røsholm informed his visitor that day—maybe later, maybe in the mines; he would think about it; he jotted down "truck driver." And then there is the hike across the Svea glacier—six days of hardships borne with Fyrand and the miner Israel Boyle. The crack of the tent canvas in the northeast storm wind, exhausting progress using crampons, and the glacier itself, hundreds of square miles of it, its ridge deeply fissured—chasms, cracks, and black wells, a dream landscape of blue and black ice, all of it just as the commander on land had described it. The loud sound of each breath, of each step that took them ever deeper into the glistening labyrinth, the oceanographer always up ahead, his eyes invisible behind disks of keratin. The oceanographer, who talked about the sluggish, inexorable flow of his river of ice, and about how a glacier thaws, feeds, and grows, as if about the pulse of a violent animal. I shall stop at that and say simply: The exertions of this and other hikes were nothing compared with Mazzini's last and greatest task, training the dogs. But whatever Josef Mazzini did or did not do, people hardly mentioned it at the post office bar. The Italian was there. He was staying on. And his existence seemed more inconspicuous and undetectable with each passing day—another proof of the power of the undertow that has its source in the emptiness, timelessness, and tranquility of this wasteland and that takes each of its victims indiscriminately, dragging them away from the warm security of a well-ordered life into silence, cold, ice.

Kjetil Fyrand was a patient teacher. He had been very hesitant about yielding to Mazzini's urgings at the start, but now he seemed to be increasingly fascinated by the idea he could teach his dogs that in obeying the orders of his pupil they were in fact obeying *him*. It was perhaps the most difficult trick against which he had ever matched himself and the devotion of his dogs.

October was stormy, like something made of metal—the driving snow was stinging chrome hail at times. The land and the sky were of iron. Whenever weather permitted, Mazzini would harness the dogs under Fyrand's supervision. The pack then had to lie very still in the snow, ahead of the sled—three pairs in a row, Suli with Imiag, Spitz with Anore, Avanga with Kingo; Ubi always alone in front—and wait for a shout that would finally break the spell and let them leap up. *Oiiya!* This was followed by the barely audible whir of the suddenly tautened reins and the abrupt jerk that yanked the runners over the snow, destroying the pattern left there by twenty-eight paws.

The first time Mazzini drove the dogs by himself, Fyrand followed the spray of the racing team on a snowmobile and shouted instructions to his pupil. In the mining town's *Trekkhundklubb*—a small, loose organization that upheld and carefully cultivated dogsledding as the most perfect expression of arctic traditions—there were repeated and lengthy discussions about the futility of the oceanographer's efforts. But lesson by lesson Fyrand and his pupil appeared to refute all the club's predictions—most of them made in the bar and with no great seriousness. Josef Mazzini was making progress. The dogs obeyed him. They did so reluctantly and were often so irritable during even the shortest pauses that they would attack one another. But they obeyed him.

A dogsledder, Mazzini learned, has constantly to create the illusion in the dogs' minds that they are moving forward, holding to a straight line; he must avoid every abrupt change of direction and try to detour around chasms and barriers in large, gentle arcs. A team could be forced to veer suddenly or, worse, to turn around only at the risk of terrible confusion.

Once they had finally been brought to pull their tamer and his burdens across the ice, they could interpret being forced to drag the vehicle back over the tracks they had just engraved only as labor lost and undeserved punishment. They therefore resisted any hasty correction in an uncertain course with all their bewildered strength. They wove the reins into braids that were difficult to untangle, and no command could touch the yelping pack. So a dogsledder had to be completely part of his team, and at the same time far ahead of them, had to see things both visible and invisible, anticipating the snow-drifted course of their route and the barriers of a hidden landscape. Sometimes, however, the dogs would scent prey deep in the ice and would storm off unexpectedly. There was no holding them back. Still linked to his team by a painter line, the tamer would shout in vain, and he had no recourse but to throw out his ice anchor, a heavy claw, to prevent the dogs from simply leaping a crevasse, dragging the sled and everything else into the abyss. But whatever happened and however mad the dogs might run, Fyrand said, a dogsledder could cut his painter line only in the most extreme emergency. Separation from his team, equipment, and weapons could mean death even on a short trip.

When the oceanographer spoke of the laws and requirements of dogsledding, he often quoted Jostein Aker, a former miner who had left Longyearbyen years before and now lived in total isolation north of the mining town, a march of a hundred or so miles. Aker was the last resident of the Spitsbergens for whom a dog team was not a sport or a passion but a necessity of life, even now. Everything he, Fyrand, knew about driving a team he had learned from Aker.

Jostein Aker was the last in many respects. His driftwood hut stood on Wijdefjord at the foot of Cape Tabor, a tongue of rock that disappeared under snowdrifts in the winter months. Polished black and shiny by the wind, Cape Tabor towered above the beach of the fjord—a rock formation from the Precambrian era, almost as old as the earth itself but with no trace of life. Apart from helicopter crews who made brief stopover landings in this desolate spot every few months, the hermit was visited only by Malcolm Flaherty and Fyrand. These two came to the cape every spring, a march of five to seven days, and once a year Aker himself traveled to Longyearbyen, cashed in pelts he had bagged with his gun or in stone traps—seals, white and blue arctic foxes—replenished his supplies and equipment, got drunk at the bar, talked a lot (and for days was himself the talk of the bar), and then returned to the wilderness with his dogs. Many of the miners thought he was crazy. In recent years Governor Thorsen had taken to calling him an anarchist, and Aker had neither contradicted nor qualified the title. Kjetil Fyrand often talked about the hunter.

Decades before, hermits like Jostein Aker had been as natural a part of the population of the Spitsbergens as miners and polar researchers were now. But with the gradual conversion of the icy wastes into national parks, the prohibition of bear hunting, and the establishment of hunting seasons, the hunters had vanished. Only their abandoned huts, half fallen in now under heavy ice, still lay strewn about the Spitsbergens—dilapidated monuments to their retreat from the inhabited world.

On October 28 the fire of the last segment of sun went out at the latitude of Longyearbyen. The landscapes of Svalbard farther north had long since lain in shadow. The first of the 110 days of polar night passed in blue twilight in the mining town—the tormenting yammer of snowmobiles, and rare silences. Kjetil Fyrand now retreated more and more into his winter work and left Mazzini alone with the dogs. The oceanographer organized the measurements collected from the Arctic Ocean over the last months, drew the conclusions expected of him in Oslo, and early in November began enameling pieces of copper for his mosaics, garish knickknacks.

Mazzini sometimes sat beside Fyrand, helping, handing him things, and talking about Lucia's hands, how they had painted miniatures, those endless rows of medallions with tiny, never-changing landscapes.

In the second week of November, Kjetil Fyrand flew to Oslo to give his annual lecture to the members of the Polar Institute. He stayed in Oslo for three days, then four in Tromsø. When he returned to Longyearbyen, Josef Mazzini's room was tidy and empty. The dogs were missing, too.

The Italian? They had seen him last Friday, no, last Thursday with the dog team. Then at the post office . . . but no, that was even before then. A trip? Nobody knew anything about that. Boyle had been in the mines and at the bar a lot, and had not been paying attention to anyone. Flaherty was in Ny Ålesund. Hmm . . . hadn't the Italian bought some things in Moen's store? Right, right, gas for the stove, canned goods, the usual . . . but beyond that. They searched a long while for Josef Mazzini, riding snowmobiles to out-of-the-way places, at first with a good deal of cursing, convinced that the idiot was sitting somewhere in a hut or in his tent with no idea that he had forced a whole army to go to all this damn trouble. Every step squeaked in this cold. But it was only their own noise, the noise of rescuers. If they stopped, there was silence everywhere. The Fredheim hut—good, secure quarters on Tempelfjord, a way station for sled teams—lay beneath drifts, unused. When the helicopter took off at last, no one was cursing. Their search flights only confirmed that the more important routes showed no tracks, either. The glaciers were empty. Then they were forced to wait out a turn in the weather for two days. Fyrand thought of Jostein Aker; maybe Mazzini had been crazy enough to try to make it to Cape Tabor. When the wind and snow let up, the oceanographer and two pilots, Berg and Kristiansen, took off for this last spot. Dark and indistinct, land fell away below them. Restless snow lay on the ridges and glaciers. Ice had closed over the fjords in ash-gray shields. Time shattered. Wastelands that the oceanographer had taken days to cover with his dog team on one trip or another now glided, faded away below them in minutes. Weeks were hours. And hours nothing at all. And then a row of dull silver sculptures revealed the soft curves of the coast; these were pyramids of driftwood the hermit erected on the beach during the short summers. Then, hardly bigger than the wooden monuments, a hut nestled in the ice. Above it all, dark and deserted, Cape Tabor. Someone was standing down below now, looking up with arms raised to ward off the curtain of crystals whipped up by the rotors. Dogs on long chains, six of them, bayed at the monster sinking down on them. And then the oceanographer ran through the roar and the stinging eddies of snow, shouted a greeting to the hermit Jostein Aker, shouted: Is he with you? Is he here? Fyrand took him by the shoulders, and Aker, who only now realized who had come, shouted and laughed back in surprise and confusion: Who are you talking about? I'm alone, I've always been alone.

17

The Retreat

On May 20, 1874, the Austro-Hungarian North Pole Expedition leaves its last refuge. It is evening. Weyprecht orders the flags of the monarchy nailed to the mastheads of the *Admiral Tegetthoff*. Decorated for its doom, the three-master now lies on a petrified swell strewn with trash. The commander orders the crew to fall in ready for travel and to raise three cheers for the abandoned ship—their gratitude. Then he gives the signal for departure.

By the light of the midnight sun both crew and officers drag the three heavily laden lifeboats—massive Norwegian whaling boats with mast and lugsails—on sledges over humps of ice and through glassy, deep slush. They advance by fits and starts, yard by yard. Often they sink in up to their waists before they find firm ice underfoot, and the boats sink with them. Their shoulders and hands are rubbed raw by the ropes, and within hours many of them are vomiting from the exertion. Four and a half tons of equipment and supplies have to be moved, and every step of the way, every barrier, must be conquered not once, but three times, because moving just one boat demands the strength of them all. They plod on through the night, dragging boat by boat away from the *Tegetthoff*. But after ten hours of hauling and pulling they have put little more than half a mile between themselves and the ship, and its beauty tempts them. How fine it must be to rest in those cabins, how much warmer and more secure than in these narrow boats covered with canvas. They miss their ship badly. But Weyprecht says no. Weyprecht will let no one back on board ship. We are on our way to Europe, he says, we have abandoned ship. And so after those first, tiny steps of retreat, here they lie under canvas, in contorted positions, soaking wet, exhausted—absurdly close to their ship. And Europe is infinitely far. Even if they could hold a straight course for the Norwegian coast, and not have to make hourlong detours around every chasm, every cliff of ice—make for the coast as the crow flies!—and not have to take to channels and ponds, ten, sometimes fifteen times daily, hitting the oars three times and then heaving the boats up onto another ice field, even if they could *fly*, the coastline for which they yearn is almost a thousand miles away. But they cannot fly.

Those who cannot bear the truth can at least comfort themselves for now with hope of a more benevolent future, of increasing strength, more passable ice, and lighter burdens. But those who have lived through the tortures of the sled trips across their new, unhappy land know that each agony will increase, can only increase. The truth is that the first day of their retreat is only a taste of the weeks and months to come, only a paradigm of a time that will ultimately seem to them the epitome of all the hardships and disappointments of their years in the Arctic. After two weeks Weyprecht, Orel, and ten sailors return to the ship, still only a few miles away, and fetch the last lifeboat. But even with the weight apportioned over four boats, they make almost no progress and lie trapped for days at a time, wedged in the rubbled landscape of the pack ice, waiting until a crack widens into a channel or the ruins collapse under a milder season and finally open a path for them. And the waiting is worse than life on board the *Tegetthoff* ever was. They clear their path with pickaxes and shovels, a week's worth of digging, and then the world of debris suddenly shatters and reassembles itself into insurmountable walls. They have to turn back and search for a different route. Their provisions and energies dwindle. When they have good luck hunting, they eat raw bear meat and seal blubber. But they are themselves being devoured by the ice. And when they finally do have a good day and think they have made some little progress to the south, the drift of the polar ice gently, very gently takes hold of them and moves them back north again, arc minute by arc minute. After two months of toil they are barely nine miles from their point of departure. The mountains of Franz Josef Land loom as close as ever. But Weyprecht's confidence seems unshakable. This march through the ice, he says, is our only hope. There is no other way to save ourselves. We will reach the coast of Novaya Zemlya and find a ship, a whaler perhaps; we will sail back to Norway; we will sail, not walk. He must tell them this again and again. And the grumblers among the sailors who believe that this drudgery is useless in any case and that a more promising course would be to return to the *Tegetthoff* and wait out a third winter if need be, wait for gracious seas, for a miracle, or at worst for death in a dry cabin . . . after one of Weyprecht's speeches these sailors grumble no more—for a few days at least. But the commander on water and ice confides to no one what he is really thinking during this period; for that he uses a pencil—his fine Italian hand is unchanged—for entries in a *Journal of Retreat*, a small notebook just the right size to fit in his breast pocket, which will be found a decade later among the papers he leaves behind:

Every lost day is not a nail but a whole plank in our coffin. . . . Dragging the sledges across the ice fields is only a bluff, for the few miles we gain are of no importance to our purpose. The slightest breeze moves us about in random directions far more than the

most exhausting day of labor. . . . I put on an unconcerned face to all this, but I am very much aware that we are probably lost if conditions do not change radically. . . . I am often amazed at myself, at my own calm when viewing the future. I sometimes feel as if I were not involved at all. I have resolved what I shall do if worse comes to worst, which is why I am so calm. But the fate of the sailors lies heavy on my heart. . . .

The officers of the *Admiral Tegetthoff* had resolved what to do "if worse came to worst" while still on board ship: If their retreat should lead only to hopelessness, with provisions depleted and all their strength exhausted, they will lay hand to themselves and advise the crew to commit suicide as well. Death by a bullet would certainly be more merciful than gradual, degrading enfeeblement, and was above all preferable to the horrors that had so often accompanied doomed arctic expeditions—the bestial battles for a scrap of flesh, the collapse of humans, and finally, cannibalism and madness. No, an Imperial North Pole Expedition could not . . . *dared* not deteriorate into a pack of emaciated wolves. They had to greet their end, once it was certain, with the same determined resolve with which they would greet good fortune. But who speaks of that now? They are now deep in the ice and have few means to survive much longer. Weyprecht writes in his journal . . .

All my thoughts and plans are now directed at depositing my journals in such a fashion that they will be found in future years. . . .

But the end? When is the end certain? Who shall decide that it is? And have they not, without ever being conscious of it, already shown that they too cling to every minute of this dreadful life, the only one they have, and will ultimately set upon one another, each against the other? Every man for himself. Marola has already come to blows with Lettis over a ration of seal blubber, and Scarpa has fought with Carlsen over a few crumbs of tobacco. The sailors have gotten into

fights over some trifle or other before this as well—loud fights for the most part, but seldom physical. But that the ice master has taken to using his fists, that even officers and commanders can no longer conceal their disagreements, their hate, that is new and strange. Payer gives Orel a dressing-down, regularly. Until at last Orel screams at him: You bastard, I can't stand you. And then comes the day when the two commanders confront one another: they have seen nothing like it before. Weyprecht records this event from their years in the ice as well, as punctilious as always, apparently without emotion, but perhaps deeply wounded:

Payer . . . is once again so charged with rage that I am prepared for some serious collision at any moment. In front of the men he made offensive remarks to me about some trivial matter . . . which I could not let pass without reprimand. I told him that in the future he should be careful not to use such expressions. . . . He then went into one of his rages, said that he still remembered quite clearly how I had threatened him with a revolver a year ago, assuring me he would steal the march on me next time and declaring outright that he would try to kill me the moment he saw he might not make it home.

If the Payer–Weyprecht expedition had failed, someone discovering whatever remained of this record of implacable differences might perhaps have interpreted it as the beginning of the end, or perhaps simply as proof of their desperate situation—but all such guesswork is superfluous, for in August 1874 the ice at last seems to have grown weary of its sport and releases them, no longer requiring that they demonstrate the commonplace that men are wolves to men.

What happens now is the "radical change in conditions" that none of them had believed in anymore, that had become the most improbable and reckless of hopes. It comes about only because the arctic summer of 1874 is mild, milder than it has been in years or will be for years to come. The black cracks and channels gradually widen and turn blue, the

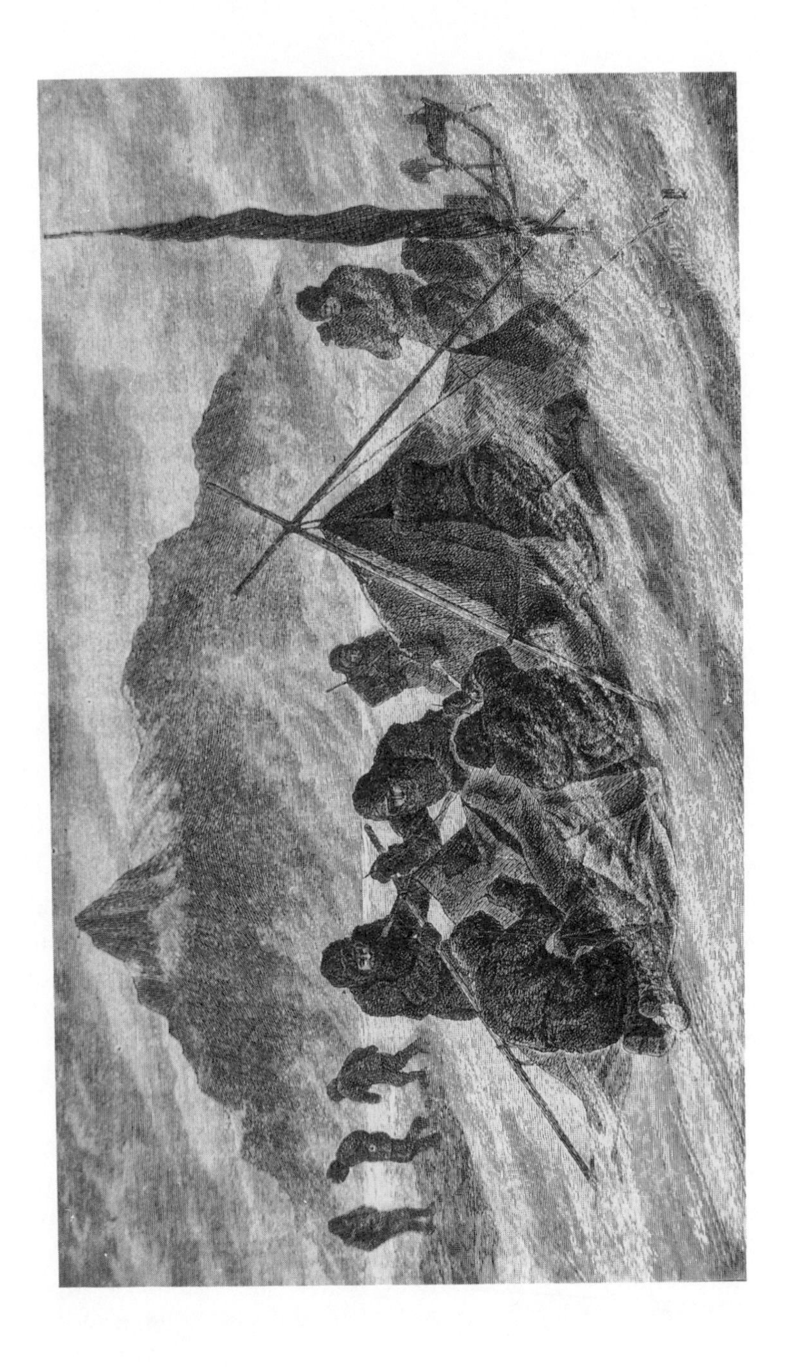

ponds become lakes. Slowly and steadily the ruins of pack ice break apart like cumulus clouds on a peaceable afternoon; the barriers open, become floodgates. Where before everything was fixed and immobile, there is now thaw, currents, progress. The hasty, shimmering shadows of gusty winds veer and shift ahead of them. But they are rowing and sailing to the southeast. They have to heave their boats up onto the ice and drag them to the next open water less and less often now. Then there are only flat fields of drift ice extending ahead of them, a large plain carved with countless lakes and rivers. The plain seems to breathe, its rise and fall is heavy and rhythmic: ocean swells. They have reached the border of the ice. On the far side of this rolling plain flocks of birds mount up, and there, under a dark sky, lies the open sea.

August 15th, the Assumption of Our Lady, was the day of liberation, and we flagged our boats as if for a celebration. . . . We pushed off from the ice with three cheers, and our voyage across open seas began. Its happy outcome depended on the weather and our ceaseless rowing; if a storm should come up, our boats would surely sink. . . . With immeasurable satisfaction we looked back at the white rim of ice as it slowly became a mere line and finally disappeared. (*Julius Payer*)

The rolling seas drive the last two surviving dogs mad. They are almost impossible to control, they snap at the oars and the spray pouring in over the sides. Torossy, born in the ice, has never seen waves, and Jubinal has probably forgotten them. But nothing can be allowed to disturb their labor against the heavy seas. The lot falls to Klotz. He must shoot the dogs.

On August 16 someone shouts *Ice!* and they stare in horror to the south. But it turns out to be only the distant snow-covered mountains of Novaya Zemlya rising slowing above the flood. There, somewhere in the lee of that land, they will find a ship. Commander Weyprecht has promised them. They row the confused waters of the coast, its weather-beaten cliffs staring down at them. The bays are empty. No ice. No ship.

On August 17 fog descends, and without knowing it they pass by the supply depot left behind on the Three Coffins two years before. When the fog clears and they realize their mistake, the Barents Islands already lie below the horizon. But they dare not row another stroke back to the north. Time shatters. For the first time in months they watch the sun setting. If there are still any salmon fishers or whalers in the vicinity, they will soon be making ready to sail home.

On August 18, the Kaiser's birthday, exhaustion forces them onto land. They have rowed for three days and three nights. They sink to the ground around the fire and toast the Kaiser with watered rum. How gentle and soft this land seems compared with the island realm they have discovered for their monarch. Short grasses, moss, and even a few sparse flowers grow on the graveled slopes that seem to pour down out of the clouds. *Forget-me-not of rare beauty,* Weyprecht writes in his journal, *so beautiful that I suspect it is not forget-me-not.*

Their sleep is brief. A clap of thunder echoes from the walls of the glaciers, and the booming does not stop—the herald of a shift in the weather. They have to move on.

Since most of Novaya Zemlya's coast is unapproachable, we were forced to continue our journey without stopping, although our arms were stiff and swollen with the constant exertion of rowing. We searched in vain for a ship . . . but all we saw was the rough vastness of arctic mountains. . . . Stormy weather came up, exhausting our strength and separating our boats, which were taking on so much water the crews had constantly to bail. . . . We rowed on mechanically through the endless flood, toward the secret of how all this would end. (*Julius Payer*)

On August 24, 1874, at seven in the evening, with only a breeze from the southwest, crews on the Russian whalers *Vasily* and *Nikolai* anchored in Duna Bay off Novaya Zemlya see four boats approaching but hear no sounds of jubilation, only the slap of oars. They recognize the flags and realize that these are the missing men who are the talk of arctic harbor towns. Some of these foreigners cannot climb the gangway of the *Nikolai* on their own and have to be helped. Without a word Weyprecht hands Captain Feodor Voronin the safe-conduct letter issued by the czar in St. Petersburg. Into the silence Voronin haltingly reads aloud that Czar Alexander II commends the Austro-Hungarian North Pole Expedition to the care of his subjects, and the Russian sailors bare their heads and sink to their knees before these emaciated strangers whose faces are disfigured by ulcers and frostbite.

18

Removed from the World—A Necrology

On December 11, 1981, a Friday, when polar night lay great and clear above the land, two dogs turned up in Longyearbyen. They were dragging a tattered harness behind them and were so savage and strange that Kjetil Fyrand hesitated a moment before he recognized these wolves as Anore and Imiag from his own team. The sled dogs devoured the food he threw them, but drew back growling and baring their teeth when he tried to free them from the lines binding them to one another. And they remained so unapproachable, so fierce and wild that on the fourth day after their return the oceanographer shot them.

Those curs. Would that barking never stop? And now the pain, the jerk of the train setting itself in motion. The wall of a pier glided past. The train platform. A mole. Passau. It got brighter. But the barking went on and bounced off a sky nailed onto cast-iron columns. Wasn't anyone going to punish those curs? Sometimes it had been enough for Payer just to write a few hissing strokes in the air with his metal rod, and then they would quiet down. But those weren't Payer's dogs. They couldn't be Payer's dogs. Klotz had shot the last two, on an ice floe drifting far out into the open water. Open water. And were those mountains out there? A coast? Land! Weyprecht tried to sit up.

Lie still, Carl, someone said softly, and bent down over him, lie still, and he sank back onto his bed, glowing, burning. But that rolling and stomping under him, that had to be the swells, and the ship flew before the wind with full sails. How near the coast was now, a green shoreline, beyond it empty fields, bare poplars. And he was lying in the darkness in his cabin. He had to go up on deck. *Starboard division, reef the topsails! Reef one! Into the yards! Brace! Halyards free! . . . Braces taut! . . . Hoist the reef tackle! . . .* Quiet now, someone said to him from the shadows, quiet now, calm down. Then it was still. The northeast wind soundless in the rigging. No dogs anywhere. He awoke when iron suddenly screeched below him—rails, wheels, brake shoes—and a distant voice shouted Regensburg!, doors banged open, a curtain at the window was carefully closed, and a ray of sun was cut off. Regensburg. But that was way off their route. It must be Berlin, Breslau, or some other station on their journey from Hamburg to Vienna. Bouquets of rockets had burned in the sky above the harbor in Hamburg, and Bengal lights along the piers, and the ships' foghorns had all sounded in unison like a massive organ as the mail steamer from Vardø sailed in, bearing the discoverers of the last land on earth. Then the hansom ride through the cheering crowds, the flags and speeches at the train station, and the platforms noisy with hurrahs—but they had lost their ship and brought nothing back except the nomenclature of islands buried in the ice, and nevertheless, at station after station, more excitement, and there was a great clamor out there now too, that couldn't be Regensburg. But why were the curtains closed, why was he lying in a salon car, why was he alone? Where were the others? He lifted his head and only now did he see his father: there beside his bed sat Herr Weyprecht, royal court attorney and estate agent to Count Erbach, so dignified and serious in his black dress coat, who solemnly said, We're in Regensurg, Carl. . . . *Our dear father has passed away,* that was the news waiting for him in Vardø; Scarpa, too, Lusina, and Orel, they had all received similar messages. Has passed away. Has been taken from us. Is dead. In Vardø he had paid the captain of the *Nikolai* 1,200 silver rubles for rescuing them. Peace reigned everywhere, people told him, Napoleon is dead. *Our dear father is dead.* Decked out in his Order of Olaf and his white periwig, the ice master leaves the mail steamer in Tromsø and stands there on the jetty, happy in the tender embrace of an old woman, and keeps shouting to his comrades the same old sailor's adage with which he has tried to banish misfortune so often during their years together: *If God is with us then nothing can be against us.* Then the cheering crowd carries him off. He has passed away. No, the man sitting there beside his bed, even though he was wearing the Order of the Grand Duchy of Hesse-Darmstadt pinned to his dress coat, that couldn't be his father, he had been laid to rest in König. He turned back to the stranger and saw that it really was his father. He was silent now and no longer wore a dress coat, but there was something shiny on his chest, not an order, but something shiny that hurt his eyes and then melted in the heat of fever.

I see Lieutenant Commander Carl Weyprecht before me again now, six years after his return from the ice, forty-two years old, sunk in delirium, exhausted by tuberculosis and near death, lying in a salon car of the Kaiserin Elizabeth Railway; at his bedside a mournful doctor, his brother, who has come to Vienna from Michelstadt im Odenwald to bring the dying man home to his mother's house in the Grand Duchy of Hesse. The hero of the Imperial North Pole Expedition shall not breathe his last in Austria-Hungary, in a foreign land that he has called his fatherland. It is a quiet journey. The brother watches and listens, is ready to write down any last words, any legacy to the world. But whatever there was to say Weyprecht said years ago amid the noise of ovations for the discoverers who had returned: *I've never been seasick,* so began one of his speeches about the Arctic and the state of science, *but it might easily happen if I have to listen to any more balderdash about my achievements, about my immortality. Immortal! With this cough?* . . . Arctic research had degenerated, he said, into a game for martyrs and was exhausting itself in the current ruthless pursuit of new latitude records for the sake of national vanity. But it was now time to break with such traditions and follow different paths that did justice to science, nature, and humankind. For research and progress would not be served by ever greater sacrifices of men and material, by more and more doomed polar journeys, but rather by a system of observation stations, by a Polar Watch, which would guarantee both consistency in the description of arctic phenomena and some minimum of security for the men involved. As long as the principal motive behind exploration remained nationalistic ambition for mere voyages of discovery and agonizing conquests of icy wastelands, there was no room for real knowledge.

I beg you, gentlemen, Weyprecht concluded in a highly regarded lecture before the Forty-eighth Assembly of German Natural Scientists and Physicians in Graz, *I beg you not to think that in saying this my intention is to denigrate my predecessors' achievements in the Arctic, for few men can appreciate better than I the sacrifices they made. In speaking openly about these principles, I am at the same time accusing myself and tarnishing a great deal of the hard-won results of my own work.*

In Nuremberg the commander of the *Admiral Tegetthoff* orders all the studding sails struck and whispers as he counts off soundings. *Sixty-two fathoms, mud bottom . . . eighty fathoms . . . a hundred and nine fathoms, mud bottom.* Then the sinker is dangling in a sea whose bottom no plumb line can reach. The commander falls silent. Breathes. On the evening of

March 27, 1881, a Sunday, the train rolls into Michelstadt. Weyprecht does not recognize friends who enter his salon car, his ship. They bear him on a stretcher to his childhood home. He has arrived. He has been gone a long time.

Gracious heaven, what a reunion it was, his seventy-year-old mother writes in a letter to Vienna in early April, *his dimmed eyes did not see my own deathly pallor, my trembling and unsteadiness. Only after I called out his name did he recognize me, but he thought I was visiting him in Vienna, and he thanked me most touchingly for my love. We had him alive with us for two nights and a day, then he found his rest, on a bier and covered by flowers—until Thursday, March 31, when he was buried in our family grave at König, beside his dear father, whom he had not seen after his return from the north.*

Weyprecht had used all his energies in realizing a dream, Julius Payer wrote in an obituary that appeared in Vienna's *Neue Freie Presse*—the dream of a chain of observation stations rimming the Arctic Circle, the dream of international research, yes, of pure science.

The efforts he devoted to achieve his lofty goal went beyond those of any single man. He struggled on with little support and no prospect of success.

It was almost seven years to the day, Payer continued, that he and a few companions had returned to the *Admiral Tegetthoff* from their journey by sled across their newly discovered land, sending their stoker Pospischill on ahead with frozen hands. They had all been very weary and there was no sight of the ship, which lay miles ahead in the darkness.

Suddenly I saw Weyprecht coming toward me among the crags of ice: a figure in white—beard, hair, eyebrows, clothing, all stiff with ice. The shawl wound about his mouth had frozen fast.

Weyprecht alone in the ice, without his furs, without a weapon, and terribly anxious for his comrades—the image would remain indelible in Payer's memory.

Everything, almost everything, was a mere memory now.

When the commander on land penned his "Necrology for a Dead Friend and Former Companion in Misfortune," the new land was already of no further value. A darkened historical photograph is all that is left of the cheering city that waits for the train decorated with branches, flags, banners, and flowers and carrying the North Pole Travelers—the Discoverers, the Masters of the Ice, the Conquerors for New Austria—back to Vienna. Only politicians, aristocrats, or those who can produce at least a Grand Cross may join the military on the platform. It takes hours for the heroes' carriages to make the trip from North Station to the center of the city.

Again and again new waves of cheers and hurrahs washed over the carriage in which the two leaders sat. It had been hung with several large laurel wreaths presented to the North Pole travelers during the journey to Vienna. Flowers were tossed into the carriage by the ladies, and both leaders and crew seemed equally amazed at this spontaneous eruption of joy and sympathy from the Viennese. The carriage could make its way only step by step from North Station onto Jägerzeile. The crowd threw itself into the path of the horses and would not allow the carriage to advance. An ever-growing sea of hundreds of thousands stood waiting for them all the way to the heart of the city and parted only very slowly. The streets were black with the throngs, every window in every building was occupied, cheers and waving handkerchiefs greeted them on all sides. In certain areas the moving crowds were indeed a danger to life and limb. It would be no exaggeration to estimate those taking part in the reception at a quarter-million. Their route moved from Praterstrasse across Aspern Bridge to Stuben Gate. There the carriages carrying the sailors turned left down Landstrasse and Hauptstrasse to reach Dreher Beer Hall, managed by Herr Ott, who has offered them free room and board. . . . The officers drove from Stuben Gate via Wollzeile and Rothenthurmstrasse, Stephansplatz, the Graben, Bognergasse, and the Hof to the festively decorated Roman Kaiser Hotel, where rooms awaited them. The tokens of the public's joy and sympathy were uninterrupted all the way to the hotel. In the narrow streets of the inner city the reception took on a more intimate quality. Compared with the colossal masses on the Ring and along Jägerzeile, the tightly packed crowd here seemed more like a large family come to fetch relatives. The old walls of the patrician homes seemed to come alive. At every window there were hurrahs and cheers, waving white handkerchiefs, and loud cries of welcome. The balconies swayed beneath the weight of so many lovely ladies. (Neue Freie Presse, *Saturday, September 26, 1874*)

But two hundred, three hundred thousand enthusiastic welcomers were not welcome enough—all the speeches, banquets, medals, even the favor of His Apostolic Majesty, were not glorification enough to save their triumph of discovering an arctic island empire from the secret powers that erode the reign of monarchies—from the idle talk of aristocrats, from gossip among the military, from rumors at court or remarks made by the Imperial Academy of Sciences and in certain circles of the Geographical Society. The sailors and hunters need not worry about this slow, secret campaign to disparage their polar journey—they melt away in the ebbing glory of receptions, return home to the Adriatic and Bohemia, Moravia, Styria, and Tyrol, taking up civil service posts that Weyprecht procures for them there. And Weyprecht, who does not even hear the gossip of the schemers, has no desire to become something more, to hold further honors in the House of Austria. He longs to be back in the ice—far from the laws governing ascending fame—and to measure what is measurable, to make the unmeasurable measurable. Only Julius Payer, the hero, who wants to be not just respected, but honored, loved! proves vulnerable—and is wounded.

Herr Payer's mapping of this so-called Kaiser Franz Josef Land is unfortunately, really quite, quite inexact, says some anonymity from the learned, fine society. Those coastlines just dwindle off to nowhere . . . so inexact, rather like fantasies, another anonymity says. . . . Beg pardon, but this Bohemian foot soldier, who permits himself the title of "Sir" only by the grace of His Majesty, probably did find a few fresh rocks . . . rocks in the sea, by your leave, not lands. . . . And the way the good gentleman goes on about his sufferings and malheurs in the best salons, that really is somewhat fantastical, purest literature. . . .

Payer does not miss a single malicious remark. He struggles to combat the gossip, to follow rumors to their source and refute them—but he is tilting at windmills. He commits faux pas, is deeply hurt. In some officers' circles this new land, his land, is considered a lie. And during his lecture at a banquet of the Geographical Society his description of the hardships of a journey by sled are interrupted by an anonymous heckler: "If only it were true!" His land, a lie!

What good does it do him if the latest fashions are Payer hats and Payer coats and Weyprecht cravats, if the brandy served in suburban pubs is called Northern Lights, Eternal Ice, or Franz Josef Land. What good are garish fame and streets full of enthusiastic crowds if the more discreet judgment of society is not unanimous, if the aristocracy's small talk casts doubt on the very existence of the land it cost him such agony to survey?

Before the year is out, a disappointed but resolute Payer says farewell to the Imperial Army and leaves behind him Vienna, then Austria, and above all his life as a conqueror. *As to the discovery of a land unknown before,* he adds in a footnote to his report on the expedition, *I personally place no value in it today. . . .* He wants to become a painter. With the same passion with which men once searched for new lands and a hidden passage through arctic seas, Payer now dedicates himself to color theory, anatomy, and perspective, as an art student first at the Städel Institute in Frankfurt, then at the Royal Academy of Fine Arts in Munich, and finally in Paris.

During this period only once does he again become the subject of gossip: Fanny Kann, the wife of a Frankfurt banker, so goes the rumor in the salons of Vienna, has left her husband for Payer and after a spectacular divorce has married the arctic traveler. Devil of a fellow, this Bohemian knight. Alice and Julius are the names the de Payers give their two children born in Paris.

I have become a painter, the émigré writes to Gerhard Rohlfs, a German explorer of the Sahara, whom he wishes to accompany on a trip through the Libyan Desert to the divide between the Nile and the Congo. But in the end Rohlfs departs without Payer, who remains behind in his Paris atelier with his pictures—large, powerful paintings of glaciered mountains, arctic tragedies, scenes of the Franklin expedition of 1847 and a winter no one survived, canvases covering a hundred square feet and more, windows on a frightening world. Ragged figures creep across pack ice, the snow-covered bodies of John Franklin's companions lie strewn about as food for bears, the sky races past overhead. This is a man who paints the terrors of ice and darkness with such cold mastery it strikes fear in the beholder. The critics applaud. Payer is awarded prizes in London, Berlin, Munich, Paris—gold medals.

In 1884, ten years after his return from the ice, the painter goes blind in his left eye. A long period of despair follows. Then he begins working again. Gradually the faces of his life-sized figures take on the features of Weyprecht, Orel, Carlsen, the crew. Julius Payer begins to paint his own drama, the years in the wilderness. He has difficulty selling the paintings; they are so large they require great halls, palaces. His diminished sight does not allow him, the painter complains, to paint anything smaller or more delicate.

In 1890, so a friend's letter will later report, Payer was seized by an all-consuming homesickness. What is certain is that the painter leaves his family that year, leaves Paris for good, and returns to Vienna. Society's reception is cordial: an entertaining guest, who still talks about the Arctic a great deal. Payer gives painting lessons to society's daughters, travels the provinces as a lecturer, and begins work on one of the largest paintings of his life. It is the scene of their retreat, their flight from the north, thirteen feet wide and eleven high. He will call it *Never Turn Back* and people will say it is his masterpiece—yet more than anything else it is a glorification of Weyprecht. Against the transfiguring light of Franz Josef Land in the distance, the commander on water and ice stands before his men as they lie or kneel huddled in the snow—a preacher with a Bible in his right hand, who comforts the weary and despairing and implores them to give up any thought of saving themselves by returning to the ship, returning to the past. *Never Turn Back.* Their only hope is the path through the ice ahead.

This painting marks the completion of many things. And now, with the resolute confidence of a dreamer, Julius Payer returns from his own memories and makes new plans. He wants to travel in the Arctic again, to Greenland and to the north beyond. Painters will accompany him, it will be an expedition of painters, a grand attempt to capture in art the magic of color and light flooding the polar wastelands. And later, later, he hopes, he may be able to join an expedition to the polar region of the south, yes, certainly, he will wander the ice shelf of Antarctica.

In the last summers of the nineteenth century Payer begins to fit himself out again, to train for the journey in the ice. He wanders the Alps and Lombardy, then the Pyrenees, and on through Spain to the Gulf of Cádiz. There is no doubt now of the existence of Franz Josef Land. Fridtjof Nansen and the Jackson expedition of the English have both wintered there, and the Duke of the Abruzzi and his companions, who spent the turn of the century in the darkness of that land, found the message left on Cape Fligely by the Austro-Hungarian North

Pole Expedition, and put it back undamaged. No, the old man who tours villages speaking in church halls about basalt coasts and amazing phenomena of light is no liar, he knows what he is talking about, he no longer needs a public that honors or ignores him depending on how the wind is blowing. The time has come for Payer to resign his honorary membership in the Geographical Society of Vienna, for him to write appraisals of inns and alpine hotels for Baedeker guidebooks, for him to avoid the salons.

Sven Hedin, one of the new heroes, a Swede, an explorer of Asia, deplores Payer's fate in a speech he gives in Vienna: *It disturbs me deeply that a man of action like Julius Payer . . . has been forgotten and is forced to live the life of a poor, neglected man who travels about like a salesman, giving lectures for small fees.*

The final total is one thousand two hundred twenty-eight lectures, one thousand two hundred twenty-eight visions of the Arctic. Payer keeps strict account: place, date, attendance, applause, honorarium. But he is deep in his future now. He will reach the North Pole in a submarine, he says. Departing from Kiel, he will float along in underwater twilight, all the way to the point where the scales on his instruments show him that he has arrived. At the top of the world and yet deep under the sea, he will ignite explosives. The ice above him will burst. Then the water will grow calm and smooth again, reflecting the sky. And he will surface, surface at last and walk upon the mirror.

In May 1912 a stroke makes an invalid of the North Pole traveler, turns him into an old man of seventy, who has trouble walking and cannot speak a word. He scribbles whatever he has to say now on bits of paper that he glues together. His questions, his memories, his complaints become a rustling, ever-growing strip of paper. He calls them his "snakes" and unrolls them for visitors. Does the mute man still have goals in the world of ice? I do not know. Whatever myths were left to be destroyed about the polar wasteland have been destroyed by now. Baron Nordenskiöld has drifted through the Northeast Passage, and Amundsen through the Northwest, the foes Peary and Cook have returned as masters of the North Pole, and it is said that Amundsen has now conquered the South Pole as well . . . but whatever has been achieved, it has been achieved without Payer, without the frail patient who spends his last summer in Velde, a spa in upper Carniola, between the Julian and Karawanken Alps. While there he receives news that a certain Jules de Payer, who lives in Paris and calls himself "Chef de la Mission Arctique Française," is preparing an expedition to Franz Josef Land. *Esteemed Jules de Payer, Esteemed Son . . .* the invalid writes as the salutation of a letter he never finishes and never sends. For time now collapses on everything. Franz Josef I, the ruler of the land named for him, has his manifesto pasted on the walls of his empire:

To My peoples! . . . After long years of peace, the intrigues of a hate-filled foe compel Me to take sword in hand for the maintenance of the honor of My monarchy, the protection of its prestige and ascendancy, and the security of its possessions. . . . Flames of hate have risen ever higher against Me and My house. . . . I place my trust in the Almighty, that He will grant My weapons victory. . . . With good conscience I now follow the path to which duty directs Me. . . .

How silent, how soft and flooded with light must the remote world of Franz Josef Land seem in this summer of 1914. Its rocky walls bear no proclamations, its coasts and mountains hear no thunder of war, its crevasses appear to be made of jade or lapis lazuli, its dark capes are feathered by flocks of gulls and auks. I say: The silent man now realizes that he really did discover a paradise.

In the years that follow, the fields of Galicia are gibbous with mass graves, the meadows of Flanders as well. By the Masurian Lakes of Prussia, in Alsace-Lorraine, in Champagne, Serbia, the Caucasus, or along the Isonzo: dead men lie everywhere as Julius Payer dies beside Veldeser Lake, with the noise of men doing their duty raging all around him. It is August 29, 1915, a hot day with no breeze. They bathe the body of the spa guest, deck him out in fine clothes, transport him back to Vienna, and there, on September 4, lower him into a grave of honor. His papers are put in order, they throw out a down shirt, canvas boots, a tattered fur—all the protection against cold that the mute man had kept in a chest, and they unroll his snakes of paper, too, note by note, find commentaries and aphorisms, as well as sketches—and somewhere, not at the end, and not given any particular emphasis, an entry that predicts *a revolution in Russia . . . and the murder of the czar, the liberation of Poland, bankrupt nations, millions of dead, the destruction of cities, of navies and commerce, the spread of plagues . . . and finally the end of the world, when our planet will be incinerated as a shameful stain upon the solar system.*

I will reach no conclusions. I will remove nothing from this world. Was I afraid my researches would end like this? I am gradually beginning to feel at home in the wealth and banality of my material. I find ways to interpret the facts of Josef Mazzini's disappearance, facts about the ice, find ever new and different ways, and I shift around in them as if in a chair, until every version feels comfortable.

My walls are covered with maps, of nations, coasts, seas, paper in every shade of blue, folded, sprinkled with islands, and traversed by the jagged limits of the ice. The same lands repeat themselves on my walls, the same empty, ragged lands—Norwegian and Soviet provinces, the Spitsbergens and Franz Josef Land, remote territories, stones in the dragnet of longitude and latitude.

Zeml'a Franca Iosifa. The old names are still valid. *Ostrov*

Rudolfa, Rudolf Island. There, I hear myself say, is where able seaman Antonio Zaninovich and his dog team fell into a glacier, where the commander on land panicked.

And Cape Fligely still bears the same name, and the islands, straits, and bays have kept their original names, too—Vienna Neustadt Island, Klagenfurt Island, Cape Grillparzer, Hohenlohe Island, Cape Kremsmünster, Cape Tyrol, and so on. This is my land, I say. But the notations on my maps say: "Restricted area." "May not be entered," they say. "Is not open to travel. No flights permitted." A forbidden land: it is as impenetrable a wilderness as ever, impenetrable even in mild summers when the ice has been nicely divvied up.

North of Rudolf Island the blue of the ocean grows darker. Those are the trenches of the Eurasian Basin. I like that blue. I linger there often, smoothing the folds in the Arctic Ocean and following them back far to the southeast, to the familiar long line of the coast of Novaya Zemlya, the coast of cliffs, the beautiful coast. There purple moss, coltsfoot, and sorrel grow. There is Cape Suchoi Nos and beyond it a broad bay where whalers once kept watch for missing boats, for lost sealers, for anything and everything that had ever disappeared in the ice. A great deal of flotsam surfaces near Suchoi Nos—the burst hulls of ships, planks, splintered masts, leached and bleached. Maybe some fragment is waiting there for me, I hear myself say, maybe some token from a glacier in the Spitsbergens has been washed free by a rivulet of thaw water, to be carried on a long stream, and left behind near Suchoi Nos.

I protect the cape with the palm of my hand, cover the cape, feel how dry and cool its blue is, stand here in the middle of my paper seas, alone with all the possibilities of a story, a chronicler who lacks the comfort of an ending.

Note

The characters in this novel have helped write their own story. All quotations are set in italic, with the name of the author noted. The following works have been used:

Julius Payer, *Die österreichisch-ungarische Nordpol-Expedition in den Jahren 1872–1874.* Vienna: K.K. Hof- und Universitätsbuchhändler Alfred Hölder, 1876.

Carl Weyprecht. Diary, letters, and manuscripts. Austrian War Archives, Marine Division, Vienna.

Carl Weyprecht, *Die Nordpol-Expeditionen der Zukunft und deren sicheres Ergebniss.* Vienna, Pest, Leipzig: Hartleben's Verlag, 1876.

Otto Krisch, *Tagebuch der zweiten österreichisch-ungarischen Nordpol-Expedition,* excerpted from the author's literary remains and edited by Anton Krisch. Vienna: Wallishauser'sche Verlagsbuchhandlung, 1875.

Johann Haller, *Erinnerungen eines Tiroler Teilnehmers an Julius v. Payer's Nordpol-Expedition 1872/1874,* excerpted from the author's literary remains by his son Ferdinand Haller and edited by R. Klebelsberg. Innsbruck: Universitätsverlag Wagner, 1959.

I would like to thank Mr. Peter Jung and Dr. Peter Broucek of the Austrian War Archives for their valuable assistance, and my friends Brigitte, Jaro, Margot, and Rudi for long conversations about the ice.

C. R.
Vienna, May 1984

Illustrations

Black-and-white photographs appear as follows: page 17, the *Admiral Tegetthoff* in the harbor at Bremerhaven; pages 18–19, the members of the Austro-Hungarian North Pole Expedition; page 21, Karl Weyprecht; page 23, Julius Payer.

The drawings on pages 31, 41, 43, 45, 205, 207, and 209 are reproduced from Julius Payer, *Die österreichisch-ungarische Nordpol-Expedition in den Jahren 1872–1874* (Vienna: Alfred Hölder, 1876).